the GLOW of FALLEN STARS

By Kate Ling

The Loneliness of Distant Beings
The Glow of Fallen Stars

Publishing in 2018

The Truth of Different Skies

the GLOW of FALLEN STARS

KATE LING

LITTLE, BROWN BOOKS FOR YOUNG READERS
www.lbkids.co.uk

LITTLE, BROWN BOOKS FOR YOUNG READERS

First published in Great Britain in 2017 by Hodder and Stoughton

1 3 5 7 9 10 8 6 4 2

A CIP catalogue record for this book
is available from the British Library.

ISBN 978-1-51020-018-0

Typeset in Minion by M Rules
Printed and bound in Great Britain by
Clays Ltd, St Ives plc

The paper and board used in this book are
made from wood from responsible sources.

Little, Brown Books for Young Readers
An imprint of
Hachette Children's Group
Part of Hodder and Stoughton
Carmelite House
50 Victoria Embankment
London EC4Y 0DZ

An Hachette UK Company
www.hachette.co.uk

www.hachettechildrens.co.uk

For N, and her fearless heart

Chapter One

The water moves around my hips as I walk, surging up against me, pulling at me. It isn't clear or blue like I expected but instead has a skin that is pale and pinkish and scaly, that parts when I touch it with my fingers then stays there as I lift them to my face and study the way it dissolves.

'The ash from the burned-up entry shield,' says Dom, watching me, then looking up at the deep red ball of the sun. 'Come on, let's go.'

Ezra is ahead of us, the closest to shore, stooped half over and blowing water out of his nose, shaking his head, yelling about something. Mariana is between us and him, walking with her arms crossed over her front, getting slower. I would be getting slower too if Dom wasn't pulling me; it's as if I'm melting, as if the water is claiming me.

Ezra turns back to us, making a face. ' ... fricking gravity ... ' is the only part of what he says that I catch over the loud hiss that fires out of the shuttle behind us as it cools in the water, shooting a screaming plume of steam into the sky.

It's only as the water gets shallower that I start to really feel it, to feel the way I am almost slowing to a stop.

'We're nearly there,' says Dom, squeezing my hand. 'Fifty metres more, tops.'

I can't do much more than look at him with my mouth hanging open. There is all this bruising under his eyes and around his mouth and, as I watch, a large drop of dark blood snakes out of one nostril.

'Are you OK?' I manage to say, but it cracks in my throat.

'I'm fine,' he says. 'Let's figure it all out on land.'

We reach Mariana just as she loses her footing and sits in the water. I push my arm in under hers, pull her up and grip her close to my side while we walk.

'This is just . . .' she says, close to my ear, but she doesn't finish.

Ahead of us is a long pale beach, backed by trees and plants that stand together so thick and tangled it may as well be a brick wall. It's hard to tell if the sand is pink and the leaves are dark purple and blue and red the way they seem to be, or whether it's just the fact that Huxley is casting everything in its blood-red glow. Looking in one direction down the beach I can see where the island ends in a point of low, pale rocks; looking in the other it is punctuated by a mountain, so black and so steep that it is more like the massive blade of a knife, towering up into the sky as if it might be about to fall at any moment. There are more giant black rocks, a forest of knives, stretching out to sea, as if at some point they rained down from space, like we just did. This must be the place for it.

Explorer 37 groans suddenly like a dying beast in a monster movie, and I turn in time to see it twist in the water, raising a shattered wing to the sky, releasing an orange jet of liquid in a geyser.

'It's sinking,' I tell Dom. 'We can't let it sink.'

'It won't sink,' he says, but before I can ask him how he knows, he is bent double, coughing a string of blood.

I squeeze his hand and use every bit of effort I have to walk, even though Mariana's weight on my shoulder feels as if it's hammering me deep into the sand and Dom is losing ground, wrenching at my hand with every step. It's only by focusing on Ezra, who is staggering into the shallows, stopping to haul off his undershirt before getting bowled on to his hands and knees by a wave, that I manage to keep going.

When a wave gets us, Mariana and I manage to stand strong against it, but I feel it take Dom, take his feet, so that he is being sucked away from me. I turn and grab his hand with both of mine, hauling him through the surf as the wave retreats and he is able to get back on his feet. In the gap it leaves we run; we run until we are knee-deep, ankle-deep, falling on to the wet sand, panting there.

The sky is a deep, vivid pink and it's snowing. But how can it be? How can it be when the air around me is so hot I can hardly bear to breathe it in?

'It's snowing,' I tell Dom, watching a flake fall on his cheek, just below his closed eyes. 'It's snowing,' I say again, looking up at Ezra where he lies on the beach, just above us, his feet close to my face, propped up on his elbows.

'It's just us,' Ezra says. 'Just our debris.'

Mariana lies on her side a metre away with the surf moving in and out around her, letting it arrange and rearrange her hair. I watch her twist on to her front and lever herself up to vomit something dark into the water.

'Come on,' I tell her when she's done, offering her my shaking hand.

The beach is sloped up from the water in three steps and I get us to the middle one, too afraid to be any closer to the water, too afraid to move any closer to the trees. I go back for Dom and manage to get him to his feet, get him leaning on me for the few heavy steps before he lands on his back.

'You need help?' I ask Ezra but he shakes his head, stays where he is, turns on to his side to face away from us.

I sit in the sand next to Dom and Mariana and look

at Huxley. She is morphing and melting into a dark red puddle on the horizon, as if she is becoming a part of the sea.

'Sunset,' I try the word out. 'Nightfall.'

I look around the sky, at the way it is blue, red, yellow, lilac, and as I follow it up all the way and over to the opposite side it darkens to a deep blue and shows the first stars.

'There were moons. Weren't there moons?'

But nobody answers me, and there aren't any. Not now.

I look at Dom, touch the deep purple bruising under his eyes, which makes him open them and roll them around a little before he manages to look at me. They are oddly dark, though, not lit like usual, and that feels so painful it hurts my throat. I smile anyway. The words 'you almost died' are still on my lips but I can't, won't, say them. He lets his eyes fall closed again.

I've seen this sunset before, watching out of the window on Ventura with my hands cold against the glass while the sun slid behind the flank of the turning planet and for a moment it was orange, its light broken into strands through the atmosphere and mirroring on the surface of the water before it disappeared.

I used to see that and imagine myself here, right here, watching it with my toes in the sand. As I pan down to my feet and flex them it hardly seems real, especially because it is all so different from how I imagined it would be, Huxley so big and close, divided in half now and shimmering in flame.

Suddenly the air surges. It sucks and pulls at us, tossing the trees, swirling the falling shreds of debris and scattering sand into my face, burning my eyes so that I have to close them. Mariana buries her face against Dom and screams.

'What is that? What is it? What's happening?' I hear her say.

'It's just the wind,' says Dom, stroking Mariana's hair. 'I guess it's probably normal.'

I lie down next to him with my head on his chest.

'It's getting dark,' I tell him.

'Yeah.' He swallows.

Huxley is now just its very top edge, melting, melting, and then gone, leaving only multicoloured ghosts of itself in the sky.

'What now?' I ask Dom.

He moves his hand down my hair. 'We should try to rest and work out what to do in the morning.'

Even though there is such a bone-deep ache in me I can hardly move, I know sleep is impossible. For a while all I do is tremble even though I'm hotter than I've ever been. The heat is so thick I can't dry off; if anything I'm just getting wetter. It's lucky, really, since we all left our uniforms at the bottom of the sea to swim here and are only in our undershirts and underwear and a coating of sand.

6

The first noise from the forest makes Dom jolt so hard in fear he knocks my jaw and I bite my tongue and taste blood.

'Oh my God, what is it? What is that? What is it?' shrieks Mariana.

'Be quiet a minute so we can listen,' says Ezra, up on one elbow, squinting at the treeline.

'What is it what is it what is it what is it?' Mariana can't stop.

'Man, just be quiet, will you?'

We lie listening to it. *Meep.* Silence. *Meep.* Silence. Then we listen as it is joined by another voice, almost the same, just a couple of semitones different, chiming together.

'Insects?' says Dom. 'Right? I mean, like, remember those movies? Don't insects on Earth make noises like that?'

'Why should anything be like it is on Earth?' says Mariana, lifting her head. 'We're millions of miles away from Earth.'

Ezra lowers himself back on to the sand. 'Insects seems a reasonable guess, but I'm pretty sure the life scans we ran on the recons showed up nothing beyond microbial level.'

'Deadly microbes,' I say, without meaning to. 'Deadly microbes is what we were told.'

Nobody answers me but we all just sit with it for a few moments.

'Well,' Ezra sighs eventually, 'noisy microbes I guess,' and he wraps his arms around his bare chest and rolls back on to his side.

I am listening to the sounds so hard that I exhaust myself and slip into some kind of unconsciousness completely against my will. The next thing I know I am waking and it is maybe hours later and I am staring up at the sky, at the gigantic banner of hot blue universe bearing down on me, coming for me, coming to claim me back. I swallow the fear and watch it for a while, realising it is moving, parts of it breaking away to streak all across the sky in pale lines, heading for the horizon, perfectly silent but streaming, beautiful and terrifying all at once. I start to shake again and it wakes Dom, stirring him into stroking my arm.

'What is it?' he murmurs.

'Shooting stars?' It's a phrase I've heard but never understood.

He opens his eyes and watches them in silence. 'Wow,' he says, and it calms me.

'Maybe it happens every night?'

He shakes his head. 'I think it's us. We made it. Our dust in the atmosphere.' He lays his hand on my hair. 'Our little way of saying, "Hello, new planet."' I feel him smile and it makes me do it too. I turn my face to him and we kiss and it is warm and soft and oddly metallic tasting and I never want it to end, but when it does we stay nose to nose and study the wet of each other's eyes.

'So scared,' I say.

'I know,' he says.

'Are you?' I say with a tremble in my voice.

'It'll be all right,' he says, but at the same time he looks at something over my shoulder so fixedly that for a moment I am covered in terror. 'Look.' He nods at it, and I turn my head.

Something huge and dark pink is appearing out of the sea, a bigger version of the sun but with all its light bled away and all its power gone; a ghost of Huxley, bringing with it only a profound silence that overwhelms us.

'One of the moons,' I breathe.

We watch it rise, filling the sky with its broad face. It becomes hard not to feel watched.

'Moonrise,' whispers Dom.

I turn back to look at him. 'Is that a real thing?'

'It is if we say it is. It's our planet.'

I think about that, blinking at the moon. It only takes a few minutes for the other to join it, peering over the edge of the world, smaller but closer, tucked into its side like company, a friend, a lover, a child, both watching us closely to see what we'll do next.

Chapter Two

We've almost given up on it ever being daylight again by the time the dawn creeps in, at first just a paleness that is so delicate we don't dare believe it, then colours that finally make it true and undeniable. We have just begun to feel cold when Huxley herself makes the horizon, and streams her heat and light on to us as if she's bringing us to life.

37 lies offshore, shining and silver and blackened and burned, already looking like a chunk of another world, another life. It is barely staying afloat, and of course it has drifted somewhat further out. So this is the point at which we realise we will be totally screwed (Ezra's words) if we don't do something about it.

The sea is so different this morning, pulsing in waves every few seconds, great curving sun-glinting arcs of water that look easily twice as tall as us. They pulverise themselves into a wall of foam when they hit the shallows – mesmerising, beautiful, petrifying.

Squinting out at it, I say, 'It wasn't like this yesterday, was it?' and Dom shakes his head in my peripheral vision.

'I guess something had just crashed into it. From space and everything, so . . .' He shrugs, then looks at me. 'At least we can swim.' He puts his arm around my shoulder. 'Swimming lessons on a space traveller finally come in useful for something,' he says, and he is smiling.

We swim out there in a line with Dom at the front until he is treading water and waiting for us. Once I get close to him I realise how tired I am, how flooded with pain every muscle in my body has become, and I try to tell him but I can't, because every time I open my mouth water fills it. Dom lets me grab at him a few times, lets me dig my nails into the skin on his shoulder, and then he pulls me into the shelter of his body and says, 'You need to not panic, Seren – you're wasting energy, and we need you.'

Which makes me want to be better at it, but not actually any more able to be so.

'I'm going to get you inside so you can operate the winch,' Dom yells about fifty times before I manage to get him to understand that I have no idea how to go about it. 'I'll give you a boost. Just look for it on the On-Planet Utilities menu.' He tows me right to the side of 37, where the waves batter me repeatedly against the blackened metal. Somehow Dom gets me up to where I can grab the bottom sill of the hatch and I lever myself up, even though my arms are shaking and the whole thing is almost impossible. But finally I get the top half of my body over and I am hanging there, staring down into the nose of the shuttle where I can see the back of our seats and a whole bunch of stuff that has slid down to the front because 37 is pitched forward in the water.

'We need to do this fast, Seren – release the winch cover panel and start unspooling it. The electrics are probably flooded so it may have to be manual, OK?'

I manage to get the bottom half of my body up over the sill but then gravity takes over and I slide, face first, all the way down the floor into the nose, face-planting on the control panel and mashing my lip into my teeth. While I am trying to get the systems screen to boot up, Mariana drags herself up and over the edge and sits with one leg either side like a sensible person would, and then looks down at me.

'Oh my God, what have you done?'

I touch my face and see the blood.

She climbs down to help me figure out the winch release but nothing happens, so we end up watching through the front windscreen while Dom dives down to find the manual release lever, kicking past us like a fish, then rising back up to the turmoil above. He does this four times, then Ezra tries but has to haul himself down using the nose cone because he's nowhere near the swimmer Dom is. We are staring at the drifting upturned soles of his feet in the blue light when we hear the grind of the lever and the breach alarm sounding. The OPU screen shows that the unspool is in progress so we climb up the seatbacks to where we can hang out of the back door.

They are swimming away from us, Dom in front and Ezra behind, the thick metal cable slung over their shoulders making their strokes laboured and slow, getting closer to where the waves curl and demolish themselves.

Once the waves take hold of them they disappear. All we see is the cable tightening and slackening in the broiling foam, and sometimes a leg or a hand. This happens for so long, Mari has to stop me jumping in.

'They're OK,' she says, after what seems like eternity, pointing out Dom as he stands, hair all plastered over to one side, eyes wild, fishing Ezra out of the water by his wrist, waving an arm at us. We watch them struggle out on to land, weighed down by the cable. They haul it to the treeline and stand arguing about something for the longest time before they feed it round a trunk and then Ezra makes this weird circular hand motion at us, and I look at Mariana.

'You know what to do?' I ask her, clambering down towards the control panels while she shakes her head.

I pull down menus and make selections until we hear it start, grinding at first, whining, as 37 begins to turn in the water, shunting round.

'Well that was easy,' I say, but it only lasts as long as it takes for us to hit the sand.

By this time we are close enough to see the disappointed expressions on Dom's and Ezra's faces as they watch us crunch to a halt about thirty metres out, the winch mechanism screaming as if in frustration. It keeps going for a while, squealing harder, a rending creak in the front panel, 37 inching forward painfully slowly. Then there is a new sound – a high clean cracking that none of us understand until we realise it is the tree splitting, coming apart, exposing its pale insides, severed by the cable, which whips off down the beach as if it doesn't give a damn, nearly taking Ezra out in the process.

Mari is quicker on the uptake than me and has already gone back to the control panel to stop the retraction, which gives Dom and Ezra a chance to unspool it again and look for something that might be strong enough. They're in the treeline, gone for a while before they appear again and Ezra does that same weird hand signal, but Dom is motioning something else.

'He wants us to come in,' says Mari, just after I've started the retraction. 'Lighten the load, I'm guessing.'

We forget about the waves. The second I've jumped in Mariana shouts and I look over my shoulder to see it – a wave like a wall, towering, curling, shattering with sun and breaking right over my head.

And this is what I am thinking: *I made it out, I made it out of Ventura, all of that, only to die here, tumbled in the seawater of this alien planet, all because I can't find up, all because every time I get my head above water there is another giant wave, a wall of water, bearing down on me.* It is only Mariana coming to me, catching my wrists, going under with me, tumbling, doing hopeless, awful, sickening somersaults before emerging momentarily to shriek, 'Get up, get up, get up,' that makes me do it, that makes me find sand with my feet, only to be knocked away from it again, and again, and again, as if I'm being punched.

And then I am on the shore, weeping, yelling, coughing hot seawater against my hands while Dom crushes me against his chest and says nothing except, 'You're OK now; you're OK now.'

I watch 37 make it to the sand through my tears.

Half an hour later we have almost everything from the storage unit laid out on the sand.

'I think this is a tent.' Dom pulls out metres and metres of thin orange material from a bag, and scratches his head.

'A tent?' Ezra makes a face.

'Yeah.'

'That's all we have for shelter?'

Dom looks around him at the forest of boxes and bags punctuating the ten metres of sand between him and where Mariana and I are standing. 'Looks like it.'

Ezra flaps a hand. 'Doesn't matter. Let's stick it up. We won't be here long.'

Mariana looks at him in horror. 'We won't be here long?'

He starts hauling the contents out of one of the boxes: little packs of freeze-dried food from the look of it. 'As soon as we can get the boat functional, we need to set out for the continent.'

Mariana frowns. 'Wait – what? Why?'

Ezra doesn't stop sorting the packs into lines in front of him. 'Reasons. Too many to go into right now. Let's get organised before it gets dark.'

Mariana and I find four bagged-up work uniforms and hats and four rec uniforms, all size medium. They're more or less OK for her and Ezra but too small for Dom and too big for me, which in the end doesn't matter that much because I put a work one on for two seconds before I realise we're never going to be able to wear them in this heat. It's funny because on Ventura I was always cold, always wondering why they hadn't made the uniforms warmer or thicker, but now the density of the fabric, the way it hugs my hips, heats me up so intensely I have to tear it off within seconds.

Mariana watches me kick it into the sand and then studies the one in her lap. 'We'll have to cut them up, I guess. One rec uniform each isn't going to last long.'

I look around at the bags. 'Underwear?'

She shakes her head.

'Seriously?' I stand with my hands on my hips and

watch Dom and Ezra connecting the long looping strand of a tent pole with its component parts. 'Also, I hate to say this, but I need the toilet.'

She laughs. 'You'd better get digging a latrine pit then.'

I swipe sweat off my face with my forearm and study the treeline, the way the red and blue leaves knit together to hold the darkness in among the dusky pink tree trunks with thorns like knives. Up above, the tops of the trees fan out flat in a plane, meaty and enormous.

'I'll help you dig one in a bit. But help me work out the solar still first?' says Mariana.

'The what?'

She points at a brushed steel and glass pyramid sitting on the sand.

'I managed to build it but I can't figure out how it works. It says it can make fresh water out of salt so I'm thinking we need it.'

I squat next to it, but if Mariana can't master it I doubt I can – every day I spent working alongside her on Ventura showed me how much better she is than me at anything technical. But, miraculously, it gently hums into life twenty minutes later once its cell is charged. By this time we've already moved on to the ration packs that Ezra left in the sand, trying to split them into days to see how long they'll sustain us, realising that they all need to have hot water added to them so we're going to have to figure out a way to make water hot.

'Hey.' Ezra, sweat-soaked in only a pair of rec shorts, shades his eyes as he looks at us. 'We need help if we're going to get this up before it gets dark again.'

All they have so far is a lot of shining poles and the orange material laid out across the sand.

'Where are we putting it?' I frown at Ezra.

He raises his eyebrows. 'Um, here?'

'Here?'

He looks around. 'You've got a better idea?'

I feel one shoulder rising in a half shrug. 'Well, shouldn't we work out a bit more about the island first? It's not very sheltered here and we don't ...'

He's already shaking his head. 'Hemple, we're not staying here long enough to worry about it. We can't.'

'Lomax ...' says Dom, then to me, 'We'll put it up here for now. Come and help me.'

I walk over to him and notice the red skin across the top of his cheeks, his nose, and reach up to press my fingers to it.

'Yeah that's sore,' he says, flinching.

'What is it?'

But he just shrugs.

The tent is a complete mess by the time we get it up and not at all how I suppose it's meant to look. It's lumpy and half collapsed on one side, but by now the sun is leaving the sky again so we spread the sleeping bags out open on the sand as a floor inside and pile everything else on top, trying not to think about the fact that it's our home now, the only home we have.

I head to the waterline to wash some of the sand and ash out of my hair, trying to ignore the night coming on. Behind me, Dom and Mariana are using the laser lighter on a tiny swirl of dry leaves, in an attempt to start a fire. Up the beach a little, Ezra is walking the treeline, stopping every few metres to look at something in the sand or peer into the forest.

Suddenly Mariana is squealing, leaping to her feet, arms in the air.

'*Por fin!*' she tells the sky.

Dom stays to feed the fire a little before standing too, all smiles, pulling her into his arms. Then they remember themselves and squat back down, tending to the tiny smoking bundle on the sand.

We end up sharing two of the food rations because none of us can remember the last time we ate. Then we just sit and watch the fire as it begins to die. None of us have ever seen a fire before, not in real life. There are these lights in it, colours I never expected, little dancing spirits within that flare up and then die just as quickly.

The last of the sunlight from our second day here is leaving the sky. Dom sits behind me so that I am between his raised knees, and he yawns against my shoulder. Ezra throws a handful of sand out to the water.

'Need to get that boat inflated tomorrow,' he says.

'Not the priority.' Mariana shakes her head. 'Food is.'

'That will be easier on the continent, I swear to you. I flew over it, remember.'

'How far away is it?' asks Dom.

Ezra doesn't answer.

'You don't even know? It would be crazy, man. You saw what that ocean did to us today.'

'I can use the computer to figure it all out before we set off anywhere.' Ezra throws more sand at the sea.

'We haven't even checked out the island properly yet,' I say and just then, as if on cue, the noise from the forest starts up again and we all freeze to listen to it, that one lonely voice that peeps away in the forest, soon joined by another, then another.

'In the morning we explore,' says Dom, close to my ear.

Mariana turns from the fire to look at him for a moment.

'What?' he says. 'Stay here if you like, Mari – we need someone to organise things anyway. Seren can stay too.' He kisses my neck.

I twist to him. 'I'm not staying here. I'm going with you.'

He smiles slowly. 'Well OK, then.'

'Water,' says Ezra.

And Mariana says, 'You'll have to see if there's any in the still.'

He shakes his head. 'No, I mean, we need to look for

water. We can't rely on the still. What if it breaks down? Surely life on Ventura taught you that tech is unreliable. We had entire teams of people spending their lives going round fixing stuff as it broke.'

'Yes, Lomax,' says Mariana. 'We are probably a lot more aware of that than you.'

He scowls at her over the fire, but doesn't say anything else.

I look up at the stars that are beginning to appear. None of them are shooting tonight.

Chapter Three

I hear footsteps squeaking in the sand behind me while I'm standing in the shallows splashing my face the next morning. When I turn it is Ezra.

'I'm going to check around the base of that mountain. It seems like a place there could be water.'

I look down the coast to where the mountain of black rock is painting its shadow across the island. 'I thought you were going to stay here and work on the boat.' I cut a sideways glance at him.

'I still say we should go. While the still is working, while we have supplies – we should go. But it's high-risk, for sure, so I'm willing to give the island a chance to change my mind first.'

I watch him disappear down the beach in the heatwaves shimmering off the sand. Dom arrives next to me.

'Are you ready?' he says.

I slide my arm around him and knock my hand against something tucked down the back of his shorts.

'Careful,' he says, stepping away and reaching around

to pull out a short curving sword. Both of us stare at the glare of sun on the blade.

It makes me laugh nervously. 'What the hell is that?'

'Bush knife,' he says, turning it a little to admire it. 'I'm quite impressed that it was in the On-Planet toolkit. We're going to need it.'

'For?' I almost swallow the word.

He points it at the treeline. 'Making any headway whatsoever in that.'

Mariana's inside 37, stripping it for anything else useful, so we just call goodbye to her when we leave. We walk along the coast a little looking for anything that might look like an easier access point into the forest. Dom takes my hand, and it's weird because for a moment it's almost as if we're shy with each other.

'We made it,' he says, a little out of breath from walking in the sand.

The first thing that comes into my mind to say is that we almost didn't – *he* almost didn't – but I bite it back. Instead I move on to the next scary thing and say, 'What are we going to do now, though?'

He smiles. 'Figure it out as we go along.'

'Figure it out?'

He stops and takes my head in his hands, holds it there. 'I love you,' he says, which doesn't seem relevant at all but makes me smile, and when he leans in close I kiss him, say I love him too.

The red skin across his nose is getting worse, peeling up a little, and his lips look cracked.

'What's happening?' I ask, running my thumb along his cheekbone.

'I think it's the sun.' He touches the places on his chest and shoulders where the skin is starting to pucker and I notice the way the rest of his torso is darker too, browner in varying tones, like the shading on a drawing. It's lovely, actually.

'Suntan.' I remember the word from books and movies. 'Sunburn.'

'You're getting it too,' he says, touching my cheek so that I flinch away in pain and it makes him laugh. 'The good news is that you're also getting freckles, and they're incredibly cute.' He kisses me just under my eye. 'You never told me you had freckles.'

'I didn't know myself.'

'What other secrets do you have, huh, estrellita?' he purrs, his lips close to mine, and for a second all I want to do is pull him against me, down into the sand, and show him everything he doesn't yet know. But he just kisses me once and says, 'You should wear this,' pulling a Ventura cap out of his pocket, pushing it on to my head. 'To keep the sun off.' Then he takes my hand and half winks. 'Let's go.'

We walk along the solid wall of the forest for half an hour before we reach the headland that reaches out into the sea. We step over low, wet rocks until we round the point and find ourselves in another long sweeping pale bay, also walled by forest. The only difference is that the sea here is as smooth and glassy as the pool on Ventura.

'Zero waves,' I tell Dom.

'Yeah. Weird,' he says.

'Angle of the land?' I wonder, then I see something offshore, just under the surface, lumpy and pale. 'Or maybe those rocks are protecting it. Either way, I already like it better here.'

He squeezes my hand.

Halfway along its length it gets even better. We find a gap in the forest wall, and a reason for it – a stream running out of the forest. Dom squats and tastes a drop while I squint down the gap into the solid darkness of its tunnel.

'Fresh,' says Dom, rubbing some on his face. 'Jackpot.'

I fill my hands with the coolness of it, and I'm just about to gulp it down when Dom says, 'No, estrellita, don't.'

I frown at him.

'Lomax was saying this morning we shouldn't drink any water we haven't boiled first.'

Just then I spot something over his shoulder, gleaming dully just inside the tunnel, next to the stream. I crawl along the rocks until I can get to it, close my hand around it, and it is so meaty and soft and warm that I drop it in horror.

'What is it?' asks Dom.

I reach for it again, pull it out into the light. It's purple, shining, slightly bigger than my hand, drawing into a deep red point at either end.

'It's fruit.' I look up at him. 'Right?'

He raises an eyebrow. 'I mean, it looks like it.' He takes it from me, plunges his thumbs in and parts it, revealing pink flesh, red pips. It is almost horrifically like a body part. He raises it to his face and sniffs. 'Smells good.' He goes to take a bite.

'Dom, don't!' I push at his hand.

'Why? I'll just try a bit – how else are we going to know?'

He sucks it a little against his lips, then bites, chews thoughtfully, before looking up at me, smiling, a bit of it still stuck on his front tooth.

'It's good,' he says, going for another bite. 'Really sweet, actually.'

I take it from him and he watches me bite it, filling my mouth with a taste that is so strong my brain doesn't even process it at first, I just feel it behind my eyes.

'I guess that's about what fruit should be like,' I say and then I look up above us, at the inner ceiling of the tunnel, where I see them, in among the branches, shining in the gloom, loads of them. 'Let's pick some and take them back.'

Dom's tall enough to reach so he twists them off the stems and fills the bag while I walk up the stream about ten metres, listening to the silence, straining my eyes in the darkness.

'Estrellita, come and look at this.'

I walk back to him where he is standing on the beach, gazing up at the sky, which is blooming with cloud, thick and dark. There's loads of it, bunching together, getting a little purple underneath.

I feel my mouth fall open. 'Where did it come from?'

He shrugs.

'Does it mean it'll rain?'

Another shrug, but he smiles down at me as he says, 'I kind of want it to, though, don't you?'

I love this thing Dom does sometimes, like right now, where he moves in as if to kiss me but stops just short, lips parted, his mouth maybe not even a centimetre from mine, waiting to see if I'll come the rest of the way to him. I will, I always do, I always will.

We get back to camp mid-afternoon. Mariana is digging a hole near the broken tree when we get there, covered in mud, wiping her mouth on her sleeve as we offer her a fruit. She eyes it suspiciously before taking it and peeling it carefully with her fingers.

We sit watching the clouds and eat a whole fruit each, dripping juice into the sand between our knees, before Mariana and Dom start on a fire again. I'm looking along the beach for Ezra when I see this weird pop of light in one of the clouds that scares me, and then hear a noise that makes me cower against the ground and hold my head, wondering if the shard-mountain has picked this day to fall. But it hasn't. Lightning and thunder. Something that's only ever been theory to me until now.

I turn to Dom to find him coughing dark blobs into the sand. 'OK, don't eat any more fruit,' he laughs, before running to Mari's half-dug latrine.

It gets to me next, of course, first only as a cramp that cleaves my body in two, then as an icy sweat, then as vomit that forces its way out of me, then the rest.

Ezra arrives back just as Mari makes it halfway to the latrine pit before puking in her hands, and then he watches Dom and me groaning and shivering on the floor of the tent.

'What did you eat? And why the hell didn't you sample-test it first?' He dumps an armful of firewood on the sand at the doorway.

'Did you find anything?' Dom manages to ask in a feeble voice.

'Nothing we didn't already know about. Impenetrable jungle, unscaleable cliffs, rancid soil.' I notice the scratches all along Ezra's arms, probably from the thorns on the trees. 'On the plus side, there's some pretty amazing surf if you had a board and, you know, a death wish.'

This is when we hear a hissing, sizzling sound almost like something rising out of the ground, growing into the air around us.

28

It's raining.

And, I mean, this is the first time it has actually done this, the first time any of us have ever seen rain at all, so we sit up, knees brought up to our chests, watching it come down, watching it puckering the beach, listening to it hissing in the trees, watching it puddling nearby and making the sand swirl, and finally I say, 'Wow.'

Dom laughs and says, 'I know, right?'

Mari runs back in from the latrine just as it intensifies on the tent roof. She's already soaked through, wringing rain out of her hair. But it's just too exhilarating somehow, and so even though I'm still feeling sick, I say, 'It seems as if we should dance or something.'

Ezra laughs and Dom says, 'You've always said you hated dancing.'

I look back out at the rain.

Dom stands, takes my hand and steps out backwards so that I watch the rain fall on him first, soaking him instantly like a curtain. He doesn't flinch, just smiles, looks down a little as it flows over his hair, flattening it on to the sides of his face. And then it is battering at me, pounding at me like a million little fists, coursing over my skin. I'm shrieking a little until he pulls me in against him and everywhere his skin touches mine I feel it. He links his fingers through mine and pulls my arms out to my sides and up over my head, leaves them there while he traces the runnels of water down the insides of my wrists, my inner arms, my ribs.

Back in the tent, I watch him rub the water off his face and push back his hair, watch the way the drops sit on his brown, goosebumpy skin like beads of glass. I reach to smooth them off his shoulders and chest and the side of his neck, all the time feeling his eyes on me, turning me into something beautiful. He leans in as if he'll kiss me but just before he does Ezra says, 'Man, guys, get a room.'

Dom shoots him a look, but I guess all of us think about that for a minute. I know I do.

Halfway through the night, we're woken by the thunder which has moved right overhead, so close that it rattles in our chests. The wind is whipping at the tent so fiercely that Dom ends up having to lie across me to hold it down. The sleeping bags are completely soaked, streams of water flowing in under the walls and collecting beneath us.

Ezra gets up.

'Where are you going?' yells Mari.

'We need to lash it down better,' he yells back. He's gone before we can tell him he's crazy.

Dom gets up too and I follow him to the doorway. Outside is a kind of hell: the rain swirling horizontally, the clouds on fire, thunder so loud it's as if the planet is unmaking itself, the wind so strong it's impossible to stand. Dom and Ezra fight against it all while they pull at the ropes of the tent and kick clods of sand around before giving up and coming back in.

It feels as if we'll wash away, blow away, be burned by

lightning, crushed by thunder. The weight of Dom across me feels as if it's the only thing keeping me alive. I curl my arm around his head and try to breathe. Mari moves in close behind us.

This is why, when the morning comes, and the world is white and still, and we are crawling out of the tent to find that two of the poles have snapped, it is easier to convince Ezra to move to the next bay, the one with the stream.

'The storms swept in at us this way, just like the waves do. Even if we're not here long, we need to be more sheltered,' I tell him. 'And there's water there.'

He shakes his head. 'We should just go, man.'

'And get caught in a storm like that at sea? When none of us have even been in a boat before?' Dom shakes his head as he's pulling the tent down. 'We go round there, where it's safer, and get the lay of the land.'

Ezra gazes silently out to sea for a full minute before he gets up to help.

It's a truly horrible amount of effort getting everything we need over the point but, once we do, the sun has come out and the world is steaming and brightly coloured and the bay looks even better than it did, fallen jungle debris notwithstanding.

The tent no longer pitches without being strung into the trees, but we manage to get it looking OK. It's while I'm helping that I kick something out of the sand and lift it into my palm, pulling it into halves so that it exposes a silky lining and a smooth green nut the size of my thumbnail that slides apart into hemispheres at my touch. I show it to Mari, who raises an eyebrow.

'After you.' She smiles.

'I was wondering whether we should cook them first.'

There are a lot of them, brought down out of the jungle canopy by the rain, so I gather them in our retractable bucket while Mari coaxes a fire and sets up stones to balance the frying pan. We're just watching these sea nuts, as I decide to name them, turn pale and then brown in the pan and debating about when to get them out when Dom and Ezra return from their second trip back to the first bay to carry more stuff over, right in the middle of an argument.

'I'm just saying it's a stupid point, and not even a little bit relevant right now,' Dom says, dropping bags on the sand.

'I, on the other hand, think it *is* relevant,' says Ezra, clearly under the impression he's winning. Although neither of us asks, he says to us, 'I'm just pointing out to Suarez here, *once again*, that having seen the continent—'

'Look what Seren found,' interrupts Mariana.

'Great. More poison.'

'I think they're done,' she says, pulling the pan out on to the sand, before looking round at us. 'Who's going for it?'

'I will,' says Dom, picking one out. 'They smell good.'

'Well, if you are, I am,' I say, grabbing one. 'If it kills you it better take me too.'

'That's so beautiful,' says Ezra, pretending to wipe away a tear before he takes one as well.

In the end we all eat one, Russian-roulette-style, watching each other. Ezra even pretends to fall over and grab at his throat as if he's choking on it at one point, but he's the only one that laughs.

At sunset there's no sign of rain tonight. I watch Ezra messing with the fire while Dom and Mariana stand in the glossy shallows.

'Funny, isn't it?' Ezra says, as if I've been inside his head the whole time.

I look at him blankly.

'It's just that we've lived all our lives on Ventura, a situation which by its very nature meant we had no choices. And we desert, only to find ourselves in another situation where we basically have no choices.' He carries on kicking at the fire with his trainer but flicks his eyes to me. 'Pretty ironic, when you think about it.'

I look out to where the bottom edge of Huxley is meeting the sea. 'We only just got here,' I tell him. 'We'll figure it out.'

He raises an eyebrow. 'Optimism? From you?' He shakes his head. 'Now I know we're doomed.'

Chapter Four

On the day I turn seventeen, Dom and I wake up early and get ready as quietly as we can. It's been more than three weeks since we got here, which is plenty of time for the camp to have turned into a mess in which we can't find anything, so it's far harder than it should be. We never said we would sneak out without the others, but somehow I think we both knew we would. We're halfway up the beach before we look at each other and smile.

'Where are we going?' I ask him.

'Wherever you like,' he says.

'Anywhere as long as it's with you,' I tell him, and when he kisses me I feel it in every part of me, like a breeze stirring on my skin.

The headland at this end of the beach is made out of the exact same rock as the shard, but lying horizontally instead of vertically. It's been eroded into rough steps by the sea so it's not actually that hard to climb to the top of the headland and look down into the next bay, which is much smaller, a narrow half moon of pale sand and placid sea, completely surrounded by towering jungle at the back, horizontal shards of rock on either side.

'Race you down,' I tell him, starting before he has time to react.

I leap down the rock like a staircase, two at a time, and hit the warm sand. Dom chases me down, gaining every second, then catching my hand and pulling me back so that I fall on to my backside and he lands on his knees right behind me, his face against the skin of my neck as he says, 'Got you.'

I turn until I am kissing him, kissing him as I keep twisting my body, as I hook my leg over one of his and he sits in the sand and I am in his lap, flexing my hips against him. He makes this noise in his throat, closes his eyes, then opens them so that we are watching each other, both half smiling. I pull off my salt-crusted vest, feel him watching my hair drop out of it on to my shoulders, before I ditch it and unclip my bra. There's this half second of stillness while he looks at me and I look at him, at the heat in his eyes that makes me feel as if I am beautiful, beautiful, so, so beautiful, and then he is kissing me across my chest while I enclose his head in my arms and breathe into the sweet-salt of his hair. Almost as if I am willing him to, he leans forward, all the way over, lowering me into the sand on my back. It's so warm and soft there that I arch into it, feeling it on every part of me, as I look up at him where he holds himself above me, face made slightly different by the gravity. I reach for the buttons on his shorts and pull at them, connect my ankles together behind his back, tighten my legs around his hips and look into his eyes while I feel him against me. His mouth opens a little, and he is breathing hard, and I smile. There is sand clinging to the side of his face and it sparkles in the rays of the sun, like stardust, before sprinkling down on to me, fine as salt. He hooks his fingers into the top of my trousers and I lift my hips so he can pull them down, and then I see the way he glances up and around at the trees that line the bay.

'They won't come after us,' I tell him, and at the same time I am using my hands and then my heels to move his shorts down his hips until he takes over, hauling them down and kicking them off.

We're naked together then. Suddenly and completely. And for this moment we are just lying there, pressed close, while his hand travels all the way up from my leg to my hip to my ribs to the side of my breast to my throat to my face.

'Estrellita,' he says against my lips.

God, I want him. God, I want everything. I move against him and when he shifts his weight I reach for him, for the heat of him, manoeuvring my legs and hips. When he realises, he says, 'We can't,' but I know how much he wants to really. I can taste it on him, I can feel it burning under his skin, I can hear it in the hitching of his breath.

I move my hands on to the smooth skin of his back, and I can hear the way I'm breathing, my chest heaving hard and heavy so that it almost hurts. He holds himself up on his arms and studies me, super serious, a slight shake of the head, but it's more like disbelief than refusal.

'We can't,' he says again, eyes sad and beautiful and lips swollen, so I kiss him, deep and long. None of this stuff even made any sense to me until there was him. I can't wait any longer to be with him this way. I just can't. I won't.

Even though there's a deep ache to it, it's mostly an intense relief. As if every tiny bit of desire I have ever felt in my life was just a precursor to this. He sighs that way too. As if he was waiting for this, wanting it for so long. We breathe into each other's ears for a long moment, overwhelmed by it, stilled by the beauty.

'Am I hurting you?' he whispers, and I shake my head.

I would never call it pain, even though it hurts. It's more like hunger, or need. It's all I can do to bite against the skin of his shoulder without passing out, or yelling, or maybe crying. And then the strongest instincts I have ever had take over and I forget about anything else, everything else, except him.

Afterwards he trails the backs of his fingers over my hipbone as if I am something so precious, and I smile against his smile.

But then he says, 'We shouldn't have done that.'

And I swallow my fear and say, 'Why? Didn't you like it?'

He takes my face in his hands. 'It was amazing, estrellita. The best thing. Ever.' He shakes his head. 'Ever.' And I feel so full of him right then, so possessed by him, every inch of me smelling and tasting of him, that I'm amazed I can't feel what he's thinking without him having to say it. 'We just can't . . . we can't take risks like that.'

I hook a hand over his shoulder. 'It's OK – I had my eggs harvested on Ventura.'

He shakes his head. 'It's not a hundred per cent, though, is it? It's like eighty or something, tops, right?'

I think back then, back to my sister Pan, back to Deborah, conceived as a natural after her egg harvest. Deborah. My arms still ache to hold her.

'Being pregnant here, giving birth . . . I can't put you in that kind of danger, Seren,' says Dom. 'God, I'd never forgive myself.'

I sit up, away from him, arms across my chest. Suddenly I have this solid memory of the moment Deborah arrived in this world, the buckets-worth of blood hitting the floor around my feet. Dom sits up behind me, curving himself over me, chin on my shoulder.

'Mari says there are ways to be safe,' I say.

He laughs through his nose and speaks against my skin. 'She doesn't have the best track record.'

I feel my mouth drop open. 'I can't believe you just said that.'

He shrugs. 'It's true.'

'Ronaldo Benitez had his part to play in it.'

'For many reasons, you know that I am fully aware of that,' he sighs. 'Which is why I'm saying this, even though I really, *really* don't want to.' He runs his hand through his hair, leaving it standing up and sweaty. 'I mean, right now the consequences for us are worse than they were on Ventura. It'll be different once we're established here.' He looks down to where he plays with my hand.

I sit there with that, with what that means, with what this all actually means. I smile, though, because even though it's too huge to think about, I still love that he talks about our future like that, as if we're heading somewhere good, as if he can see beyond this to where there is an actual life lying out in front of us.

Later, we walk along the treeline, collecting the branches that last night's storm brought down so we can take them back for firewood. It's only maybe the fifth storm we've had since we got here, sweeping in off the sea with no warning in the middle of the night, but three of them have been in the past week. By contrast, the days that follow them are beautifully clear – whitecaps visible far out to sea, the sight of plants clinging on the high ramparts of the mountain – as if the colour's been turned up on everything.

As we walk along the beach I spot plants I haven't noticed before leaning out over the sand – fine feathery red leaves on blue stems. I take a leaf in my hands and stroke at its pattern, before noticing its thick root, just next to my foot. I get on to my hands and knees and smooth it out of the sand. It fills both my palms, is brownish, rough-skinned, and gives a little under my thumbnail.

'Dom,' I say. He turns from where he is breaking up wood. 'What do you think?'

'I think we need to see if we can find more of those.'

I can see more a few metres into the forest and there seems to be light there, maybe some kind of hidden clearing, so Dom starts trying to cut a path, but we can hardly take a step without having to stop and hack our way through a wall of creepers and tangled branches with the bush knife.

'Here.' He hands me the bush knife and picks up the bottom hem of his T-shirt, wipes the sweat off his face with it, before pulling it all the way off. 'Arms are aching so bad,' he laughs. 'Take over for a bit?'

We only make maybe five metres of progress, but I manage to find two more of the root vegetables, neither as big as the first. I'm just starting to ache myself, covered in the sticky sap that weeps out of every cut creeper, itching and sore with it, ready to quit, when I hear something and stop, motionless for a moment before I turn back to Dom, who is watching me.

'Do you hear that?'

He nods.

Water. Running water. Or falling water.

I squint up through the high canopy at the blinding blue of the sky but still ask, 'Rain?'

He shakes his head, steps past me, and falls.

I reach desperately for him but he plummets, down, straight down, while I am snagged in a tangle of creepers and can only watch him drop away from me. There's this slow-motion moment when I hear myself screaming as if it is someone else and I have time to think, *I am watching him die. This is the moment when I watch him die.*

And then he hits the water. Hits it and disappears in a spreading plume of foam, gone for a thousand years while I listen to myself begging, 'Pleasepleasepleasepleaseplease be OK be OK be OK,' and then watch him surface, hear him say, 'I'm OK.'

And I let my head fall forward on to my arms and breathe there, so hard it pops something in my throat and leaves a taste of blood.

Once I recover enough to look around and to listen to Dom as he calls up to me, I realise that it's a sunken pool, fathomless and dark, at the bottom of the most incredible waterfall spilling off a towering ridge of shard rock that is hidden back here in the forest. As I make my way carefully down the sheer slope to the edge of the pool, Dom stands in the shaded water and watches me, calling out about where I should put my hands and feet, until I reach the bank and can put down the bush knife to help him clamber out.

He folds me into his arms and laughs. 'Yeah, that didn't feel so great. Pretty much wondered if that was it for me.'

But I don't think it's funny.

I tilt my head to look beyond Dom's shoulder to where water chases itself off the rock, falling in this long smooth curtain that breaks apart into a lacy spray somewhere in the middle and then comes back together again at the end. There's something terrifying about being way down here at the bottom of a rocky hole, only a circle of sky above. Suddenly all the fear overwhelms me and I tighten my arms. 'Oh God, I thought I'd lost you.'

Dom doesn't speak, just runs his hand once down my back.

'I used to lie there on Ventura feeling as if I were this living thing,' I tell him. 'This little living thing surrounded by layers of metal and layers of air and nothing else. Nothing to protect me from space, from the cold and the vacuum that would kill me instantly. It seemed so cruel always. Didn't it to you?'

He pulls away slightly so he can look at me. 'I guess I never thought about it quite like that.'

'I never imagined ... ' My throat tightens up and it's a moment before I can finish. 'I used to read and watch movies and whatever and I longed so hard for all the things that make life *life*, and I never thought I'd know them. Never thought they'd be mine. But now ... now they are.'

'We definitely got lucky,' he says.

I find his hand and bring it to my face, breathing in the salty smell of the spare bits of string and cloth he's started to keep around his wrist in case they're useful.

'The problem with having a life you love,' I say into his wrist, 'is that suddenly you have something to lose.'

He tightens his arm around me. 'You're not losing anything.'

It takes us a while to climb back up out of the well. The walls of it are draped in leaves and plants and creepers and dark blue beards of slippery moss. At one point, halfway up, one of my footholds shears away from the wall and I only don't fall because Dom sees it happening and plants his hand on my butt, pressing me against the wet earth and rock just in time. We share a look.

Huxley gets lower in the sky, and in here under the jungle canopy it gets dark sooner. Which is probably why, at this point, we hear the *meep*ing sound start up. But this time, for the first time, it is loud, clear, close. So we stop climbing, and look around.

All I see are these clumps of white flowers perched on the rim of the far side of the well, little fleshy trumpets in threes, dark leafed but somehow slightly incandescent, glowing discreetly, a little blue, and it is them; I can tell immediately that it is them making the sound.

'It's the flowers,' I tell Dom, touching his hand.

It's not as if they're moving, so I don't know how it works, some kind of combination of chemicals or whatever, but there is something in that moment, us in that clearing with those weird *meep*ing alien flower pods, and I know that probably I should be scared, probably my reaction should be fear, fear of something so totally unknown, but it isn't, and instead I am utterly floored by the amazing beauty of it all, of this planet, of Huxley-3, and I am smiling so hard it makes my ears ring. So we keep climbing. I had been right on the verge of giving up when that happened, but it renews me.

We reach the top of the headland just at the moment that Huxley is setting. Dom pauses, reaches out and pulls me in close to watch the deep red bottom rim of it sink to caress the horizon.

'When I pictured my seventeenth birthday, I never pictured it like this,' I tell him.

He tilts his head. 'What did you picture?'

I try to think, try to remember, but I can't. That other life is much too far away, too far gone, for me to ever know. I just shake my head and take hold of a lock of his hair, playing with the end of it between my fingers, where it is beginning to fade from dark at the root to a deep honey blond at the tip. 'Do you ever wonder whether we're just dreaming all this?' I say.

He laughs. 'No, why?'

'Doesn't it just ... sometimes seem a little ... too good to be true?'

He makes a face. 'It has its moments, like today ...' He leans down to kiss me. 'But ... there's something distinctly not dreamy about the smell of the latrine pit, don't you think?'

I laugh, even though I am studying the sun damage, the broken-up scabs and shiny pink patches of new skin on his chest, and there is something so sad and sharp inside me.

'What if ... we never really made it? What if we got shot down, decompressed on the way here, or ran out of air, crashed into the sea and sank?'

He presses his broken lips to mine, then watches me, cups my face in his hand. 'Do birthdays always make you so ...'

'Miserable?' I supply.

'I was going to say philosophical.'

I laugh at myself while he pulls me close.

'Only happy thoughts today,' he says, and I hear it through his chest wall.

Huxley has been halved now, and the sky is lit in stripes of lilac and gold and pink. This is my favourite moment of every day, any day, by a long way; over the past few weeks

I've religiously stopped whatever I was doing to watch Huxley go down, as if I was trying to make up for all the sunsets I've missed out on in my life.

Across my chest, Dom's forearm is smooth and cool and golden. Whether this is a dream or not has never mattered less.

Chapter Five

When we get back to camp Mariana is just getting the fire going, eyes narrowed, face centimetres from the sand where she can watch its variations in light and heat. She's really good at this now, better than any of the rest of us. She's developed an instinct for it, or maybe woken one up that she had all along.

'Nice day?' she says, a smile in her voice as if she knows, as if she can sense it, which makes me want to die a little bit.

'We found these.' I show her the roots, changing the subject.

She raises her eyebrows. 'Not exactly a birthday cake, but close enough.'

'Where's Ezra?' asks Dom, looking up and down the beach, hands on hips.

'He's asleep,' says Mariana, not looking up from the nuts in the pan.

'Asleep?' Dom makes a face.

'He was tired.' She shrugs, almost sheepish.

Then Ezra steps out of the tent behind us, pulling on his T-shirt, sleep crumple lines decorating one side of his face, hair all to one side, saying, 'What'd I miss?' in a half-asleep voice.

After we eat, they sing me the birthday song. I had forgotten how much I miss Dom's singing voice.

'I wish I had my guitar,' he says afterwards, but this is something he says a lot so I just squeeze his wrist with my fingers while he sighs.

'I'm glad you *don't* have your guitar, Suarez, if that's any consolation,' says Ezra.

Then suddenly Dom says, 'Oh my God,' and sits up straight so quickly he takes me with him. We are both looking along the line of his arm as he points to where they lie, marking the edge of the tide, like fallen stars.

'What are they?' Mariana asks, though it seems as if none of us are breathing. 'Are they ... alive?'

We go to them then, but slowly, feet squeaking in the cool sand. They are intensely purple-violet orbs of light, more of them carried in with each gentle lap of the sea and only visible as they touch land, twinkling there.

Dom is the first to scoop one on to the end of his finger and look at it, so close he is cross-eyed, face lit by its shine.

'What is it?' I whisper as if I'm in church, but he only squints at it.

Ezra gets one on to his finger too, shakes his head at

it, pinches it between thumb and forefinger so that the light spreads suddenly like glowing paint. He laughs, gets another, paints a stripe of light along his inner forearm, scoops a few into his palm and walks towards me as he picks one out, showing it to me.

'Happy birthday, Hemple,' he says, before pressing it against my cheek, painting it there so that some of its light bleeds into my field of vision.

'But . . . what are they?' I ask him as he mashes another on to my wrist, streaking it up on to the back of my hand. 'Aren't they life forms?'

Dom nods, shooting Ezra a look. 'They're animals.'

'Tiny little aliens,' says Mariana, kneeling in the sand next to the line of them and peering.

I study the streak of light on the back of my hand as it begins to fade. 'So aren't you . . . crushing them? Killing them?'

Ezra shrugs. 'I guess so, but it's still beautiful,' he says, only dimly visible in the starlight, moonlight. 'It's just another unlived life, Hemple. The universe is full of them.'

And I look from him back to the line of beached stars, legions of them, lighting, fading, being replaced with every breaking wave.

'Is this it?' says Mariana, gazing at the light she cups in her hands. 'First Contact?'

Ezra laughs. 'First Contact of the algae kind.'

'But . . . ?'

'Let me enlighten you,' says Ezra. 'Since you don't seem to have learned an awful lot in your life. Definition of First Contact: meeting of two cultures who were previously unaware of each other. Two cultures. Two races of *sentient* beings. Weren't your ancestors Spanish? Shouldn't you know this? You guys practically invented this when you busted in on the Americas.'

She rolls her eyes. 'Earth history was never my specialist subject.'

He looks amused. 'What *was* your specialist subject?'

'Wouldn't you like to know?'

'I think I would, actually.' He steps closer to her and for a minute I am completely distracted, watching the way he gets right in her space before she shoots him a look and turns away.

He laughs it off. 'Look, what I'm saying is, it's beautiful, but it's not significant enough to get excited about. These are chemical reactions, basically.'

I watch him before saying, 'It must be nice to know everything.'

He laughs again, stretches his arms above his head, exposing pale underarms. 'Oh man, you never miss an opportunity to take a shot at me, do you?'

'You make it so easy, Lomax,' I tell him and he grabs hold of my leg so quick I don't have time to react, and he scoops me, carrying me as he runs into the water and throws me out to where the moons are reflected. I shatter through the surface, only just taking a breath before I go under.

By the time I stop coughing and stand back up he is next to me, laughing, hip deep in the water, taking my hands to steady me.

'I can't believe you did that.' I shake my head at him.

'Hemple, it's your birthday – what do you expect? And you're not going to die from a bit of water, jeez.' But then he's frozen, frowning, staring out towards the horizon, face lit, and he says, 'What the . . . ?'

I push my wet hair off my face and turn to follow his gaze, out to where the water is pale and lilac and lit from below.

It's the reef, no doubt about it. We've seen it before. We've taken the decompression masks out there to look at it and it has been blue and purple and white and bristling and beautiful as a forest, but it has always been the day so we have never seen it doing this. We have never seen it glowing; shining from under the sea like a second set of stars.

'Come on,' says Ezra, before striking out for the horizon, turning back to me, treading water, calling to the others. 'Guys, come out here!'

'Ezra, no, it's rough out on the reef,' I tell him, feeling the water surge around me.

'It's not!' he calls, just as he gets to where light begins

to illuminate him from beneath. 'Get out here – seriously, you have to see this.'

Dom passes me easily, so I follow him out, ten or more full strokes before we stop, just on the inside edge of the reef.

It glows like a galaxy beneath the water. Amazing. Like the most amazing thing I can imagine. As if a universe of stars toppled out of the sky into a pile just here. It's only annoying that no matter how much I try to stay still to gaze at it, I can't, because of the way the water here surges and sways.

'Stay on this side, yeah?' says Dom, disappearing under to dive down the side of the reef for a closer look.

But I get so distracted by it that I swim across it, staying on the surface because the coral is less than half a metre below us. Only now do I realise that I'm at the edge furthest from the shore, near Ezra, who has his head down, face in the water. He lifts it out to say, 'It's amazing ... so cool ... it is literally the craziest thing I have ever seen.'

And that is when the wave catches us, both of us at the same time, sucking us up into its mouth before dumping us on to the reef, hard. He yells right at the moment I do, right at the moment I feel it catch my hip and carve a deep scrape along it. It happens in an instant and, in the aftermath, is as fiercely hot and sore as a chemical burn.

'Oh man,' I yell at the moons, and when I look at Ezra,

lit from underneath, he is flinching and breathless and down in the bright water between us there is a blooming cloud of red.

'You're bleeding, I'm bleeding, someone's bleeding.' Fear in my voice.

He tries to laugh but stops right away, winces.

'What happened?' shouts Mari. Dom is only just surfacing from a dive under the water.

I take hold of Ezra's wrist and strike out for shore, hauling him after me. Something builds in me and I'm too scared to even name it panic. When I finally find sand beneath my feet, I shove my toes in and climb for dry land, dragging Ezra behind me. Once we are out on the beach he falls and I turn to see his blood leaking on to the pale sand, where it forms dark clumps.

'Ahhhhh-ha-ha-ha-ha,' he says while he's lying down. 'It really, really hurts.'

Dom splashes out next to us, dripping on me. 'What happened?'

I can't seem to get it together to talk so he has to ask again before I say, 'A wave dumped us on the coral,' and then, seeing the flaps of flesh hanging off Ezra's ribs, I do the only thing I can think of and pull my vest off over my head, ball it in my hands, press it hard against him.

He shrieks and fights me off. 'Get off me, Hemple! What's wrong with you? You're hurting me!'

'I'm sorry but I need to stop the bleeding!'

He lets me and there's this moment where we're face-to-face, eye-to-eye, him yelling out in agony, spitting in my face when he does.

'I'm sorry,' I tell him again. 'I'm sorry but if I don't push hard it'll just keep bleeding.'

'OK,' he says, puffing out breaths in rhythm. 'OK, OK, OK.'

I hear Dom say, 'You're bleeding too,' and feel him touch my hip.

When I peer down there is this messy graze right on my hipbone and blood running down the side of my leg, diluted by seawater so that it seems orangey and loose.

'I'm OK,' I tell him.

But he's pulling his own T-shirt off and pressing it on to me, and Mari's running to the tent.

Ezra tries to laugh again, the sound becoming a yelp and then, 'What is that reef made of? How does it cut so deep? Man, it kills.' He falls back into the sand, letting his muscles go slack so that only the trembling remains. Between my fingers blood creeps into the far corners of my balled-up vest, dark in the moonlight. I spot Ezra's shirt a metre away and hook it close with my foot, folding it over and crushing it into place instead of my sopping vest that falls away like wet meat. He puffs heavy breaths, squirms and writhes away from me while I shush him.

'It's OK,' I tell him, my voice steadier than I could have hoped for. 'Just stay there, stay still for now; it's stopping,

54

it'll stop.' And then, because Dom's pulling on me and making it difficult, I say to him, 'I'm OK, just leave me, I'm OK; he's the one who's hurt; just wait, OK?'

And he lets go.

Ezra blows out more air, blows out all of it, laughs right at the bottom of his lungs so that it sounds strangely deep. 'OK, going out there was stupid,' he says, smiling a watery smile.

'It's a small victory, but I'll take it,' I tell him.

Dom helps me gather up the courage to ease the shirt away a little so we can take a look. It's pretty much a mess all along the side of his ribcage, torn-up flesh from just below his armpit right down to his hip. The good thing is the blood is darkening, getting sticky, beginning to slow up and crust. Now I'm pretty sure he's not going to bleed out I feel something flood out of me, energy draining into the cool ground, and I sit and clasp my head.

'Let me take over,' says Mari, getting back with the first aid box, pulling something out of it and giving it to Dom as she tells him, 'You need to clean Seren's cut, then bandage it.'

I watch Dom's face for clues when he peels away his T-shirt to check my wound.

'Am I OK?'

He nods, and I can tell from the fading fear on his face that he is beginning to believe it.

In the end it takes both Dom and Mari to bandage

Ezra, while he shakes and cries out in pain. Afterwards they leave us lying side by side on the beach in order to fold out the cot beds we finally figured out how to set up. I turn to Ezra, look at his face, the half of it I can see that isn't pressed into the sand, anyway. His eyes are closed, lips parted, all tension gone except for a crease between his eyebrows.

'Are you OK?' I ask him.

'Yeah, of course,' he says, not opening his eyes, clearly falling into the deepest part of shock-induced sleep, irresistibly. I carry on watching him, trying to stop shaking while my hip burns. The light of the reef illuminates the night from under the water like something impossible to imagine, big and blue and relentless.

I don't realise I've fallen asleep until Dom comes back for me and scoops me up out of the sand, carrying me to bed. Being close to him like this makes me remember something suddenly and I smile up at him and say, 'Was that only this morning?'

And though he is straining under my weight I can tell from the way he smiles that he knows what I mean.

I don't know how much later it is that I am awake again, and I am shivering.

It must be bad, because it wakes Dom on the camp bed next to me, and he frowns in the dark before he whispers, 'Are you cold?'

I have to think for a second. 'I ... I don't think so.'

'You're trembling.'

'Maybe it's ...' But my teeth are chattering, and I am suddenly so weak, and I feel it then, I really feel it. A cold that's in my bones.

He notices. 'Do you want a blanket?'

My teeth are chattering so hard I can hardly get the words out. 'It's f-f-f-f-f-freezing.'

'It's really not.' He rubs at the top of my arm, but the cold has taken over, so even though I can feel that Dom is hot, sweaty, it doesn't warm me even slightly.

He stretches across to rummage a blanket out from one of the storage boxes, then drapes it over me, tucks it tight, and I realise how hard I am shaking, how much my bones are rattling with it. He takes my face in his hands and studies my eyes.

'You caught a chill or something,' he says.

'I'm fine!'

He shakes his head. 'Seren, you're not.'

'I'm just tired,' I tell him, feeling it suddenly, feeling it in my eyes that want to close again, in my body that aches, in my head that won't think.

He wraps me in his arms and spoons in behind me.

'Seren,' he breathes into the back of my neck, almost as if he's telling me off, though I know he isn't.

'What?' I try to keep the fear out of my voice but it is there all the same, spiralling.

He props himself up on one elbow and I can feel him watching the side of my face as I shiver. 'I'll get you some water.'

I don't know how much later it is that I hear Mariana's voice, speaking in Spanish for a long time before she adds in English, 'He's not right, *primo*, look at him – he can hardly breathe.'

I try to turn towards her but it's as if the air has thickened and I'm stuck. Something beeps behind me and I hear Dom say, 'Temperature of 40.2 – is that even possible? This thing must be broken.'

I feel him lay something over my forehead and try to open my eyes, fail. Another beep.

'Hers is 40.1.'

'You think maybe it had ... I don't know ... venom or something?' says Mari. 'The coral?'

I feel Dom's hand along my hairline, then the rush of air as he sighs. They go on talking for a little while after that, but in Spanish so I can't follow it. In that strange space between asleep and awake, I am opening my eyes, I am looking up into the trees, looking up at birds that line every branch, every creeper, a metallic shine on their wings, all of them watching me.

Chapter Six

Just as morning breaks, a fire starts inside me that nothing will put out.

'Estrellita, just try to drink some water, please.' Dom rubs at the back of his neck, and I want so much to tell him I'll be OK, but all I can do is make a noise that couldn't even be called a word.

I am soaked in sweat; there are actual puddles on the cot bed that my elbows slip in when I try to raise myself up and Dom has to help me into a sitting position. The messages from my brain just don't seem to be activating the muscles I need them to. He is so gentle as he holds the bottle to my lips, so sweet, that I find myself smiling at him afterwards, which makes him do it too, then he kisses me super softly on the mouth and says, 'OK?'

And I say in half a voice, 'Thanks.'

He lowers me back down and though he doesn't hold me very hard it feels as if he is crushing me.

'You're doing well,' he says, studying the way I am racked by shudders.

I don't know what really happens after that, but I come round and it is night, and Mariana is touching my shoulder to get me to drink water again and I shriek at her and scramble away into the corner, tangling myself in my blanket.

'I don't … I don't … I don't …' I pant while she shushes me, and Dom kneels next to me and takes my hand. Over their shoulders, in the dim illumination from the solar light, I see Ezra, lying flat on his back on his bed, slack-faced, ribs bandaged, shoulders shining with sweat, completely out, so lifeless it is hard to believe he isn't dead.

I let them settle me back down and Dom stays with me, playing with my fingers and frowning at me the way he does when he's worried. I still haven't stopped panting, I can't seem to; it's so hot I can barely breathe. When I twist on to my side it feels as if it's the hardest thing I've ever done and as if I could potentially break my hip by doing it. I peer over the edge of my cot bed and blink and pull away from Dom as he searches the fear on my face. How is it that the ground is gone, that we are flying, that there is nothing beneath us? Then there's the sound, a thrumming, suddenly so loud it flows through my ears into my head, filling it completely and making me clasp at it.

'What is it?' Dom takes my hands away, replacing them

with his, one each side of my face as he makes me look at him.

'Where's the ground?' Even in this state I know that it sounds stupid but I don't know how else to ask.

'Where's the ground?' he repeats, but he doesn't leave more than a beat before he puts his hand down and touches it, disturbing the surface of what I now realise is a huge puddle, swirling with motes of sand and flecks of moonlight. 'It's right here. We just got a little flooded, that's all. There's a storm tonight.'

I lay my cheek against the edge of the bed and stare down at it, watching the surface shudder as Dom moves his fingers. He lays his other hand on my head, pressing my hair flat over my ear, blocking the sound for a moment.

'That's better,' I say, closing my eyes, my own voice super loud in my head. 'The engines are so loud tonight.'

'The engines?' He half smiles. 'It's the rain, estrellita. Just the rain on the tent. Will you try to drink some water?'

He helps me sit up, then holds one of the bottles to my lips. I manage two painful gulps before turning my head away.

'Please,' he says, but I shake my head, curling into an aching ball, the shadows of former shudders gripping me for a minute, or maybe the whispers of ones to come.

He arranges the blanket on me and lies on his front

next to me, propped up on his elbows, watching me through the dark for a moment before pressing the heels of his hands into his eyes.

'It's you,' I say, surprised by my own voice. 'You brought all this water. You always do. You always did. You brought water into my life. You brought everything that I can't live without.'

He makes a noise – half laugh, half something else – then lies flat.

'Plus a whole load of things you could have lived without,' he sighs.

I shake my head. 'No, that was me,' I tell him. 'That was all me.'

And then I close my eyes, and when I open them it's light, and Dom is gone.

Mariana appears in the doorway of the tent, water running off her as if she's been swimming, and she sniffs and rubs the drips off her face, before coming in and sitting on the end of my bed.

'Are you with us today?' she asks.

'I think so,' I tell her. 'Kind of.'

'Then please eat something.' She gets up and clatters through the boxes.

After barely getting myself to the edge of the bed on quivering arms, I sink my feet into the tepid puddle beneath me and look up at her. 'I don't know if I can,' I tell her.

'You can.'

I hear the breathing then and look across at Ezra, in his bed, arms crossed over his rapidly rising and falling chest, as pale and waxy as a dummy of himself. Dom and Mari's beds are folded away so I slosh across the water between us and sit next to him. His skin is cold to the touch, his face slack.

'Ezra?'

'You won't get any sense out of him.' Mari hands me a bowl of something brown before looking down at him with a deep crease between her eyebrows. 'He's even worse than you.'

'What is this?' I look up at her.

'It's the last of the root vegetable we cooked last week.'

The smell coming off it burns in my nose. 'Couldn't I just have some sea nuts or something?'

She sighs, leans against the tent pole behind her, looks up at the orange roof, which is holding a big blister of water that she pokes at with her finger. 'We're running out of those too,' she says. 'We just ... ' She shakes her head down at her feet, almost ankle deep in brown water. 'We're struggling to keep things dry. It hasn't stopped raining since you got sick.'

Dom appears in the doorway then and stands looking at me as if he's seeing a ghost. 'You're up,' he says, squatting down near me, hand hovering close to my shoulder before making contact, as if I am something inevitably breakable.

Even though he's a little behind me I twist to him so I can see the way the water streams off his skin, as it drips off the tips of his hair on to my shoulder and makes its way down my arm.

'You're eating,' he says.

'Um,' is all I say, studying the cold brown stuff in the bowl and wondering if I can be sure of keeping it down.

Ezra moans just then – a weak, husky sound I've never heard from him before.

'He's not doing well, Dom,' I say. 'Is he?'

He shakes his head.

'What are we doing about it?'

'What are *we* doing about it?' Mariana laughs suddenly. '*We've* been busy wondering whether you were about to die, Seren, or hadn't you noticed?'

I watch her push her way back out into the teeming rain before Dom leans close to my neck and says, 'Don't worry about Mari; she's tired, and she's been so worried about you. And about, well, everything.'

I turn to him a little and he sighs through his nose, no smile, his long hair making beautiful wave shapes where it is stuck to the new hollows under his cheekbones.

'I'm going to her,' I tell him, using his slippery shoulder to struggle to my feet.

I pull back the tent flaps to look out at the world of water. The rain is pelting out of the sky, puckering and repuckering the sand, making a screen that blocks out

64

everything except the grey-green view of itself. I half walk, half stumble into the treeline and find Mariana, sorting through husks in the sand under the vague shelter of overhanging limbs. I sit in the sand opposite her and watch the way she picks up sea nuts and splits the shells, black liquid pouring out of them into the bucket between her knees.

'What is that?' I ask her.

'It's what happens to a sea nut when you don't keep it dry.' She looks up at me. It's our first real moment of eye contact since I woke and it seems to soften her. '*Por dios, amiga*, you really scared the crap out of me.' The corners of her mouth pull down. 'And now everything's just ...' She indicates the mottled, rubble-strewn beach.

I look around, then back at her. 'I'm OK now. I can help now.'

She is shaking her head. 'I don't know if you can,' she says.

I pick up one of her pile of nuts and pull the hemispheres of shell apart, watching the glob of black and grey slime that drops into the bucket.

Suddenly she makes this face as if she's going to cry, but she shrugs off my hands when I reach for her shoulders.

'Lomax just seems to be getting worse,' she says. 'It looks a horrible mess.'

'What does?'

*

Back inside, Dom moves Ezra's arm while Mari holds the solar light.

'Lumpy, see?'

I lean forward into the light, press my fingers into his side where there are these purple ridges creeping into the flesh around the sticky mess of his coral wound, marbled blue skin bunching and gathering around the edges. He makes this noise then.

'Hernf,' is how it sounds, and he swings his arm out at me, batting me away.

'It hurts him,' Mariana says into the hand that is clamped over her lips. 'He'll barely let us touch it.'

Dom frowns down at it. 'This looks seriously weird, doesn't it? It's as if there's something . . . '

'Living in there?' I finish for him, before watching him look at me, face pulled into a grimace, not even having to nod.

Ezra lies there, mostly still, but every now and then he wakes up just a little, sometimes even starts talking, but always something totally weird that doesn't make sense, such as asking us to slow down because we're moving too fast (when we aren't moving), or telling us to get the fish out of the room (when obviously there aren't any fish) or even talking to his mother (when clearly she isn't anywhere nearby).

Later, we sit him up, Mariana getting in behind him like a chair, while I spoon cold root vegetable into his mouth, but he won't wake enough to manage chewing, and he ends up just coughing it out on to his chest and fighting us off, and we have no chance of giving him any more painkillers or anything to bring his fever down.

He shouts and moans in his sleep almost all night, which in a way I'm glad about. It's his periods of stillness and silence that scare me more.

Chapter Seven

'He looks better,' I offer Mariana, lying of course, as the sun crests the horizon the next morning and I step across to where she is sitting on Ezra's bed, hers already folded away, or maybe never even having been laid out at all. I tell her I'll stay with him, hoping she'll go to my bed and get some sleep, but she doesn't move from next to me.

'We have to do something about his wound,' she says.

'Like what?' I ask her.

'I don't know – cut it out?'

'Cut it out?'

'I don't know, *amiga*, something.'

I move his arm to peel back the wet piece of gauze draped there and study the wound. There is no point denying that there is something alive in there, something making inroads into his flesh.

I stand and touch my hip, where I can still feel my own wound, sticky against my shorts. I haven't even looked at it since that night. I turn away from Mari before I pull down my waistband, peel off the edge of the patch bandage gently and brace myself before looking down. It's mostly orange, weepy and yellow, but around it there are these traces of what Ezra has, purple edges, a lumpiness to the touch. Mine is so much smaller and shallower a cut that it is like a ghost version of his.

I am swallowing when Dom appears next to me, kissing my shoulder, and immediately I pull up my shorts and say, 'There's no two ways about it. Mariana's right. We need to cut it out.'

'Cut it out?'

'We need to get him free of this, whatever it is,' insists Mariana.

Dom studies Ezra's exposed side, pushing fingers against his lower ribs, making Ezra moan and turn on the bed, shucking off the damp, yellow gauze on to the floor.

'We have no idea how to do something like that though. We could kill him.'

I watch Dom, watch him watching me. 'He might die anyway if we don't,' I say.

'We didn't cut it out of you, and you made it.'

'I wasn't anywhere near as badly hurt as him.'

'How is yours now?' He reaches for me, but I lay my hand over it.

'It's fine,' I tell him, holding his eye.

He bites his lip. 'You . . . ?' he starts, doesn't finish. 'You would be confident to actually ... do that? Cut it out of him?'

I swallow, making a clicking sound in my throat, turn to Ezra, look at him, not at the wound but at him, at his face.

'No,' I say. 'Not even a little bit. But I'd rather try it than have him die on us.'

Dom spends a while going through the medical box, then moves on to the general storage boxes. It is something from one of these that he brings to me in the end, eases into my hand before walking away a metre, then turning to check my reaction.

I only look at it then, at the small paring knife he has handed me, and I sigh.

'I don't know,' he says, sighing too. 'We don't seem to be in possession of any actual scalpels.'

I fight a wave of nausea and say, 'OK, but, it's just ... really?'

'We're screwed, man. I mean, seriously, what are we going to do? One cut from the coral reef that is right there on our doorstep, and we have no idea what to do, and it looks as if we're losing someone.'

Mariana gasps so hard it makes us both jump. 'We're not losing him!' she yells. 'We're not losing him!'

'Whoa, OK,' Dom says, and then, 'I'm sorry. Of course we're not. Don't worry, *prima*, please. *Todo estará bien.*'

We debate how we're going to do it for a while. In the

end, it seems clear that we'll just have to hold him down –
Mari at his feet and Dom at his shoulders.

And so it falls to me to be the one, and for this minute
beforehand I am breathing through the fear. I take the
knife in both my hands and I decide. I DECIDE that this
is what I am going to do. I am going to cut around every
trace of it, every trace of this thing, and that is it. After
that we will hope that his skin, his flesh, remembers itself
and grows back. I try not to think about the possibility
that he could die from the trauma of it.

I am just about to do it when Dom says, 'Wait – stop.'

And when I turn to him he says, 'I think I remember
something from a sea life documentary I watched once.'

I wait.

'It was all about how if you stood on a sea urchin –
which is this, like, spiky underwater creature . . . Anyway,
if you stood on one and got its spikes inside you, it said
you should beat it with a rock, break it up, give your body
a chance to deal with it in smaller parts.'

I blink at him.

'What if we try that? If it is growing, living, inside
him – that'll kill it.'

'Bashing at it?' I find myself saying. 'Dom, have you
seen it? Have you seen the state of him? He's . . . he's in
such a bad way.' I sit down then in the water and sand
next to the bed, with my knees up where I can lean my
forehead against them, and in the dark place I create there

my breathing is ragged and noisy. I feel Dom's fingers on my shoulders, squeezing.

'Look, we don't know what to do for the best. Of course we don't. We're on an alien planet. There's no frame of reference. We're just going to try. We're just going to keep trying and trying until we figure out what to do. We're just going to refuse to give up. And we'll work it out.'

And I reach up to my shoulder and take his hand, lace my fingers through his and pull his palm to my mouth to kiss it.

We find a rock and spend a while cleaning it, mostly to put off the inevitable. Then we stand looming over Ezra, holding the rock and looking down at him where he sleeps, covered in sweat, utterly motionless, that scowl of his in place.

Dom and Mari take their places again to hold him still, while I kneel next to the bed and peel back the gauze, flinching when it sticks a little. I pick my spot, right at the edge of the wound where it invades the healthy flesh. Then I raise the stone and bring it down.

Ezra's scream seems like the loudest, most terrifying sound Huxley-3 has ever known, and it probably is. It tears open the day, and it comes from the deepest part of him.

Mariana has gone white. 'God, *primo* – we're torturing him. We can't do this.'

'We're running out of options,' Dom says, and then, 'Aren't we?'

72

So they take hold of him again, while I hold the stone in my trembling hand and make myself do it, make myself hit him with it while he screams, wide-eyed, while the wound opens back up and bleeds, splashing on me so I can taste it, so that I am blinded by blood and pus, until I feel Dom's hand take mine and still it in the air so that I drop the stone in the rainwater I'm kneeling in and the screaming subsides, leaving only Dom's voice saying, 'OK, I think that's OK now.' He pulls me into the shelter of him. 'Well done, estrellita,' he says, touching my face, his hand coming away streaked with blood.

I am out in the rain, down at the water's edge, shouting at Huxley, pulling the seawater against my face and chest again and again and again, but it'll never be enough, so I plunge in, dressed, because it is the only way to get it off me.

By the time I get back to them, soaking wet, they've cleaned him up and bandaged him and he is sleeping, and they are sitting side by side in the doorway of the tent. Dom has his hand on Mari's back.

'We got him to take some painkillers,' says Dom. 'It's progress.'

'We should clean him with hot water really, but we can't make a fire,' says Mari, gesturing at the endless puddles and looking so tired.

'Eat something?' Dom offers me the pan, where two cold lumps of forest vegetable look dark and floppy. 'It's the last of it, until we find some more.'

But even though I'm emptier than ever, I can't imagine eating. Instead I go to Ezra, squat next to him, watch the way his eyes move under the lids, dreaming. There is blood speckled over his neck and face, like paint spattered on canvas. Just as I start feeling sick, Mari comes over and stands behind me.

'I don't know why he's bothering, but Dom's gone to look for wood,' she says, and then, gazing at Ezra, 'I haven't been this scared since ...'

I turn to her. 'Since ...?'

She shakes her head. 'I don't know if you ever got how close we were to losing him.'

A coolness creeps across the skin of my back. 'Who?' I ask, but I know she means Dom.

She sniffs against her hand. 'When Lucas was killed I knew, we all *knew*, that it was supposed to be Domingo. And I knew they weren't going to give up, which is why they recommissioned him down to Factory the next day. They said it was for misconduct, but it was just another way to arrange an accident for him.'

I lock eyes with her, barely getting the words out. 'They recommissioned him to Factory? He never told me that.'

She shrugs, blinks once, super slow. 'You know him – he wouldn't see the point in telling you something that's only going to make you sad.'

I look down at my hands. 'He loved working in Farm and Fishery.'

I'm aware of her nodding in the edge of my vision.

'I went down to Factory to see him on his break on his first day. He came out in a face mask and noise cancellers and covered in orange grease. He said it was the meat proteins. It was in his hair and everything. It stank, like something dead. And I just *begged* him to pretend to be ill, any excuse, anything, so I could get him out of there, so I could keep him safe. He wouldn't come. I could tell he was scared too, but he thought it would only cause more problems. And instead he just kept talking about you.' She almost laughs, just a sound in her nose. 'He wanted me to go and see you in Correctional. He was worried about you and about how you must be feeling. They were trying to have him killed and all he could do was worry about you.'

'Wait, when was this?'

She looks up, thinking. 'About a week before we left, I guess, a little more.'

'I'd already seen him then. I saw him at View.'

She watches me. 'Yeah, that only made him hassle me more. Every day he didn't see you bothered him. Every hour.'

She looks up at the ceiling of the tent before she says, 'I guess I was angry with you at first for doing what you did at the wedding and putting him in so much danger.' She swallows, pushes away a tear and looks back at me, arms folded. 'But he just kept telling me and everyone who would listen that it wasn't your fault. He just kept telling everyone that you were ready to go through with it – you were the one who had made that decision in everyone's best interests – but that he was the one who turned up the night before the wedding and upset you, reminded you about everything you had tried to forget.'

In the silence that follows we look at each other.

'He never really told me what happened.' I shake my head.

She laughs, but not as if something's funny. 'A lot. A lot happened while you were in there. It was pretty much a version of hell. Ventura hell.'

I swallow. 'In what way?'

'Security seizing everything, questioning everyone, and I mean *everyone*. They even had Domingo's parents in, my parents, my grandmother, even though they knew nothing. They had me in there. They had Annelise.'

'Annelise?'

'Of course. And man, her family were so upset about all of it. Her dad laid into Dom in North Cantina – did you know that?'

I shake my head, but I remember that bruise on Dom's face, just before we left.

'There was this whole ugly scene with him telling Dom that he'd never been good enough for Annelise while everyone watched. He lost it big time. "I've always known you were nothing." That's what he kept saying. "I've always known you were nothing." Dom didn't fight back, he just let him get it out. It was ... ' She gulps. 'Horrible.'

Dom comes back right then, carrying armfuls of wet wood. 'Telling bedtime stories?'

'Just talking about Ventura,' says Mariana, looking up at him. 'About how it was just before we left.'

He nods but says, 'Why?' and then, 'Come and help me work out if we can make a fire instead.'

We can't, of course, not in the teeming rain, on waterlogged sand, with wet wood, but at least it distracts us for a while.

A little later, Mari and I check on Ezra and, even though he is in a deep sleep, there is something better about the colour of him, about the way his skin feels to the touch, and even though neither of us say it, I think we both dare to wonder if it might have worked.

Dom is lying face down on my bed, his hands linked over his head as if he's bracing for something. I sit next to him and he shifts, coils an arm around my waist, opens the one eye I can see to look at me. I lay my hand on his long hair, pulling it off his face and neck, tidying it behind his ear lock by lock while he watches me. I'm about to ask him about Factory when he says, 'Thank God you're OK,' as if he's only, just now, finally believing it. 'Please don't ever scare me like that again.'

'You make it sound as if I did it on purpose,' I say, and then, 'You must be so tired.'

He tightens his arm around me and his elbow puts pressure on the wound on my hip, making me yelp.

'I'm sorry,' he says, raising himself on his forearms. 'It still hurts?'

'Yeah.'

'Let me see it.' He pulls at my vest, but I take his hand, press it between mine.

'Don't worry – please don't worry. Let's just be happy for now. Let's just do that, even if it is only for a little while, OK?'

I lower myself next to him even though there's nowhere near enough room for us both on one of these beds; we've learned this already.

'Roll over,' I tell him, pushing at his hip until he turns on his side away from me, facing the wall of the tent, and I fit in behind him, big spoon to his little one even though he's so much taller than me that this ends up with my face between his shoulder blades, where I smile against his skin. He takes my hand and threads it up under his arm and past his chest to his lips, where he says, 'Are you comfortable like this?' into my fingers.

'I'm perfect,' I say, as he falls asleep in my arms, and I watch the dark creep in.

Chapter Eight

It's another two days before Ezra properly wakes up. I open my eyes in the morning to find him standing there, scratching his chin while he looks down at me, horribly pale and about half the size he was, bound around his middle by stained bandages.

'I guess, as it turns out, I'm not going to die,' he says on an outbreath, wincing in pain as he sits on Dom's bed.

'Yeah,' I croak, trying to sit up. 'That's good.'

'Although it's still up for some debate, evidently.'

I look at his pale scalp through the greyish strings of his filthy hair, down at the white knobbles of his shoulder joints and knees.

'But hey,' he continues, hugging his arms to his sides as if he's cold, 'I'm only guessing. I have no clue what's been going on these past ... '

'Six days,' I supply.

'Six days.' He nods, managing to look impressed, and

79

then adds, 'You attacked me with a rock, Hemple.' He is half smiling.

'I'm sorry,' I say to my feet.

'No, I think I owe you one,' he says. 'I'm still here, aren't I?'

I go to find Dom, out on the beach under the vague shelter of the trees, packing things into a bag and tucking the bush knife down the back of his shorts.

'I'm going upstream to look for food,' he says.

'I'll come with you.'

He shakes his head. 'You need to rest.'

I shake my head back at him. 'I'm better at finding things. You know I am.'

Mari and Ezra watch us leave, ankle deep in surf as we tread carefully into the dripping cave of the forest.

The stream gets narrower, the overhanging trees and creepers denser, until there isn't even enough space for us to duck and edge along the way we have been, and Dom starts having to hack at branches with the bush knife until he is running with sweat and out of breath. When he takes a break, he accepts the bottle I offer him, shakes it once and says, 'Why didn't we bring more water?'

And suddenly I'm so thirsty I could cry. I squat low and squint into the wall of leaves that hem in on us.

'We'll find something soon,' I say, just before he hands me the last sip of water from the flask. 'We're close – I can feel it.'

Like a miracle I see them then: the fine spray of red leaves atop deep blue stems. I know them, and I know what lies beneath. It seems a portent, somehow – a sign. If there are these then there are more. If there are these then there are probably other things somewhere in this mess of life that we can eat, and that can sustain us. I set about digging one out with my bare fingers. But I am only just getting to it, just getting ready to lever it into my hands when it pops. Literally pops like a bubble, as if it were never really there in the first place. As if it were a dream. I raise my fingers to my nose and mouth then, but all there is is black slime that reeks. I scoop in the depression that the rupture has left, but there is nothing.

I look at Dom in horror and he looks back the same way but says, 'Probably just a bad one,' and starts prying at the next one with the bush knife, only for the exact same thing to happen, only worse. This time it kind of hisses as it blows, leaving behind a rancid, stinking ghost of itself. There's one left, and even though I know both of us are scared to do it, I reach for it, tenderness in my fingers as I seek out its shape, quiet prayers on my lips as it crumbles, annihilates itself silently, leaving only decay.

And suddenly it seems so sad. So, so, bottomlessly, achingly sad that I can't help but cry. And Dom can only watch me as I start to weep and as it gets worse he pulls me in against him and I leak these massive strings of snot against my hands and I dribble and moan and there is no point to it at all but still I can't stop.

'Let's go back,' says Dom, his voice so sad.

'NO!' I yell, surprising myself, and him too. 'We can't go back with nothing.' I push my tears away. 'You know we can't.'

He nods, and a little further on we find them, a patch of the *meep*ing flowers, but they are closed and sad and utterly devoid of light and life, meaty flesh inert and dull under a fine coating of mould. I fight the urge to panic, but it happens anyway, and there is so much fear in me that I run, run away, down the stream, away from Dom, away from all of it, until I am falling.

And then it happens. I am here and then I am there. Or maybe I am in both places, all at the same time. Because suddenly I am surrounded by light, by colour I don't recognise. I look up and the sky is flaming orange, all the treetops erased to show me its beauty more clearly, the moons riding high at their apex. I pan down, around me, expecting the forest but not finding it, finding instead a close-cut field of grass, and a path of neatly tessellating stones curving away under my feet. I am breathless, so lost but so utterly sure of it as I turn to take a step along the path.

And then it is gone.

And Dom is standing there, my hands in his, pulling me up out of the stream where I am wet, wrecked.

'Estrellita, what are you doing?'

I look around at the solid roof of trees above, the thick cloud above that, the deep gloom.

'I ... ' But there is no way to respond. 'I ... ' I try again. 'I was just ... I just saw something ... '

He holds my hands tighter. 'Talk to me,' he says.

'I could see ... I wasn't here. I was somewhere else. Different. And there was a path.'

I look around at the tight tunnel of the stream and then back at his frowning face.

'A path?' he says. 'Like ... the stream?'

'No, it was ... ' I cover my face. 'Suddenly I was just in another place completely. The trees were gone and there was this ... path.'

Dom stands with his hands on his hips, not speaking.

'I don't know.' I shake my head. 'I really don't know. That was so weird.'

He curls his arm around my shoulders and goes to pull me close, shushing me, but I resist, push back against his chest so I can look at his face.

'You don't believe me?'

'I do,' he says, but I can tell he doesn't. 'Estrellita, I'm not saying ... it's just that it's been so stressful, hasn't it? All of this has just been ... and maybe you're just ... I don't know ... wound too tight?'

'No.' I shake my head. 'It's more than that. It's not in my head. It's this place. I know it sounds nuts but I feel as if it was Huxley-3, talking to me. Trying to tell me something.'

'Well, OK, what was it saying?'

'It's not as if it was talking to me in words. It's more like ... ' I touch the plant next to me, spear the surface of its stem with my thumbnail. 'Oh, I don't know – it's hard to explain.'

'Estrellita, please, we should head back so you can get some rest.' He takes hold of my arms but I shrug him off.

'I wish I'd never told you now.'

'Don't be like that.'

'Silly me, I actually thought you'd believe me.'

'I do, I do believe you. It's not that I don't believe you. It's the exact source of it that I'm questioning, that's all.'

'You mean, whether it's all in my head or not.' I walk away from him, back towards the beach.

This is why I don't tell the others about it, and they don't notice that I'm being quiet. Since we have no food there are lots of reasons not to want to talk.

I run into Ezra on my way back from the latrine pit last thing that night. He has his bandages off for the first time and is just in his underwear and though I don't make a point of looking I see it anyway.

'Oh man,' I say. 'It glows.'

He looks down at where his wound has morphed, grown bigger if anything, parts of it now branch-like, creeping under the skin of his torso, lighting him from the inside out, blue and pale in patches where it is close to the skin, darker and redder and illuminating veins from behind where it isn't.

'Yeah,' he says.

'Yeah?' I say. 'Yeah? There's something inside you, glowing, and all you can say is "yeah"?'

He shrugs, watching me step closer.

'It's growing in there,' I tell him. 'It's ... still alive.'

We meet each other's eye in the light from it, finding only fear.

He shrugs again. 'I guess,' he says, and then, 'Does yours glow?'

I shift my eyes to the side, fingers moving to the bottom hem of my vest and pulling, but slow. Maybe the longer I don't know, the longer I can pretend it isn't true, or something like that. But I roll it up eventually, and peel back the stick-on bandage, pull it off. I see it then, glowing, pink, pale, as if I swallowed a star.

'Oh God,' I say. 'Oh God, get it out of me!' My fingers are prying at it, pushing into the hard lumps of it that have begun to make inroads into the flesh around its core. Ezra's voice comes to me as if from far away even though he's still right there.

'I don't think it's hurting us,' he says, taking my hands. 'I don't feel as if it's hurting me any more, anyway, do you?'

I shake my head.

'Things just glow here on Huxley-3.' He laughs. 'We're just, you know ... blending in with the locals.'

I try to laugh at his joke, maybe I even do a little bit, but I don't feel as if it's funny. I run back to the tent, to bed, to Dom, and then I'm almost too scared to get in with him, now it feels as if there's something living inside me.

He wakes up and sees me standing by the bed, reaches for me.

'What is it?'

But somehow I can't begin to explain. We watch each other in silence and I notice his mouth pull down on one side the way it only does when he is worried about me, before he takes hold of my shoulders, folds me into his arms, sighs against my head.

Chapter Nine

Everything is rotting, covered in stinking black webs, even the clothes we are wearing, even our blankets, even the inside surfaces of the tent. Nothing gets dry; whatever we hang up under shelter just stays wet, gets wetter. The most pressing issue is our food supply, which now only amounts to four food ration packs and the last thirty sea nuts we've been able to keep dry.

Thunder rolls so hard and heavy all day we barely get time to speak between the claps. I see Dom standing out at the waterline, and I go to him and we are both watching walls of water sweep in off the sea and letting the rain run down us, run off the end of our noses and into our mouths and drag our hair flat against our necks and we are yelling over the roar of it all as he says, 'We need a new plan.'

And I say, 'What you got?'

And he shakes his head. 'Not a lot.'

Ezra's lying on the sand near the tent door when we get back, but when we ask him for his ideas he sits up, knocking over the bucket that is collecting the crystalline string of water that has been leaking through the perished seam in the roof for days.

'How many times do I need to tell you that we need to get off this island?'

Dom growls. 'No more times, please.'

'We need to get to the mainland.' He looks at each of us in turn, while Dom leans forward and holds his head in his hands. 'I've always said we have no future here,' Ezra persists. 'This is not the kind of place we will ever get anything to grow, or anything to live. I mean, look at this. Look at it. This place is just ... it's toxic. It's too hot; it's too wet. This kind of place, in an equatorial zone – this kind of rainy season could last a long time. Like, probably, half a solar year.'

'Half a solar year?' It comes out of my mouth before I can stop it.

'Maybe more,' says Ezra, wide-eyed.

'Or maybe less,' says Dom, but Ezra ignores him, leaning forward, animated.

'I flew over the continent. I saw it. It was the kind of land that can be farmed. I don't know for sure, but I don't think it would rain like this. The boat is the way forward, Suarez. That's what we need to be doing.'

Dom starts to lose it. 'But you admit that you don't know how far it is! Or how to get there! It's just too risky, Lomax!'

Mariana has been quietly sitting cross-legged but she suddenly slams both hands into the wet sand. 'Why do you do that?'

They both look at her.

'Why do you act as if you two are the ones who get to decide what we do? There are four of us here, and we all have an opinion.'

'OK,' says Ezra, leaning closer to her. 'And yours is?'

She doesn't answer right away; she just looks back at him for this long beat.

'Mari?' says Dom. 'The whole time you've been against the idea of the stupid boat.' He picks up a handful of sand and throws it down again.

'The boat *is* stupid. The boat has always been stupid because there are so many unknowns, which would get us nowhere except killed. But getting off this island ...'
She bites her lip and stares at the sand.

Dom watches her for a minute before turning to me. 'Seren?'

'Oh man, don't ask her,' says Ezra. 'What's the point in asking her? She'll back you up, of course she will. She always does.'

'So I don't even get a vote?' I ask him.

'What's the point?' He shakes his head. 'If he said we should fly to the moons you'd agree and ask questions later.'

'Why do you feel the need to be so rude to me?'

He sighs. 'And now we're wasting even more time discussing whether I'm being rude to you or not.'

'You are being rude,' says Mariana.

There's silence then.

'We should go to 37, to at least be dry for a while,' says Dom, 'and decide from there.'

The hike back over to the first beach doesn't actually take more than about forty minutes, but it seems a lot longer with how hungry we are, and with walking in the sand feeling as if every step gets you only about half as close as you think it should, and also with Ezra still not really being up to anything above the slowest pace imaginable and having to stop all the time. We are sandwiched between the bellowing sky and the unspeakable rain, and we are so, so wet that it is impossible to imagine ever being dry again. Our bags and clothes become so heavy that we're staggering under the weight of them. We can't talk without shouting, roaring through the grey sheets that roll in and in with the thunder that tosses at the trees.

I stagger up behind Ezra just as he sits heavily in the sand.

'Come on, man!' I have to shout to be heard. 'Just . . . come on . . . it can't be much further.'

He turns to look at me but can't because of the rain beating into his eyes. Instead I can only see the top of his head, the way his scalp is pale between the thick strings of his hair, the way water runs off his chin in a stream.

'Don't even know if I can stand back up,' he yells, shaking his head. 'Just . . . I don't know . . . weak.'

Dom arrives next to me then. 'What's wrong?'

'Says he can't walk any more,' I tell him, nodding at Ezra's slumped shoulders as he kneels in the sand.

Dom squats next to him. 'I can see where we need to get to – it's ten minutes more. Max.'

'Leave me here,' says Ezra. 'Leave me here and I'll follow you later.'

Dom laughs, hauls Ezra to his feet and takes some of his weight as we move forward again. 'We can't do that, much as I'd like to.'

Mariana goes ahead just before we get to where the beach curves out of sight, stepping out in the shallows a little to see better, and when she yells something none of us catch and starts jumping up and down and running, we know, even before we see the green and black and grey streaked bulk of it, half buried in the sand at the water's edge, looking smaller than I remember, that we have made it to 37.

Luckily the main entrance hatch is on the inland side and raised, and even though it's caked in sand and salt it still opens pretty easily so we are all able to get inside, into the first truly indoor place we have been in for weeks. When we pull the heavy hatch closed there is this weird silent moment after we have all clambered to our seats, the ones we sat in on the journey here, almost on instinct, and we are sitting there, dripping onto the floor, sniffing, glancing at each other.

'Here we are again,' says Dom, the only one who's smiling as he presses his dark hair flat against his head and water issues down his neck.

I'm looking past him at the front window, which is completely blacked out by sand.

Ezra has already pulled off most of his wet clothes and is now flicking switches to see if anything will come online, while Dom brings the main systems screen to life.

'Amazing,' he says, shaking his head. 'The solar cells are full. They must store.'

'Of course they store,' sneers Ezra, which I think is a little off, considering, but whatever.

Fast forward and we have managed to dry off a little, even got some music on and it has been SO LONG since we heard any that it is almost like a foreign language to me now, almost as if the notes don't make sense. And there's something really nice about being in there with the rain battering away outside but not on us, not on us for the first time in so long, but when Dom and I finish going through the storage lockers without finding anything to eat, I feel my stomach drop away, right away into the floor.

'Um, so,' Ezra says. 'Dare I ask how the completely futile Mission Find Food is going?' He raises his eyebrows and waits for what seems like for ever while we both sit there motionless until eventually he gets it, looks back at the nav computer and says, 'Yeah, that's pretty much what I thought.'

'I'm going to go out and set up the water collection funnels,' says Dom, and I don't know how he can bear to go back out in it but he does, kissing me on the head as he passes.

Mariana says, 'No connection to source,' and when I look at her she is studying her pod.

'They have no functionality off-network,' says Ezra.

'I know that,' she says. 'I was wondering if you could access anything on its built-in memory.'

'Why would you want to do that?' He makes a face.

A frown creases her forehead. 'Don't you miss anyone?' she asks him. 'Don't you even miss your brother?'

And when Ezra doesn't answer, and there's this silence that could be sad, she laughs into it.

'I always thought it was weird, you know, how much he looked like you. Like, I don't know, two people who look exactly the same. It's weird, isn't it? Freakish.'

He rends the front off the nav screen. 'Moreno, I think you'll find that's kind of the way it works with identical twins.'

'It's still eerie,' she says, shuddering, then to me, 'What about you, Seren? Who do you miss?'

I don't have time to react before Ezra says, 'Emme Wong?'

I laugh and shake my head.

'Who's Emme Wong?' Mariana asks him, but he seems lost in thought for a moment and doesn't answer.

'She was my best friend all through Education,' I say, and I remember something then. 'She was so hot for you, Ezra – did you know that?'

'And you tell me this *now*?' he says, but there is something in his tone and the way he smiles.

'As if you didn't know.'

He doesn't miss a beat. 'OK, I knew.' He smirks. 'She made damn sure I knew.' He notices the look I give him. 'What? You're not seriously going to act like you care.'

'I don't,' I say, too fast. 'Of course I don't. I'm just surprised she took that risk, to be honest.'

He laughs. 'I'm worth it. Besides, some of us know how to be discreet. Some of us know how to go about our business without letting the whole world know about it.'

I'm too distracted to notice the dig. 'So you . . . you and Emme . . . '

'Cool it, Hemple, it was never a big deal. It wasn't some kind of star-crossed, true love, Romeo and Juliet thing – you and Suarez cornered the market on that one.' He forces this weird laugh and says, 'It was, you know, casual. More like a friendship with benefits. Just the way I like it. You let yourself get in too deep with someone on Ventura and you were asking for trouble. You sure found that out the hard way.'

I frown at him. 'You say that as if we decided to do it. As if we set out to fall in love, but that isn't what happened.'

'I'm not saying you decided on it, but you didn't do much to prevent it.'

I'm shaking my head. 'You can't prevent something like that. We started talking that day and it was like . . . ' I can't think of the words. 'So inevitable. I hardly knew him but already I couldn't stop thinking about him. Whenever I wasn't with him I would think of all these things I wanted to say to him, to talk to him about, and I just . . . I'd never felt that way about anyone before.'

I turn to Mariana and she is watching me, this look in her eyes that is so gentle I hardly recognise it.

Ezra laughs. 'Yeah, and I mean, of course, it had nothing to do with him being this tall, dark guitar-playing Latino love god? That was all irrelevant, right?'

'Shut up, Lomax,' says Mariana. 'Just because you don't recognise feelings that emanate from anywhere above the waist, you don't need to bring us all down to your level.'

'What's your problem, Moreno?' he says. 'Whatever else it becomes, *every* sexual relationship starts out ninety per cent based on a desire to jump each other's bones – that's just a fact of life. That's called being a human. Personally I don't even think there's anything wrong with that. You think Hemple and your perfect *primo* have been elevated on to some higher plane by this love story of theirs but the truth is they're just like the rest of us. They're just animals. They're just looking for the best way to continue their line like an animal does. Yes, even them. No, actually, wait, *especially* them.'

'What are you talking about?' says Mariana, making a face. 'Stop picking a fight just because you're hungry.'

But he isn't listening. 'She hardly knew him,' he says, jabbing a finger at me. 'She hardly even knew him when she decided she –' he makes quotes in the air – 'loved him. What was really going on was that she *wanted* him. She wanted him *bad*. And the upshot is, because of that, a whole load of ridiculous things happened in such a way that now, half a year later, here we are – sitting on a beach on some backwater alien planet, in the hammering rain, with nothing to eat and no plan, and it's all because you and Suarez wanted to get into each other's pants.'

Neither of us speak, we just watch him, before he adds, 'It's a hell of a butterfly effect, when you think about it,' and laughs.

The hatch opens and Dom lowers himself back in, dripping on the floor and saying, 'What'd I miss?'

Chapter Ten

So later we're sitting watching this movie, one Dom chooses because he's seen it before and he thought it was good, and it's about these people who get to visit other people's dreams so that they can put ideas in their minds but they have to be careful or they get stuck there and because it's a dream they experience it like an eternity even though in the real world it's only about ten minutes or whatever, and it is super hard to follow and really needs concentration but at a certain point I get totally distracted. Because I am sitting on Dom's lap and he's wearing his old hooded Ventura jacket, and it's been so long since I've seen him in it and yet it is so familiar, it is the most familiar thing in the world, and I still love the way it looks on him, especially since he's bare-chested under it. I bury my face against it and trace my finger along the lines of the Ventura logo and the place where his surname is stitched neatly underneath, and it is making me remember so completely how it was in those first days and weeks when I was realising I was in love with him.

'I didn't know you still had this,' I tell him.

'I guess I left it here. Yours is probably here too, somewhere.' He looks around.

I breathe against it some more and then ask, 'Do you think about it? Ventura?'

'Of course. But ... less often now, I guess.'

'Do you ever wish you were back there?'

'Nah.' I can feel his fingers where they play along the top of my shorts, slide along to the small of my back, and then he turns to me more and says, 'Do you?'

And I shake my head. 'You were the only thing I ever really liked about it and I've got you here.' We smile at each other, and I let my head fall back on his shoulder before I add, 'But sometimes I think back to you and me then, to when being together was the only thing that mattered to either of us.'

He looks at me sideways, frowns a little, before he says, 'It doesn't matter to us now?'

And I say, 'Oh, of course it *does*, it just ... there are so many other things to worry about now, you know?'

He pulls my head in against him and plants a kiss on my hair, then says, 'It's still the most important thing to *me*, estrellita.'

And though he says this and I know I should be happy that he does, I can't help wondering how true it really is, with things the way they are.

When the movie finishes he gets up to switch it off and I stand behind him, stretching and yawning.

I glance over my shoulder to where Mariana is curled over on her side, snoring gently, and two seats away is Ezra, the worry somehow erased from his face now that he's asleep. When I turn back to Dom he leans down to me, kisses me. And I pull him close and open my mouth even though I know it'll make us both crazy, and it does. I feel his hand move from my jaw to my throat to my chest, down my side to my waist, sliding in under my vest and on to the small of my back and we are both breathing hard through our noses and he disengages a little and speaks against my mouth, 'I love you so much, you know that, right?'

And I am nodding as I bite at his lower lip, pushing my hand inside his jacket and down his chest and stomach, round to the muscles that flank his spine, down under the back waistband of his shorts, and he is pushing me against the wall of open locker doors, making them clang.

'Jeez,' says Ezra, stirring. 'Don't mind us, guys – just go ahead and pretend we're not here.'

Dom sighs hard. 'Come on,' he says to me.

'To where?'

'I don't know. Out.'

He looks at me and I look at the way his lips are still shining from where I've been kissing him and I want to kiss him again so bad, want to be alone with him more than anything, and this is the only reason I let him lead me to the hatch, even though I can hear the way the rain is drumming on the outside of the shuttle. And it's only because I happen to glance back at him as I pull myself up and out that I notice the way Ezra is peering around the seat at us and rolling his eyes.

Outside of the shuttle it is a kind of hell, pouring insane amounts of water out of a starless black, but actually weirdly warm. I start to tell Dom something but give up when he picks me up and pushes my back against the slick hull of 37, his lips on my throat. I know exactly what he wants and I want it too, want so much to make him know how much I feel him in my bones, my flesh, my soul. But then some small part of me remembers, and I say, 'But we can't.'

And he says, 'We can,' and kisses me so sweet, sucking the water off my chest and shoulders and sliding my vest up with his thumbs.

'We can't, Dom,' I tell him again, shaking my head. 'We can't.'

'Don't worry about it,' he breathes.

We end up down in the sand where it's hard and wet and warm and alive beneath me and because he's on top of me the rain doesn't pelt on me but where his hair touches me it runs on to my skin in tiny rivers, and when I slide my hands to his back I feel the way the water hits him like bullets. And when he kisses me on the part of my chest which is rising and falling with my breath and I push my hands down the back of his shorts, pull him to me and hear the sound he makes against my ear, it is impossible to remember the reason this can't happen, when it feels as if this is something I need, like nobody ever needed anything before.

But somehow I find the will to push at his chest, slide back, pull myself out from under him until I am sitting with my back against 37 and looking at him in the dark, as water streams sideways off his chin and he is bruised in patches with the sand and panting a little and there is this look in his eyes that makes me say, 'You know how much I want to,' and because of the rain I am shouting.

'So what's the problem?' He's shouting too.

I'm so shocked I hardly know what to say, waiting for his face to show me some sign of recognition, which it doesn't, so that in the end I say, 'Dom, you know what the problem is.'

He just looks away, into the darkness, as he pulls my legs from either side of his hips, passes them back to me, and shifts position until he is sitting. He tilts his head back, eyes closed, letting the water batter his face.

'Man, Seren, the way things are going we won't even survive another nine months, so why worry about it?'

I shudder and, past the solid mass in my throat, I manage to shout back, 'What are you saying?'

And he looks at me and says, 'Well I'm sorry, but we

won't,' and shrugs. 'It's just ... come on, let's face it. Things aren't looking great right now.' He laughs. 'And that's an understatement.'

And the water pours out of the clouds and soaks us with it, with the truth of the life here that we could never have known or predicted and which we have no way out of. And the hardest truth of all of them is that Dom doesn't believe any more, that his hope is gone, because mine is so fixed to his, and without his I can feel mine drifting away. He must see it on my face even in this seething darkness because he moves closer, takes my face in his hands, starts to say something, but I am shaking my head, pushing at his shoulders, and saying, 'Let's just go back inside – it's horrible out here.' And even though he tries to stop me I haul myself up to the hatch, shunting it open and dropping through, only realising once I am inside again how wet and how coated in sand I am.

Ezra is watching me as I pull my vest down over my stomach and put my hand into my sand-filled dreadlocked hair and he says, 'Classy, Hemple. Really classy.' But I hardly even hear him, because Dom is landing on the floor next to me and pulling the hatch closed, and we are eying each other, and at the same time we both freeze listening to the weird noise coming out of the speakers.

'What is that?' says Dom, just as I'm thinking it.

'The shuttle's com,' says Ezra, as if it should have been obvious. 'I just turned it on.'

And so we just listen to the noise of the com, still tuned to the Ventura's frequency, as it beeps. Three beeps, a gap, three beeps again, a gap. Out of range.

'Turn it off, Ezra, it's annoying,' says Dom, pinching the bridge of his nose and going to his seat.

'What's the frequency of the Eridani signal? Let's see how those guys are doing.'

'Don't be ridiculous – you'll never pick that up on this.'

Then, suddenly, Ezra sits up straight, leans forward, stares at the screen. 'What the . . . ?'

'What is it?' I ask.

'It's picking up another signal.'

I feel my scalp creep under my hair as Dom does this breathy laugh and says, 'Whatever, Lomax.'

'No, I'm serious,' says Ezra, and you can tell from the look in his wide eyes when he turns to us that he is.

'A signal?' Dom says, leaning over Ezra's shoulders to look at the screen. 'From what? From where?

Ezra shakes his head. 'I don't . . . I'm not sure. How would I . . . ? Can you even . . . ?'

'Well, tune to it,' says Dom, and I swear we are all holding our breath while he moves his finger over the screen and it comes on over the system.

A hiss, some popping, like something frying, and underneath it a whine.

'What is that?' says Mariana, just waking up and squinting in the cabin light. I go to her chair and sit on the arm of it, next to her.

'A signal,' I manage, watching her frown.

'Like ... but ... ?' is what she says, which is exactly what we're all thinking. So we sit there and listen to it.

I watch Dom run the side of his thumb back and forth along his lip the way he does when he's thinking. 'It's some kind of magnetic ... interference thing or ... I don't know ... ' He shakes his head. 'It doesn't sound like anything to me.'

Ezra squints at the coms screen. 'It quite clearly says here that it's a signal.'

Dom shrugs it off. 'Yeah, but listen to it.'

We do for a few minutes more and it's just hissing, a two-tone whine that runs underneath, a sporadic crackle, and you can tell that Ezra is thinking about switching it back off when Mariana says, 'Unless it's data?'

It takes a few seconds before we all turn to her, before we let it register, before Ezra is clipping the coms screen back into its dock so he can switch the receiver into data mode. We all move over to stand behind his seat, leaning in over his shoulders to look at the pale loading progress bar on the screen, and then *bang*: data. Thousands and thousands of lines of it, filling the screen and scrolling endlessly.

'Holy crap,' says Ezra.

And no one else says anything at all. We just sit there watching it fill the lines many times over, the pixels purring with it.

'What . . . ' I say after a minute or so. 'What does it say?'

But nobody answers me.

'What does it mean?' I try again. 'What kind of data is it?'

'I guess . . . ' Ezra tries a few buttons. 'I mean . . . I don't think we can read it or decode it or whatever.' He swipes at the screen with all five fingers to freeze the view and we all peer at it, into it, as if it's some weird window.

Most of the letters, symbols, whatever, aren't even anything I've seen before.

'Is it Eridani?' asks Dom.

'I don't think so,' says Ezra. 'Eridani's a long range radio signal, using electromagnetic pulses, and this is . . . ' He makes gestures in the air but doesn't finish.

'Can you get a fix on it?' asks Dom. 'A source, or . . . ?'

When Ezra doesn't move, Dom eases the screen out of his hand and pulls menus down with a fingertip, choosing different options until a black box pops up and seems to run some kind of scan. Because he stands back up to his full height, screen held in one hand and the other on the ceiling, we can't watch the scan finish. We only hear it beep, watch the way his expression freezes.

'Local signal,' he says. 'Within two hundred kilometres.'

My hair lifts at the roots and a cold creeps down my arms, prising flesh from bone.

Mariana shakes her head. 'It's . . . it's impossible. It must be a mistake, right?' She looks round at us all.

Ezra takes the screen back and starts messing with it again.

Mariana keeps talking. 'I mean, there can't be . . . people or aliens or whatever here on Huxley-3, can there? I mean, how can there be? We would have known about them before. The recons – there were the recons . . . ' She turns to Ezra. 'You! You were on the recons.'

Ezra cuts her a glance. 'Yeah, Moreno, by the way, there was a huge alien civilisation here and I just forgot to mention it.'

'We're jumping to conclusions.' Dom shakes his head, still leaning against the ceiling. 'It's not . . . it must be a mistake. It's just . . . '

'Too huge?' supplies Mariana.

'Too terrifying to comprehend?' I try.

'I can't deal with this,' Mariana says. 'I can't deal with any of it. I mean, what are we talking about here? Aliens? Aliens with computers? I mean, this is an uninhabited planet! We know it is. There is nothing living here. Nothing bigger than an amoeba, anyway. Well, except weird plants and glowing coral and stars that live in the sea. And now we're actually . . . ' She runs out of words for a minute, shakes her head. 'I thought it was how alone we were that scared me more than anything, but now . . . '

Dom leans his head to one side. 'It might not be what it seems.'

'Well, then what could it be?' I ask.

'All I know is we've seen some pretty freaky things on this planet so – who knows?'

We watch it come through in silence, with no ideas that make any sense.

After a while Ezra says, 'OK, most logical explanation? My thoughts would be that it's something Ventura left here for some reason, a beacon producing an encrypted data stream. It could be something as simple as a research tool for Science, a communication relay . . . something for my mother's own, darker ends . . . I don't know. What I do know is this: there's only a very small chance that it's aliens.' He laughs. 'There can't be life forms intelligent enough to communicate digitally on this planet. If there were it would have made way too many dreams come true to ignore. It's something else . . . ' He considers the purring pixels in silence. 'Only one thing's for sure. We have to go and find out.'

He looks at each of us in turn but none of us speak.

'We can get a fix on it, take the boat, track it to source,' he adds.

I sigh. 'But why would we do that? Take that kind of risk for something that could be a beacon or a relay or just nothing?'

He widens his eyes. 'Because we have no better plan, Hemple,' he says. 'And, I mean –' he turns back to the screen – 'it has to be something . . . '

I look at Dom, who laughs and says, 'Well, whatever. At this point, we are so screwed it doesn't make much difference.'

He's standing close to me, his arm around my shoulders, but I lean back so I can see him, the cold, unfamiliar look on his face. He notices, and says, 'What?'

'I'm just not used to hearing you talk like this.'

'Well, I guess you're probably going to have to get used to it.'

'I just want to go to sleep,' I tell him, suddenly so tired I can taste it, can hear it in my ringing ears. I go to my chair and, even though he follows me, I curl over on to my side away from him. After a minute he puts his hand on my leg.

'You mad with me?' he asks, but I can hear a smile in his voice.

'Why would I be?'

'No idea, but, you know, there are times you're still a mystery to me.'

'Amen to that,' says Ezra, reminding us he's listening.

Dom leans over to peer at my face so I close my eyes and pretend to be asleep, swallowing something, but I'm not sure if it's anger, or fear.

Mariana curls up on the next seat, but I can hear

that she isn't sleeping any more than I am. Too much shifting, her breathing too shallow. So even though we are both there with our eyes shut and pretending to be asleep we are actually just listening to Dom and Ezra, who are sitting in pilot and co-pilot, talking in circles about the signal. After a while, Mariana makes this one short sound, almost like a sob, and I realise she is falling asleep but dreaming already, slipping straight from the nightmare we're living in into one of her own making.

Chapter Eleven

In the morning it isn't raining.

I know this because I notice the sound, or lack of it, when I wake up, unstick myself from my seat and sit up, wondering what's different. I'm looking over at Dom, face down on the co-pilot seat with his arm hanging, fingertips touching the floor, and then I realise.

I pop the hatch as quiet as I can and lift myself out, easing it closed behind me. I just want the beach to myself for a bit, the hard wet sand steaming beneath my feet. There is sun breaking through clouds, fiercely hot, baking the moisture out of the sodden world, filling the air with heat and a damp so rich I can taste it. The sea is completely flat, almost viscous, easing in and out like soup, and all along the beach the trees are tattered and there are broken-up bits of tree-fall and driftwood lying in the sand like fallen soldiers on a battlefield.

I pull my mouldy trousers off my legs where it feels as

if they are welded and leave them in the sand, walking down to the sea in my underwear. I'm sitting in the hot shallows, thinking about my headache and my hunger and how sick I feel, and I have absolutely no idea how long I've been there when I hear something moving in the water behind me and when I turn it is Dom. He is up to his knees, scooping up water and splashing it on his face, rubbing his hands there, while the water runs away down his chest and stomach and he groans.

'Man, I'm so hungry I could be sick right now,' he says, laughing, squinting at me, and shaking his head.

'Nice morning, though,' I say, looking up at the patches of blue.

'Hmmm,' he says, but I get the feeling he doesn't trust it and I know why when I look out to the horizon and see the clouds that practically bubble up and billow as we watch.

He sits, soaking his shorts as he lowers himself into the water and crooks his knees up either side of my back, swiping his hand down my spine.

'That signal's still going.' He shakes his head. 'Crazy.'

I am watching him over my shoulder and I nod but then I turn back round, look out to sea, even though I feel the way his fingers stay on my good hip, putting just this tiny bit of pressure on me there to make me slide back against him, which I don't. I feel him look at me, feel him study the sliver of my profile he can still see for clues, but I guess he doesn't find them, and I feel a little sad about it.

He sighs again, and so do I, and then he says, 'Since there's a break in the weather, we should really get started on sorting out the boat.'

'Yeah?' I say. 'You want to?'

He shrugs but says, 'I guess it's all we've got,' and he gets up, pulls me up, leans forward and kisses me, a kiss that lands on the very corner of my mouth. I feel myself fall into him; I pull him close and smooth my palms along the small of his back. It's annoying, the way he does this to me; even when I'm mad at him, I want him.

'I still have faith, you know,' he says, mouth right against the skin near my ear, just as the sun goes behind a cloud.

'Faith?'

'I still believe in Huxley-3, the way you do, the way you always have. I still believe we'll find a way to a good life here.'

'You didn't last night.'

'I was ... let's call it a dark moment.' He takes my hand and squeezes my fingers together. 'We just haven't managed to make it work yet. But I am not giving up. Not as long as there are any options left. I pretty much hate Ezra's plan, but we can't give up. I won't. I never will.'

'OK,' I sigh, and then add, 'But for the record, I've

never believed in Huxley-3. It's you I believe in. It's us,' and I walk towards the shore, pulling him after me.

Considering how much time he's spent thinking about it, Ezra is amazingly light on actual plans.

'What we need is to rig the nav screen to this solar cell,' he says, sitting in a selection of detritus on the beach. 'You know how to do that, right, Moreno? You're a technician.'

'Are you for real?'

He laughs. 'I'm counting on you,' he says, and then, 'It's the only way we're going to be able to track the source of the signal, as far as I can work out.'

The boat self-inflates, so we lay it out flat and hit the button, watching it puff up like a beast coming to life limb by limb. But the wind is picking up again, and we watch in horror as there's suddenly a gust and it soars into the air and does a sickening series of vaults down the beach, stopping upside down two-hundred metres away with an alarming crack.

'Let's just hope that wasn't the on-board motor smashing itself to pieces,' says Mari, watching Dom and Ezra take off after it before we follow them, a little slower.

We pack light; we have to. No spare anything. Just the food we have, the water we have managed to boil and bottle during the day, plus the still. Spare solar cells. Blankets. The silver rain canopy as shelter. The nav screen that Mari managed to rig to a solar cell and to the receiver/transmitter that she pilfered out of 37's dash. Looking at it all, it seems like way too little to show for a life, never mind four lives. But here we are, standing on the shore, waves marching in and us with no clue how to get past them and, I swear, it's like trying to escape Ventura all over again.

As if he's reading my mind, Dom says, 'Ever feel as if you've been here before?'

I turn back to look at the island. Pinkish sand, the purple wall of the jungle, the shining black of the shard mountain – when did it start feeling like home?

Dom's arm passes across the front of my chest. 'We tried so hard, estrellita,' he breathes against my ear.

Something makes me think of the moment when I ran away down the stream. That path. 'I still wonder if the island was trying to tell us something,' I say.

'Maybe it was,' he muses. 'Maybe it was telling us to get out of here.'

We nearly don't make it out alive. The boat is way softer and more flexible than I was expecting, so that it is bent almost in two by the waves as we power our way out. We have literally only been going for a minute when Ezra gets dumped clean out of the front, and is under the sea before he can even make a noise, and we spend these horrible moments circling back to haul him out of the surging foam.

All this, and we are still in sight of the island.

All that day the wind seeks us out along the surface of the ocean like an angry monster. It whips the canopy, wrenching it from our hands, seizing it, jerking it.

Then there are the waves. Climb and crash, climb and crash. A relentless and brutal rhythm, but one we somehow adjust to. Even when the gaps widen, even when the climbs get steeper and longer and the drops sharper, the time in the air longer, we manage to cling on. Each wave is a hill, then a mountain. A mountain of water that we are falling off the top of. The sickness comes then, but it's nowhere near as hard to deal with as the fear. And then night falls, and the solar-powered engine cuts out, and it's impossible to know if we're moving forward or being washed uncontrollably back towards the island.

But, with dawn, the storm seems to lose heart. I pull the canopy off to find an endless expanse of blue with no island in sight. The rising sun almost seems to be lighting the way.

Ezra checks the nav. 'We're two hundred and eight kilometres out from the signal source.'

'Isn't that further than we were in the first place?' asks Mari, and it is the very thing we are all thinking.

'Yes, it is,' says Dom and he sits and starts messing with the still. 'Drink some water,' he adds, handing me the bottle.

'What do we have to eat?' asks Ezra, and Mari stretches herself across the base of the boat, rustles, produces something to which his response is, 'Oh man, this sucks so bad.'

There's barely a drop of rain all day as we take it in turns to steer and navigate. I can almost believe that we've got beyond the storms, but it's not something I'd dare to say out loud.

Later, when night falls and the engine cuts again, we manage to think things through enough to drop the anchor, and there's something weird about hearing it scrape on the seabed, far below. Everyone falls asleep pretty much instantly, rocked in the hammocky base of the boat, but in the darkest part of the night something wakes me. I lever myself up on the boat's spongy edge and peer into the dark water to find it lit in a streak, mirroring almost exactly the galaxy above, stretching away in a long, long line, beautifully violet: a shoal of sea stars.

'Hello,' I breathe to them. 'You're here.' I hear movement close by and realise Ezra has woken up too, and is watching them with me.

This goes on for a few minutes, peacefully, but then, 'Look,' he says suddenly, and there is so much in his voice. 'Along there.'

And so I look, along the line they describe in the sea, and off into the distance, to where there is something new, something odd, all lit in pink light, a long, low shape on the horizon.

'Is it . . . a boat?' He sounds unsure, sitting upright. 'Has to be,' he adds, and then, 'Suarez!'

Dom wakes quickly, and I haven't even managed to still the hectic, sickening coursing of my blood from the shock of seeing this thing by the time he and Mariana are both sitting and saying, 'What? What is it?'

And Ezra is pointing at this pink shape and his face is partially illuminated by the light from it, but the weird thing is that both of them just turn back to him and say, 'What?'

And so Ezra says, 'Well, grab an oar, genius, because we need to get to it,' and he has his oar in his hands.

But Mari says, 'Get to what?'

And Dom takes hold of his oar but just squints out at the horizon and then back at us. 'What did you see?'

'That,' I tell him, pointing. 'That right there.'

I watch his amber eyes scan the horizon before coming back to me again. 'What am I looking for?'

I laugh. 'That right there, Dom. That long, pink . . . '

Which is when the entire sky lights up in shades of orange and red and even blue and green. A chorus of it, so beautiful it is like music. Ezra and I make so many noises watching it, it is as if we're joining in. Curtains of it, waterfalls. Movie firework displays, bouncing off the sea. And then just as soon as it began it is over, and Ezra and I are left laughing at the sheer exhilaration.

'Oh man.' Ezra is the first to speak. 'That was wild. That was just so wild.'

But Dom and Mari are sitting on the other side of the boat, looking like two people who have no idea what's going on.

'What are you talking about?' asks Dom. 'What was wild?'

'The sky,' says Ezra. 'Those lights.'

'The sea stars, you mean?' says Mari, peering down at the water.

'Screw the sea stars.' Ezra laughs. 'Those lights were intense, man.'

Dom and Mari share another look, then turn to me.

'They were amazing!' I yell. 'How could you not see them? Wait, never mind, we need to get rowing – we need to get to the . . . ' And it's only now I scan the horizon for it again that I realise it is gone. 'Wait, where's the pink thing? Where is it?'

'Where the hell did it go?' asks Ezra, head turning almost all the way around.

'We need to get some sleep, guys,' says Dom. 'It's actually really important, survival-wise, that we do that.'

I look at him in amazement. 'But didn't you – there was something – didn't you . . . ?' I realise then. 'You didn't see anything?'

He frowns, shakes his head. I turn to Ezra. 'But you did?'

He's still scanning the horizon, sitting up on the edge of the boat, oar ready, so much so that he only turns back to me briefly to say, 'Oh I saw it. I saw all of it. There's something out there, for sure.'

I go through the bags then until I find them – this little set of binoculars in the tool kit. I hate using them because I never seem to be able to see through them properly but I check the horizon anyway, the whole three-sixty of it, while Ezra refreshes the scan on the nav screen.

'Anything?' I hear him ask.

I shake my head. 'You?'

'No.' He takes the binoculars from me.

It's only now I realise how tired I am, how weak, that my lips and fingertips are numb and buzzing with exhaustion and hunger. Dom and Mari look as if they've already fallen back asleep, heads together against the back edge of the boat. I lay my head on Dom's lap and feel his hand on my hair.

'There was all this light,' I whisper, watching Ezra sweeping the horizon.

'Rest,' I hear Dom say, which is actually annoying enough that I sit back up and am about to call him out on it when I see how asleep he is, how tired, how thin he looks, dark depressions dividing his cheeks from under his eyes all the way down to his jaw. I look back at Ezra, still using the binoculars and balancing his oar across his lap, and because he has no shirt on I can see the way his coral scar is lighting up the side of his torso gruesomely in pink and blue branches, despite the heavy shadow of dark bruising and scabs that I inflicted on him. It glows so hard that he almost has his own source of light.

I sneak my fingers down to my hip, to where it is hot to the touch, and lift my top, wincing with the prick of sharp pain I have been feeling a lot but mostly ignoring. It casts its bluish light beneath my skin. Is it bigger? There's definitely a pale branch of it that's new, reaching along my stomach. I press and it is hard against my fingertips. There is so much in it that I can't bear, all I can do is shut my eyes tight, curl into a ball, tremble.

The solar motor starts up by itself at dawn and Mari sits steering it, yawning so hard her eyes stream. The waves are small, a fresh wind skimming along everything, but all there is is us and endless water, endless sky. She sees me awake and says, 'Pass me the nav.'

I lean over Ezra where he is curled away from me and pry it out of his hands.

The signal source is still to our north-north-east, closer but barely. I let her see it too.

She raises an eyebrow, managing to seem amazingly calm about it.

'A hundred and eight kilometres to go,' she says. 'Man, I feel sick.'

There isn't a lot to do that morning except take our turns steering and then lie in the bottom of the boat, feeling the way the water moves beneath us like something living. When the sun is straight above, the high humming sound I wasn't even noticing purrs to a stop. I lever myself on to my elbow and look at the still, reach to touch it. When I start pulling off pieces of it Dom notices and rests his chin on my shoulder.

'What are you doing?' he says, voice sluggish.

'I think it just stopped,' I whisper, glancing at the other end of the boat where Ezra steers and Mari sits at his feet, studying the screen.

We pull the still apart in the end, at which point the others obviously notice. By the time we conclude that it is dead the sun is beginning to set again and there is this stillness falling on all of us.

'How much water do we have left?' asks Mari.

I show her two half-filled bottles. It sits there, like a physical weight in the centre of the boat: doom. The stupid doomed plan. The inevitability of it all. In the end, Ezra himself says, 'Come on then, let's hear about how stupid my plan was and how you knew this was going to happen,' but none of us say anything.

Another night. The engine gives us about half an hour of travelling in the dark before it stutters to a stop and we have to drop anchor again. We ration out sips of water and bites of sea nut. The sea is oddly calm, flatter than we've ever seen it. It's colder, too, but the sky is clear and full of stars.

I watch the light of the nav screen on Dom's face. 'We

should be close. To whatever it is. Thirty-seven kilometres. Let's just hope it's . . . I don't know . . . *something*.'

'What do you think it is?' I ask him, laying my head on his chest and watching the moons.

'Um . . . Beautiful piece of coastline with a little house on it. Cosy little kitchen with cupboards full of food. Situated by a lake full of fish. Something like that.'

I lift my face to kiss him and hurt his broken lip doing it. He squeezes my hip and aggravates my coral wound.

'It still hurts?' he asks.

'It glows, too.' I swallow, glad to finally admit it.

'Show me,' he says, and I can hear in his voice that he knew already, and maybe just didn't want to think about it. He's seen Ezra's, after all.

He watches while I move my clothes so he can see. I feel his breath on it as he leans close, studies it, then lies back down, and all he says is, 'I'm sure it's nothing to worry about.'

And I say, 'Really?'

And he doesn't answer.

'I think I'm going to gouge it out with the bush knife,' I tell him, finally giving voice to something that's been sitting inside me for a while.

He leans up on his elbow to watch my face before saying, 'No, you're not, estrellita. I won't let you.'

'It's not up to you,' I tell him, watching him frown in

the dark, reaching to smooth the crease from between his eyebrows. 'It's up to me.'

The next morning I wake up slowly, slower than usual. It's the hunger, I suppose, getting to me. It's weird, with hunger, the way it starts in your stomach but spreads out until it's occupying all of you, aching in your bones, pounding in your head, messing with your mind, making it hard to open your eyes and face another day where you can't stop thinking about it. I know it's also partly that everything is so broken, and I guess I'm just putting off opening my eyes when all I'm going to see is things I can't fix.

Maybe this is why it takes a minute to look to my left, to the spot where Dom was sleeping, and find just his blanket, pressed flat, like a map of where he isn't.

Because he's kneeling, leaning over the edge of the boat, even though dawn is only just showing itself in the edge of the sky, staring so hard and so completely that he doesn't notice when I join him.

Because there it is. As if it arrived there overnight, crept there, lay down and waited. Coastline.

Chapter Twelve

At first, as we get closer, all we can do is stare at it; we watch it like a movie, one that might be about to disappear. Like the island, a wall of trees stands guard, but these are twice the height, dark and draping, casting caves of darkness in their shade. Far away, far beyond them, almost fading into sky, a backdrop of beautiful, towering, impossibly high mountains, covered in snow – something I never thought I'd see in real life.

After we get over it a little, Ezra says, 'The continent,' and we let him be slightly smug about it. We even let him say, 'I told you we would get there,' even though it's ridiculous.

The waves here are huge, rolling, curling and white, and once we get on the inside of them they buffet and shove us, crash over us, fill us with bubbling foam, wash most of our stuff overboard, then eventually capsize us completely in the sizzling shallows where we almost drown trying to rescue what we need and hauling the boat out on to the sand.

We lie on the beach soaked to the skin and coughing while Ezra tries to rescue the waterlogged computer and solar cell, but it's no good.

'Jesus,' he yells into the sand. 'Jesus, Jesus, Jesus.'

'Just give it a chance to dry out,' says Mari to the sky. 'What did it say the last time you checked it?'

'Another nine,' he says. 'Straight inland.'

Dom gets back from the walk he has taken to the treeline. 'There's a river down there.'

It sweeps out of the forest in a broad, smooth curve, water flowing silently to the sea, ushered by the epic trees. Each has easily got a ten-metre circumference and their tops seem to almost touch the clouds.

'How tall do you think these trees are?' I ask Mari.

'Yeah, I don't know,' she says, before staggering away a couple of metres to vomit into the mud by the water.

'God, Mari, are you OK?' I call after her.

Ezra happens to be standing just there and he watches her cough it out, steps close, lays his hand on her back, and I wait for her to shrug it off. She doesn't.

We set off upriver even though walking feels harder than ever. The world is greyed out. I spend all this time wondering why everything hurts so much, why everything feels so hard, before I realise that this is how it must feel to starve. The interference in my vision, in the way sound reaches me, feels as if it's getting worse. My connection to everything is breaking up, getting patchy.

At one point I stop so I can pull these hard little orange pellets growing in clusters off a spiky, blue-leafed bush that I haven't seen before. Dom watches me do it.

'You think we can eat those?' he asks, raising an eyebrow.

He watches me for a moment while I break one open with my teeth, touch it to my tongue. It's so bitter I immediately spit it out again.

'Maybe not,' I say, the lost hope of food deepening the ache in my stomach.

The sun gets low and we are all so tired that we stop.

'I think we could eat these,' I tell Mariana, smoothing a leaf flat along my palm that I have just picked off a creeper climbing up a tree trunk. 'But we'd probably need to cook them.'

Even though it's not raining here, the floor of the forest is damp enough that we can't find much that's burnable. Mari tries to light some moss and lichen, while I cup my hands and blow when she tells me to and feed the tiniest dry strings of bark on to any meagre flame she can raise, only for it to sputter back out almost right away. So in the end, wordlessly, just through the looks we share, we decide to give up on it, and watch Dom wading in the gentle waters of the river, sweeping at it with his hands, pulling up weeds.

'Hey, look at those,' says Mariana, from her position on her back.

A group of little, I don't know, bugs, maybe, have appeared between us and the leaves above, similar to the sea stars but airborne, following each other in a line from the depth of the forest behind us out on to the river, slow and silent and steady through the air.

'Glow-flies,' I say, trying the word out, knowing it's not quite right but also that it fits.

I watch them move overhead and away into the forest on the far side of the river.

'Guys, come and look at this.' It's Ezra, up the slope behind us.

When Mari and I get to him he is staring through the trees, pointing.

'I think it's a kind of cave or something.'

I follow the line of his finger to where I can see an opening in a ridge of land a hundred metres off, something reddish glinting within.

'Where?' says Mariana, next to me. 'I don't see it.'

'You need glasses,' snorts Ezra. 'I'm going to get a torch.'

I spend a while trying to get Mariana to see what we're talking about. When Ezra gets back with the solar light I turn to him and he is frowning.

'Wait, where's it gone?'

And when I turn back I can't see it either. Where the ridge was there's just flat land, forest fading into darkness.

'Did you move?'

I can't make words for a second so he stalks a few metres away and then back before repeating, 'Did you move?'

'We're right where you left us, Lomax,' sighs Mari, turning to leave. 'There was never anything there in the first place. You're losing it, man.'

Once we're alone he stops shining the torch around at the trees and aims it at my face, blinding me, so that I shade my eyes with my arm.

'You saw it, right?'

I nod, and he beams the torch back out into the gloom, murmuring, 'That is so weird.'

We string the canopy to this gnarled, dead-looking tree, trapping the other end under a rock so it is a loose wedge, flapping in the wind like a flag. The solar lights aren't charging very well so they barely shed any more light than the distant stars.

'What happened to the fire?' says Ezra, eyes fixed on Mariana.

'Why're you looking at *me*?' she says.

'You're the fire girl, you know you are. I thought you were on it.'

'Ground's too damp.'

He picks up a stone and throws it. 'What? I was looking forward to sampling the delights of Hemple's boiled leaf feast.'

Mariana rolls on her side and growls, surprising us all so much that Dom and I share a look. 'I don't have the energy for you tonight, really I don't.'

Suddenly she sits, hitching over sideways to puke on to nearby rocks, and then says, 'Sorry,' as she lies back down.

I edge close to her and say, 'Don't be sorry.'

We lie side by side by side under the only blanket we have left. We watch the stars that we can see at the edges of the canopy and all the way up past the distant treetops and between the passing banners of cloud. I can tell Mariana is asleep from the way air escapes between her lips in a tuneless whistle.

Dom settles on to his side next to me and I turn my head to look at his face in the darkness. He puts an arm behind his head to angle it so he can look back at me. I keep noticing things I never noticed before at the moment, as if the volume is turned up on everything, or as if time is happening slower. Right now I am noticing the way, in his resting expression, his mouth doesn't seem to be able to close completely over his teeth, so that his lips are always slightly parted. It makes him seem younger, somehow.

'How long can we go on fighting to stay alive?' I ask him, feeling so weak.

'Always,' he says, touching his forehead to mine.

I watch the stars again, appearing and disappearing.

Chapter Thirteen

A cold and windy dawn. Everything is so heavy. I'm struggling to see straight. Pain rattles through my guts like knives, but I get up anyway, pull on my trainers.

Ezra is awake too, messing with the filthy hair that now lies down the sides of his face and clearly irritates him. 'Nav's completely screwed.' He hurls it on to the ground next to him. 'There's only so many times you can dump it in the sea.'

'What does it matter though, really?' yawns Dom, pulling the blanket off and sitting. 'It got us to land. And though it pains me to say it, you may have been right about it being better here than the island. Let's just concentrate on finding food.'

Ezra narrows his eyes at him but he carries on.

'I mean we must be pretty close to it, whatever it is, in any case, so if the signal was something ... significant ... We'll find out soon enough, right?'

This makes me look around, in the creeping sunlight that barely makes it through the trees.

The next thing I hear is the pile of firewood hitting the ground, shedding sticks and bark across the space between us and Mariana, who is standing against a tree, five metres away, panting and sweating and leaning over to vomit in the dirt in front of her.

'Mariana!' I say, scrambling away from Ezra who shifts and stands up behind me as I go to her. 'Are you OK?'

'I guess,' she says, wiping her mouth off along her arm. 'We doing this fire or what?' When none of us move she says, 'We need more than this if we're going to cook,' in such a way that Ezra jumps and laughs and does this salute at her and she rolls her eyes but also, just after she turns away, smiles a little.

I follow Dom along the river a while, picking up anything flammable, trying not to seize up every time a stomach pain hits, or at least to get going again after I do. I stop to pull a long stream of climbing plant off a tree trunk, drawn by its new, silky-looking leaves, and that's when I hear them, Ezra and Mariana, their voices raised but not raised, arguing. I walk up into the forest a little, following the direction of their voices until I am separated from them only by a line of low, grey branches that have been brought down in a storm. Then something makes me stop; something makes me step back where I know they won't see me and I will be able to watch them.

'All I'm asking is for you to take a look at it,' he says. 'You're the one who rigged it in the first place.'

She pulls at a branch and then kicks it until it cracks. 'And I'm saying I will.' She shakes her head. 'But we have other priorities right now. The way you're obsessing about this signal is pointless. And intensely irritating. Like just about everything else you do.'

He laughs. 'Ah, you're irritated by me – is that what we're calling it?'

'I'm ignoring you now.'

'I know how hard you wish you could.'

'*Que tonto eres.*'

'I love it when you talk dirty.'

She shakes her head and seems angry, but there's something about the way she hands the broken-up wood back to him that contradicts it.

'Whatever, Moreno, just don't start puking again. You've got me worrying about you.'

'I'm not asking you to worry about me,' says Mariana. 'I never have.'

He takes hold of her forearm, pulls her back until she is leaning against the tree that stands between them.

'It doesn't work like that,' is what I think he says, and he reaches for her face, smooths her hair back from her forehead so that for a minute she looks younger than she is, almost like a child. I can't not stare; it's just too fascinating to see her, Mariana, allowing herself to be touched when she never normally would. Right now, though, she leans her head back against the bark of the tree as if this is what she's been waiting for all along; his hand moves to her ear but she turns her face into it, resting her lips against his palm. He moves in closer to her and speaks so quietly I can't hear. I can only see that he shakes his head as he speaks and then she does too as she answers.

And then he kisses her. And this is what I notice right away: he doesn't kiss her like someone kissing someone for the first time. He has his hand on her neck, under her hair, and their lips meet and it lingers, but then it ends and he draws away a little and then stops there, and they look at each other for this long moment.

I'm so absorbed watching this that I don't hear Dom arriving behind me. He touches my wrist and surprises me so that I yelp, and jolt so hard that I fall on to a nearby branch, which snaps and sends me falling into the rocks. By the time Dom picks me up again, Mariana and Ezra are watching across the gap between us as I dust off the knees of my trousers and straighten my vest.

'I'm OK,' I'm saying, 'I'm OK,' while the whole time, all of us are thinking something else altogether. I think at some point each possible combination of the four of us exchanges at least one baffled set of eye contact, and yet the silence just goes on stretching until in the end I break it.

'You ... he ... I ... we ...' I say, pointing around at people lamely, and then, focusing on the one thing I can make sense of, 'We probably shouldn't have been spying on you.'

Ezra laughs. 'Yeah, what's up with that, Hemple?'

'I guess I didn't know we had secrets.' I look at Mariana, who looks away.

'Why *do* we have secrets?' Dom stares at Ezra.

'It's not about secrets – it's about the fact that it's just not even worth mentioning, right, Moreno?'

He watches her as she goes back to snapping branches.

He carries on anyway. 'It's like that joke about the last two people on the planet. Only real. Come on, man, what would you do in my place? Or in hers? The nights on Huxley-3 are pretty long and lonely.'

Dom is so still he's like someone who has shifted out of ordinary space and time, staring at Ezra with a heat in his eyes I recognise from long ago.

Ezra shrugs, just warming to his theme. 'She's human, you know. Red-blooded. You think she could resist me for long?' He glances up at Dom. 'And, as for me, you know – maybe she wouldn't have been my first choice but . . . any port in a storm.'

Dom shakes his head, eyes narrowed. 'You're disgusting, Lomax – don't you even *look* at her again.'

'You're too funny, man,' he says. 'You don't get to decide about that. It's up to her what she does.'

'Right now I'm with Domingo on this,' says Mariana, and we all turn to watch her walk away.

Ezra studies her retreating back. 'Ah come on, I'm just telling them how it is. How else could it ever be in this situation? We're just ... making the best of it. What's wrong with that?'

I can't see it ending well if the conversation continues, so I pull on Dom's arm and make him walk away and leave Ezra there. We get back to our makeshift camp and I leave Dom packing it up when I spot a line of smoke climbing through the trees a little way off.

She is down in the shelter of a sandy ravine that cuts into the riverbank at a right angle, blowing at the fire.

'I guess I should have mentioned it,' she says, sensing me behind her without looking.

And I surprise myself by saying, 'Well, mention it now.'

'That's the thing,' she says. 'There's nothing really to tell. Like he says, in his charming way.' She raises her eyebrows. 'I guess we both knew it was inevitable that we'd get lonely in the end. Staring down the barrel of a life like that makes you do things you wouldn't expect.'

Our eyes meet briefly.

'So you ... is it ...?' I'm not sure what to ask, or how to phrase it.

'It's only been a few times,' she says, taking a guess at what I'm asking. For a moment I'm disorientated by that.

'I know you and he have history so I really should have told you.'

'What?' I blink for a minute, shake my head, try to

laugh. 'What? No. I don't . . . I'm a bit weirded out but it's nothing to do with that.' I'm pretty sure it's true, though what it is that bothers me about it is hard to place.

I kneel next to her and watch her build up the fire, layer by layer, handing her everything she asks for.

'When did it start?' I find myself asking.

'I'm not sure. Not long after we got here, I guess.'

I snap sticks in the silence.

'I think I'm just surprised that you didn't talk to me about it,' I say after a while.

'Only because there isn't anything to talk about,' she sighs. 'It's just . . . a physical thing. We don't even like each other.'

I let the wind rearrange my hair while I think about that kiss.

'Are you sure about that?' I ask her.

She laughs. 'Yes, I'm sure.' Then, 'It's different for you, Seren. You're here with the love of your life. It's the reason you're here. It's the reason all of us are here. It's your love story, and Ezra and I are just characters in it. And I guess there comes a point when you want your own story – some kind of story – even if it's not the one you would have chosen.' She scratches her head, frowning as if it hurts, and I am just about to say something when Ezra appears.

I only look up at him once, quick, before he meets my eye and I look away.

'Here.' He tosses a load of dried wood on to the ground next to us.

'So you are useful for something,' she says.

Now the fire's going, I hand Mariana the string of possibly edible leaves I collected off the tree. 'Dom's got the cooking pot in his bag. Where is he, actually?'

'Sulking, probably,' Ezra says with a smirk and then, when we both look at him, 'What?'

I go looking for Dom, picking my way back along the riverbank, wondering why he hasn't found us.

'Dom?' I call. No answer.

I don't realise Ezra has followed me until he grabs my arm, so I almost lash out at him, breathing hard.

'You scared me,' I tell him.

'I'm sorry,' he says, pushing his sweat-damp hair back. 'Mari sent me after you.'

'I think Dom's lost.' I look around at the trees.

He makes the facial equivalent of a shrug. 'One less mouth to feed.'

We read each other for a second, and then I say, 'What are you thinking right now?'

He looks surprised and then frowns as if he's trying to work it out. 'Right now? Right now, or right then, I was wondering if you were nursing your regrets about the one who got away.'

I lean my head and shoulders back on the tree behind me and shut my eyes. 'Seriously?'

He grins. 'You had your chance to sample the goods, Hemple, remember that.'

'Oh jeez, I'm nauseous enough as it is,' I tell him, climbing up the bank and peering into where the forest thickens. 'I'm happy for you, actually.'

'Don't get excited. I've told you – sex is just a necessary biological function like any other, and in a world where the only food is porridge, you're going to eat porridge, right?'

I nod. 'That's about what she said.'

'I mean, it's like . . . wait, what?' Now he's up with me, standing close enough so that I can smell the river water on him, like wet grass. 'She said that?' he asks.

'Words to that effect.'

I notice his goosebumps, the way he goes to fold his arms tight across his chest.

'That bothers you?' I ask him.

'Of course not.' He smiles. 'Why would it?' And then he double takes, squints, focusing somewhere over my shoulder, down towards the river.

'What is it?' I ask, breaking out in chills, following his eyeline.

'Saw something moving,' he says, still squinting. 'Suarez?'

No answer.

And that is when we hear the gun.

Chapter Fourteen

'DOM!' I scream.

I run, but I may as well be flying. Nothing gets in my way, nothing stops me, not the sticks that tear at my hair and clothes and skin, not the rocks that try to knock my legs out from under me, nothing.

I can hear voices. Shouting.

'DOM!' I stare around frantically at the trees as Ezra catches up to me, but I am blind with fear.

When I first see him, he is a shape through the branches, barely there, insubstantial, a ghost materialising into something real.

I crash through everything in my way until I get to where Dom is on the ground, rolling over, bent double, holding on to his leg with blood all over his hands, the reddest thing I've ever seen, as if the colour has drained from everything else in the world except that.

'What happened? Tell me what happened! Are you OK?' I am on the floor next to him, trying to get hold of his leg while he rolls and doesn't let me.

'Run, Seren,' he says through the pain. 'Just run.'

Because right then there is a forearm across my throat, cold and hard and reptilian, more strength than any human I have ever known, and I am screaming. And I have my hands on this arm, trying to loosen it, failing, kicking back at the shins just behind me, realising that this is someone, or something, almost as tall as Dom is, so I am hopelessly outclassed. Right then I realise I can hear Ezra's voice too.

'Jesus, what the hell ...?' And though I can't see him I can hear the struggle, can hear that they have him too.

I bite down, and it shrieks in pain and I get pushed, hard, right in the back of the head, and my legs are kicked out from under me.

I see our attackers for a split second as I hit the ground. I see Ezra, watching me in horror, both arms held back as he struggles against the creature behind him – a head taller, huge reflective eyes.

'Where are you?' It's Mari, screaming, getting closer, too late to warn.

And then it all goes black.

I come round to the sound of Dom yelling in pain. Once my eyes are open I don't even dare to blink, to the point that my eyes are burning, and my breathing is so loud it is plucking at a string somewhere inside me, out of tune. The panic is such that I am left with only the part of me

140

that knows how to run or fight, and because this thing has me pinned to the ground so hard I don't have the option of running, I am only able to fight.

I catch the nearest one on the leg once, but that's all, before it crushes me against the rocks, while it secures my wrists with something so hard I'm amazed it doesn't break the skin, or some bones.

'Help him,' I scream at them, popping something in my throat. 'You need to help him. He's hurt.'

'I'm OK, Seren, just stay calm,' yelps Dom, but I don't believe him, and he doesn't realise there's no talking to me when I'm like this.

Wherever the thing's skin comes into contact with mine I feel myself shrink away. It is cold, lizard-like, and I am completely freaking out and it doesn't matter that they are all desperate for me to just calm down, because I am making it worse for myself, for all of us, a fact I realise when they hold me down by standing on my thigh.

I look up at our attackers properly for the first time.

They are bizarrely tall, freakishly thin, talking to each other in some kind of language.

The aliens.

Only they aren't.

The big, weird insect eyes they have turn out not to be eyes at all – they're just reflective, wraparound sunglasses.

They are human.

Nevertheless, just looking at them makes my hair raise

in a way I am sure must be visible, so much can I feel it. And maybe it simply comes down to the fact that they are the first humans, or human-type figures, we have ever seen that aren't of Ventura and it is eerie – out and out eerie.

But all we can do is watch them while they stand there in their matching blue uniforms with their shaved heads, guns strapped around their necks and trained on us, both touching their ears and talking in their weird language and I guess we aren't sure if they're talking to us or each other or what, but it seems mostly as if they are talking to someone else on an invisible mobile com or I don't even know what.

They haul Mariana and me to our feet and drag us off through the trees. I struggle, looking back at Dom, where he lies curled up.

'NO!' I scream, battling hard. 'NO!'

It doesn't help, but I scream and kick and struggle all the way as I'm manhandled through the trees and downhill into a clearing where there are two low grey buildings. They lead us over to where the back cargo door of some kind of storage container is lowering with a hum until it hits the rocks and the one holding me pushes me in, says something in his language which almost, for a moment, seems familiar, as he moves his sunglasses up and holds my eye with his dark gaze.

Then the door hums closed again and we are inside,

alone, under strip lights and on metal grating. It is so weird how quickly dirt and rocks and sand became the new normal when for most of my life this was all I had ever known. I clamp my hands around my pulsing head.

'He's OK,' says Mariana, more to herself than to me, before taking a big noisy breath. 'He's OK.'

'They shot him, Mari,' I say, feeling tears. 'They actually shot him.'

Ezra is brought in, alone. He is pushed through the door and as he watches it close I am on my feet. 'Where is he?'

He holds his cuffed hands in the air between us. 'Chill, Hemple, I think they're going to carry him here. He couldn't walk.'

'He couldn't walk?'

He takes hold of my elbow, even though it's awkward. 'He's OK, seriously,' he says. 'I'm telling you he's OK.'

I look down to where his broken and dirt-crusted trainers are almost touching mine before he continues, 'But, man, can you believe this? This is it!' I look up at his wide, excited eyes. 'First Contact, man! We're in uncharted territory. This is history in the making. Ventura's got another two hundred plus years on the clock and we, the deserters, have beaten them to it.' He looks ridiculously delighted for someone who just got locked in a box.

Mariana raises her eyebrows. 'If your mother could hear you now.'

We hear Dom coming before they arrive. I've never heard him make noises like this – it's as if he's someone else. We are waiting when they open the door and bring him in, leave him on the floor in the middle of us and go to leave again. I'm so distracted by the paleness and pain on his face that I almost let them go. Almost, but not quite.

I follow them, standing on the door when they start to raise it.

'Hey, no!' I yell at them, trying to show them my hands, even though I kind of can't because they are behind my back. 'Cut us loose. Cut us loose so we can help him if you're not going to.'

To my relief one of them gets it, gets it and speaks to the other one, letting his gun hang slack on the strap around his neck for a moment while he pulls a knife out of his pocket and I turn so that he can cut me loose. I fall to my knees at Dom's side, grabbing at his leg and finding the bullet wound just above his ankle, relieved at how sticky it is already, the blood already congealing.

They say something to Ezra, which makes me sit back on my heels and turn, pinning one of them with my gaze. He notices, but goes to the door anyway, hammers at the button that closes it and leaves us in dim light.

'They're from Earth,' I say, suddenly sure.

'What? No way!' says Ezra. 'I don't ... How can they be? There's no way they're from Earth. Ventura got here first. No other missions left in this direction, or were due to for years. They're aliens, man! This is it. This is First Contact.' He shakes his head.

But I am pulling off my T-shirt and getting it ready to press on to Dom's wound while I shake my head and repeat it. 'They're from Earth.'

Mari is holding Dom's hand and looking into his face but she glances at me to say, 'How do you know?'

'He used to read me his father's poems,' I say, shaking my head at myself when I realise I'm not making sense. 'My grandpa,' I clarify. 'His dad was Russian.'

They all watch me in silence, even Dom, who is only semi-conscious.

'I think they're from Russia,' I say, and then to Dom, 'This is going to hurt.' He yells when I press my T-shirt on his wound, hard.

'Didn't you see their uniforms?' I ask Ezra, who still isn't having it.

He stares back at me. 'So?'

'The logo on the chest and hip? They're another mission.'

'They can't be.' He shakes his head again.

I've torn my T-shirt into shreds and tied it around Dom's leg, which has stopped bleeding. He is shaking hard with fear and shock and adrenaline, as I sit with my back to the ridged iron wall and take all his weight curled over on me, my hand in his hair.

'What happened, Suarez?' asks Ezra.

He shifts a little, licks his lips before he speaks. 'Noticed something through the trees and went for a look. Next thing I knew I was shot.'

I gather his hand into my lap, run my thumb over his.

'Well, I guess we found your signal, Lomax,' says Mariana. 'For all the good it did us.' She sits down next to me.

Hours pass. I lose it a few times and start kicking at the walls, screaming for them to let us out, to give him something for the pain, to tell us what the hell is going on. I even smash one of the dim blue lights on the wall into a buzzing cloud of powder, before the others get me to sit down.

'I told you about that boat!' I yell at Ezra. 'I knew it was a stupid plan. Is this what you wanted? For all we know they'll shoot us for desertion.'

'They wouldn't do that, would they?' asks Mariana.

'If they're another mission, they probably will,' I say. 'They'll be bound by Allied Starfleet regulation, just like Ventura.'

'They won't be,' Ezra says. 'Because they're not from Earth.'

'How long are you going to keep denying what's going on here?' I shriek at him.

Just then we hear the door mechanism as it lowers. The original two guys have changed into these crinkled white plastic overalls with hoods and matching face masks, and there's a third person now, much smaller, a woman, wearing the same gear. They manage to indicate with their guns that they want us to stand against the walls and stay there.

Dom tries to get up but I stop him.

'You shot him, remember?' I yell at them. 'You shot him in the leg.'

The woman comes to Dom, kneels in front of him, gently takes his leg and begins to unbandage it. I say, 'It needs to be cleaned; he needs medicine,' and she looks up at me.

Though I can only see her eyes through the window in the mask, something in them stops me completely, stops any words, and it freezes her, too, so that she maintains this moment of eye contact with me that seems to go on for ever.

'They said you were from Ventura,' she says, in English, her voice tinny through the filter of the mask. 'But I couldn't believe it until I saw it for myself.' She touches the battered Ventura logo on Dom's cap where it lies in his lap and then carefully puts his leg back on the floor. 'We thought we heard shuttles a few months ago and for a moment I thought ... but I didn't truly believe it was possible.'

She stands slowly and looks across at the other two, then back at me, frowning.

'Think you could tell us who you are, since you seem to know who we are already?' I cross my arms.

She just stares at me for what seems like another half a minute before she says, 'We're Concordia. Ruskosmos Pioneer Mission. We've been on-planet for nine years – we ...' She trails off. It's as if she had a whole spiel prepared that she just gives up on, or can't go on with. She reaches for me, making me step back, but when she goes again I let her hands find my shoulders.

'How did you get here?' she says, her eyes dark and huge and never apparently needing to blink, in spite of the fact that they seem to be getting wet.

'We ...' I swallow. 'It's kind of a long story.'

Does she almost smile then?

'How come you speak English?' Ezra asks from behind her, but she only moves her head the smallest bit before saying, 'That's kind of a long story too,' and when she does eventually blink, eyes still fixed on mine, tears spill out of her eyes and down into her mask. She whispers something then, too quiet for me to hear.

'What?' I shake my head, getting weirded out and wishing one of the others would come and get her off me. 'I can't hear what you're saying.'

And then suddenly I do, because she says, 'You're Seren.'

And I say, 'How did you …' and I start to wonder what's going on, whether maybe they knew about us, whether Ventura contacted them. 'How do you know my name?'

But there is something about the way she goes on staring at me, the way she holds my shoulders, the tremble I can see and feel in her, more tears arriving in her eyes, and then she says, 'Because it's me – Grace. Your mother.'

Chapter Fifteen

'What did she say?' says Ezra, stepping closer, laughing a little. 'What did she just say?'

But I don't answer him, can't.

'But …' I shake my head, shake it and shake it and shake it until it might be about to fall off. 'You can't be. She died. She's dead. My mother's dead.'

She just blinks more tears, and says, 'I knew it was you the moment I saw you. I could feel it.'

I drop to the floor without warning then, scaring everybody. My cut-out switch just goes.

'You've had a shock,' she says, this woman, whoever she is, before switching into Russian and throwing what are clearly commands over her shoulder at the two guys, meaning one of them leaves. 'I shouldn't have …' She shakes her head. 'How long is it since you ate?'

But I can't speak, all I can do is shunt away from her, back and back until I am against the wall, right next to Dom where he is slumped low into the corner of the wall and floor but reaching for me, pulling me in against his chest where I press my face in the darkness.

I hear Ezra speaking then. 'So, wait, can I just clarify? Did you or did you not just say that you were her mother?' There's no audible answer but he presses on. 'Why would you even ...? How would you ...? I don't know what you're trying to pull, or what this place is ...'

I hear her laugh, and then she says, 'You're Kat and Marshall's boy, aren't you?'

I've never witnessed Ezra speechless before now.

'We need to get this wound treated; get you all cleaned up and checked in our medical unit. You need food. Then we can ... talk, OK?'

Just then one of the first guys comes back, and starts speaking Russian to her again before coming to Dom and pulling roughly on his arm to get him to stand.

'He can't walk!' I yell.

She translates this and then helps me to get Dom to his feet gently, shooting me a look of apology. 'Don't worry about Vasily and Alexei. They've spent too much time alone out here.' She laughs. 'We've never had visitors before. You scared them.'

Outside it's the dead of night, and the only light is these little blue lamps among the grass. They help Dom over to the second of the low, grey buildings under the trees. I follow him but the other guy grabs my arm and when I turn to him I see the reflection of myself on the screen of his mask, swimming back and forth as he shakes his head.

'Go with Vasily,' says the woman. 'Get cleaned up. He'll bring you down after.' Then she says something in Russian – presumably the same message to Vasily.

I watch the way Dom turns to look for me, not even able to use his leg so that progress is unbelievably slow across the rocky ground.

'We'll take care of him,' says the woman, as if she knows exactly what I'm thinking.

Vasily takes us to the other building, to a side entrance that he has to pull open manually, door scraping across rocks. It turns out to be a tiny, dimly lit, pretty ripe-smelling bathroom, which he gets all three of us to squeeze into before yelling something at us in Russian as he points at the shower. There is a bar of soap and three dirty towels on the floor, and a bag of what looks like clothes. He doesn't close the door, but stands with his back to it, looking out at the night.

I look at Mariana then, the way she shivers next to me in the half light and stares into the corner of the room.

'Oh my God, is that a real toilet?'

Ezra has turned on the shower already and is struggling out of his T-shirt, exposing the glow of messy broken flesh and bruising that seems to be spreading towards his spine.

'It's cold,' he says, wincing as he holds one hand under

the flow, then making a whole load of stupid noises as he actually steps in.

I have so longed to have a shower these last few months I don't care that it's cold and I am being held prisoner in some strange building in the forest in the middle of the night. I pull my disgusting vest off, peel down my shorts and kick them off, keep going until I am completely naked, with absolutely no regard for the fact that Ezra is there and Mariana is watching me, jaw slowly going slack at the sight of the lumpy mess of coral creeping across my hip, lower stomach, back, in bluish lines that I can barely look at myself.

As soon as Ezra steps out of the water I step in and it hits me hard, like knives, so that I end up kind of dancing around in the horrible chill of it, fighting it off almost but also hanging my head in it, making sure it gets all of me. There is so much, so much, to wash away.

I step out and Ezra hands me one of the towels. I stand against the wall while he gets dressed because the space is so tight. Once he's pulled on the T-shirt, I do a double take at him standing there in one of their uniforms.

He shrugs. 'Well, it's better than what we had.'

Once we're dressed, Vasily brings us into the building and it is this one low-ceilinged grey room with a table in the middle, four recessed bunks at the far end, the whole thing drifted in dirt. There are four steaming bowls on the table and Ezra nearly knocks it over getting there and picking one up, only hesitating for a second to squint at its contents before shovelling it in without even sitting on one of the stools.

'What is it?' Mariana asks, picking hers up and making a face.

'Who cares?' says Ezra, through a mouthful.

I turn to ask Vasily if he'll take me to Dom but he's gone, the door just closing after him.

I pick up my bowl – it's something I haven't seen before. At first sight like porridge, but when I look closer it seems to be an Earth vegetable, or maybe a grain – hundreds of tiny brown balls that are warm and slightly salty.

Dom comes in, flanked by Vasily and Alexei, leg bandaged from the knee down to the toe.

'Are you OK?' His face looks oddly pale as they walk him over to a stool and I help him sit in it, heavily, watching him flinch.

'They just have a temporary sick bay here. They said they have an actual doctor and a medical facility and stuff down in the settlement.'

'The settlement?' I ask him.

'Yeah this is just some . . . ' He flinches again. 'Out-of-town facility. There's a settlement down the hill a little way, apparently.'

Alexei is pulling on Mariana's arm and she is resisting him.

'It's OK, *prima*, seriously,' he says. 'She only does

154

this, like, two-second blood test to check for infectious diseases. Doesn't even hurt.'

So she gets up, arms wrapped round herself and shoulders hunched, and gives me this look as if she's never been so scared in her life.

'Can't we stay together?' I ask Alexei, but he shakes his head, pulling Mari to the door that slams after him.

Dom's hand snakes on to my shoulder while I am staring at my hands twisting in my lap. I know he's asking me about what the woman said, about what I thought of it, so I turn to look at him and open my mouth, and both of us sit and wait to hear what will come out of it. Which in the end is nothing. Which in the very end is, 'You should eat something,' and I hand him the fourth bowl.

Mari is gone for ages before the door opens again. Vasily steps in and points at Ezra, and I watch him leave.

'Where's Mari?' I ask Dom, because it's what we're both thinking.

He does this half headshake and then looks me all the way up and down. 'Hey, I like your new outfit.'

I pull my stool right up next to him and I press my face into his neck where it is warm and dark, and I feel his palm on the back of my head smoothing my hair down my back. He smells deeply and richly of sweat and salt and sea and mud and river and HIM but I could just go on breathing it for ever. No amount would ever be enough. 'You smell good,' I say into his shoulder.

He laughs. 'I doubt that,' he says, and then, 'You, on the other hand . . .' and he tucks a piece of my wet hair behind my ear, but you can tell he's thinking about something. Then he says, 'Do you . . . do you think she really is your mum?'

I shake my head. 'How can she be?'

'It's just . . .'

'What?'

'It's weird – she's actually really like you.' He studies me, almost laughs.

'But how can it be her?' I hold my face in my hands.

'Yeah, it's . . . I have no idea.'

'Did they tell you what they plan to do with us?' I ask.

He sighs. 'She said they're waiting on a decision from their Command about how to proceed.'

Just then Ezra comes back in and says, 'Your turn,' and because it is the first time that one of the guys hasn't come back to escort us, I end up passing him and heading over there alone.

I cross the windy gap between the buildings and press the door release that lets me into the next building. The three of them stand around a chair at the far end and all turn to look at me as I approach. The woman reaches for me.

'Let's get this done with quickly, Seren, then I can get this stupid suit off.'

I'm not sure what to feel about that. All the same I sit

and she takes my arm, binds it round with something rubbery and clips it, all without dropping eye contact through the mask.

'Just takes a second,' she says, pricking me with the needle.

'How are you here?' I ask her, unable to hold it in any longer.

She seems to smile. 'I could ask you the same thing,' she says as she takes out the needle and posts it into a machine on a nearby surface. It only takes a couple of seconds to beep, and she pulls the hood of the suit down, prompting both the guys to do the same.

'Both of us have long stories to tell,' she says, running a hand through her hair, and suddenly there she is. I can see her. I can see the woman from Dad's photos, photos I spent my whole life looking at, that were the only thing I had of her, my mother. Eyes that are almost too big and too dark, so that she looks younger than she is, still like a girl even now. She is looking at my face as if she is learning it. She lays her fingers on my cheek and jaw so lightly I barely feel it.

'I remember the day you were born,' she says, but then something makes her gaze shift and she turns away, then back to say, 'I'm sorry, I have to get this,' before touching her ear and walking to the corner of the room where she starts speaking Russian.

It's her pod, her com, or whatever they call them here.

Now that they all have their hazmat masks off I can see that they wear them attached to their ears – small blue things that clip around.

'Where is Mariana?' I ask Vasily and Alexei, who are stepping out of their suits, but they just look at me blankly. 'Mariana?' I try again.

Grace breaks off her call for a minute and says, 'She didn't come back?' before watching me shake my head and saying, 'You should go and find her – she had a bit of a shock.' As I'm leaving, she says, 'I'm sorry, Seren; she said she was going to you.'

When I get outside the moons are casting everything in purple light. I go back over to the other building first, but it's just Dom and Ezra sitting opposite each other at the table, turning to me.

'Did Mari come back yet?'

They both shake their heads.

I get about twenty metres out into the trees before I hear them coming out after me.

'Mari!' I call into the moonlit distance. 'Mari, where are you?'

'She's here!' Dom calls, from where he's holding on to the back corner of the building, looking along behind it.

By the time I get back there he is lowering himself awkwardly on to the ground next to her, pulling her against him because she is crying, and he is saying, '*Háblame, prima*, you're scaring me.'

I squat down in front of them as she says something into her hands that none of us catch, before adding, 'I can't believe I'm stupid enough to have let it happen again.'

'Let what happen?' I ask, but when I look at Dom I see it begin to dawn on him. I see it in the tension in his jaw.

'What? You don't mean . . .' For some reason I can't get the words out. They're just too huge and they change too much. But someone has to, so in the end I say, 'You don't mean you're pregnant, do you?'

And when she doesn't answer, we know. Wind tosses the treetops right then and we all just sit listening to it. Then I see Dom look up at Ezra and I do too. Maybe it's just the light but he looks utterly white, like a statue of himself, or maybe a ghost, but just then Mari says, 'No, not him – it's from before, before we left.'

Ezra comes to life then, breaks into a weird laugh, makes all these relief noises and turns in a circle, punching the air.

'Oh man,' he says. 'I'm telling you. Scariest moment of my life so far.' He sits on the ground next to me, then lies flat.

'Who, then?' says Dom, once he's finished glaring at Ezra.

'*A quién le importa*?' says Mari quietly. 'How could it matter now?'

'Because I want to know.'

She sits away a little and looks at him, while I say, 'It doesn't matter. What matters is what we do now.'

But Dom says, 'I just don't get you sometimes,' and shakes his head at her.

'You just don't *get* me?' I can hear the anger in Mari's voice as she glares back at him.

'You never think things through. If you want to do something you just do it and deal with the consequences later.'

'How can *you* say that to me? Did you just hear yourself? *Por favor, primo* – you're such a hypocrite!'

It's awful, dizzying, to hear them fight. The only thing to do is shush them like children, but she pushes my hand away and stands.

'Look at your life, Domingo – all you've ever done is follow your impulses and deal with it later!'

'But I'm not the one standing here on an alien planet with a baby to think about.' He shakes his head at the ground. 'And if we hadn't left? God, Mari, dumb doesn't even cover it.'

'The only difference between you and me is luck,' she yells. 'I remember at least two occasions when you came to me scared out of your mind because Annelise was late.'

I don't quite get what she's saying at first, and then I do. I feel it slide into me, like a knife.

Dom's so mad he only says, 'I was sixteen, *prima*! I've realised a couple of things about responsibility by now.'

He watches her walk away before saying to her back, 'I wish *you* would.'

But she only gives him the finger as she leaves, which makes Ezra, still lying on his back, laugh.

'God,' says Dom, pushing his hair back from his face with both hands. 'She is just . . . ' But then he turns and sees the look on my face and his expression changes. He half blinks and I can tell he's realising, thinking about what to say. His hand goes to my shoulder.

'Estrellita, I . . . '

But I don't even want to hear it right now.

'I should go to Mari,' I tell him, eyes not leaving his for a moment.

He sighs through his nose but nods, and I leave, following her through the trees.

'Seren!' Grace calls to me from the doorway of the other building, then covers the distance between us. 'I got the OK from Command to put you in a spare accommodation. It's not far from here, on the way back to the main settlement, and you can get some rest there. It's been a long night, hasn't it?'

The path down there has lights along it but otherwise looks hardly used. Grace walks with me, Mariana ahead on her own; Ezra and Alexei help Dom struggle along behind.

'Just tell me . . . ' says Grace, swallowing in a way that looks like fear. 'Pandora – is she OK?'

I look at how scared she is that I might say no. 'She was when I left,' is what I say.

She breathes out all at once. 'Dad?'

'He's fine.'

'Jamie?'

I frown. 'I just told you he's fine,' I say, then, 'Oh, you meant *your* dad – you meant Grandpa?' It feels disorientating somehow. Weird. 'Everybody's fine,' I say, confused, but then I realise I shouldn't have, because they aren't. I open my mouth to tell her about her mum, and about Great Granny Bea, even though I'm not sure I will ever get the words out, but just then we get to a part of the path where trees have been cut down and we are up on a ridge, looking back down on a great wide bend in the river, bathed in the light from the moons. I can just about see a few rows of grey box buildings arranged around a central square area of churned-up red mud and beyond it, a vast bulky grey structure that looks as if it's only partly built, a skeleton of something.

'There it is,' says Grace, and I look at her.

'There what is?'

'Concordia settlement.'

I look back at it.

'I'll give you the tour, later, when you've rested and adjusted a little.' She looks ahead to where Mariana is entering the building.

Grace turns to me. 'Domingo told me you deserted,'

she says, and then, 'I can't even figure out how that was possible. So brave.'

'Isn't that what you did?'

She shakes her head.

The others arrive and stand looking down on the settlement.

'Jeez,' says Ezra after a minute. 'I thought you said you'd been here nine years.'

Grace shifts. 'Pioneering is probably a lot more complicated than you think.'

And he says, 'I guess it must be.'

Chapter Sixteen

Inside, the building is pretty similar to the last two, in that it is grey and bolted together, with dust and dirt blowing across the floor when we open the door. It is divided into two dorm rooms with six recessed bunks in each, one central overhead light. Grace points out a door which she says leads to a bathroom.

'Who lives here?' I ask her.

She shifts her eyes. 'Nobody. It was built as a farmhouse, but the farming ... moved elsewhere.'

She goes to a storage cupboard and pulls out blankets that breathe epic clouds of dust as she flaps them out.

'Nobody's been here for a while, I guess.' She looks embarrassed as she leaves the blankets on one of the beds, then turns to me. 'I'll be back, OK? You guys just ... ' But she doesn't finish, she just gestures a little, then leaves, closing the door behind her.

Ezra is studying the riveted wall and says, 'Where do you reckon they got all this metal?'

Dom laughs from the bathroom door. 'Come and look

at this!' Because there is no ceiling in there – just a toilet and shower and four metal walls and the sky.

I find Mariana lying on a bunk in the next room, damp hair spread over the pillow, hiding her face. The Concordia T-shirt is so big for her that its unbuttoned neck hangs off her shoulder and I can see the raw, red welt from where her bag strap has been sawing at her flesh. I cover her with one of the blankets and she turns her face into the pillow, presses it there.

'Are you OK?' I ask her.

'No, I'm an idiot,' she says.

'I don't think you're an idiot,' I say.

'Thanks,' she says.

I leave her to sleep.

Ezra and I check through the cupboards but there's nothing in them except blankets and uniforms, seemingly unused.

'It just doesn't seem like much to show for a decade of being here, does it?' he says, looking round, getting taken over by a yawn. 'I'm going to bed.' He heads into the darkened room where Mari is.

I listen to Dom turning the shower off, listen to him falling over and struggling to get dry and dressed with his injured leg, and all the time I'm about to ask him if he's OK but for some reason I don't.

When he eventually opens the door again he is laughing a little.

'That was harder than I expected,' he says, limping up the step and over to me. And it's so weird, because for a moment I don't recognise him. I've never seen him in any clothes except the Ventura uniform, so suddenly, in a dark blue polo shirt and matching trousers, he is like a stranger. As he gets closer I can smell the soap on him, overly sweet, and see the water drops that still cling to his neck, the tips of his hair.

'You're still pretty wet,' I tell him.

'Yeah, I know,' he says, laughing. 'No towel.' He picks up the hem of his T-shirt to rub his face with it. I watch him in a side glance then, the perfect brown beauty of the skin on his torso that I thought was only mine to know and now suddenly isn't. How is it possible to be so angry with someone and at the same time want them so bad it hurts? He's standing so close to me now that I know he's expecting a kiss but I can't, I just can't, even when I feel his hand on my hip and the way he's looking at me.

'I need to go,' I say, but as I'm turning he takes my hand and stops me.

'Where are you going?' he says. 'Estrellita, please stay and talk to me. Please. I should have told you.'

'But instead I found out from Mari.'

'Yeah,' he sighs. 'I didn't know she was going to say that.'

'So you were never going to say?'

He shrugs, looks down, pushes his hair back and looks

166

up at me with the lopsided smile he knows I love. 'Maybe not?' he says.

I hold his eye. 'How could you lie about this?'

'I didn't lie about it – it's just that you never asked. And there was no point telling you,' he says, his eyes sad. 'What was the point? It was nothing. It was . . . technical. Just technical. And look, was I going to say no? I'm a man, Seren.'

I make a face. 'What does that even mean?'

He covers his eyes with his hands. 'This is coming out all wrong. I'm sorry. I'm sorry I didn't tell you. I just didn't see what it had to do with you and me. It's in the past, and it is, literally, a million miles away, so why waste time talking about it?' He takes my hand in his.

'Because I want to talk about it,' I say.

'OK.' He widens his eyes, looks scared, but nods. 'Then let's.'

'How many times?'

He makes a sound in his throat and looks up at the ceiling. 'Oh man, I don't know.'

'Too many to count?'

'That's not what I mean.'

'How many, then?'

'I just . . . didn't know I needed to count, so I didn't.' He rubs his face before looking at me.

'Where?'

'Her quarters, mostly. Her parents both worked first

shift in Information. Her sister was in Education B. She and I were both on third shift, so we ... had the place to ourselves quite a lot.'

'When was the last time?'

I see him freeze. I see his eyes shift. And I know. I know right then that he is thinking of lying.

'Don't you dare lie,' I say through my teeth. 'I need to know I'm getting the truth from you right now, so think hard before you answer.'

'OK. Can I just ... sit down first?' He indicates his leg before backing over to the nearest bunk and sitting there, letting his legs fall open and leaning forward over them, studying his hands. It takes me the longest time to realise what he's actually doing is bracing himself. And then he says, 'I think it was the day before the wedding.'

I am motionless while I let it sink in. 'My wedding?'

He makes a noise that is almost a laugh as he looks at the floor between his legs. 'I just felt so sad that day. So, just, hopeless. I wanted so badly to feel as if there was a life for me without you in it, as if I could ever be happy without you. But ... ' He shakes his head. 'That's why I ended up coming over. I couldn't help it. I couldn't stay away from you even though I knew it was the wrong thing to do.'

He leans across to take my hand but I pull it away so fast that he is left with his hand just hanging there while he looks at me and I look back.

'So that night, when you came to me, you had been with her?' There's a tremble in my voice.

He doesn't reply, just blinks once and goes on looking at me.

'You actually had sex with her? Like ... hours before you came to me?'

Still no answer.

'You had sex with her, and then you came to me and told me you loved me and you couldn't live without me?' I feel myself making a face. 'God, Dom, it's awful. Not just to me but to her. It's ... disgusting.'

'Now do you see why I didn't tell you?'

'So that you didn't have to own up to who you are? So that I wouldn't know how cruel you can be? That you could lie like that and let someone love you and let them think you loved them back?'

He's shaking his head. 'Annelise never thought that. She knew how it was.'

'How do you know that? You don't know that! Why would she have sex with you unless she cared about you and thought she could trust you?'

'You know how it was on Ventura. Or ... well ... maybe you don't.' It's as if he's had an idea, and he takes my hand and pulls me until I am on the bunk next to him. 'I don't think you ever really knew what it was like. When we met, you and Ezra had been assigned to each other for what, just a few weeks?'

'Three days.' I swallow, eyes on the floor.

'Exactly.' He moves closer. 'You have to trust me when I tell you that being assigned to someone is ... different ... to falling in love. Completely different. I'm not saying what I did wasn't wrong. It was. But being assigned is like an arrangement that you both accept, and you, I don't know, you look for ways to be happy and to make each other happy in this ... situation that you have.'

I look at him then; the fullness in his lower lip when he's sad like this always makes me want to touch it, tilt my head and touch it. But I don't this time.

'Annelise and I were assigned for three years, Seren,' he says. 'Three years. Whatever our real feelings were, we had definitely become friends by that point. And you know how lonely every *day* was on Ventura. Every minute, even.' He sighs. 'I was just trying to live some kind of life. I was just trying to be happy. Once I knew you, everything was so different. And so much more complicated. It stopped between us then, between me and Annelise. It made her pretty suspicious, actually. And then of course she started hearing the rumours.'

'The rumours?'

He makes a noise that is half laugh, half something else. 'We were terrible at keeping it secret. You know we were. So many people ended up knowing, or suspecting. Someone got to her, I'm not sure who, but she started calling me, upset. I couldn't face her, and she ended up going to my brother with it. Obviously he saw through everything right away. He kept on about how stupid I was to let myself get involved with this. You, the granddaughter of the Chief of Security, assigned to the captain's son. I mean, it was supremely stupid, even for me.'

I look at him then and he reaches for me as if it's all he's been waiting for.

'When you went back to him, I was ... ' He tails off, shakes his head. 'I thought about it all the time. ALL THE TIME. Drove myself nuts with it. Then the day before the wedding I saw you waiting for a transporter and the sight of you just ... broke me into pieces. Like, I literally couldn't even stand, my legs gave out. People were walking past me like, what is wrong with this guy? Once I could walk again I followed you, all the way to Fertility. Found myself on the floor again – couldn't think, couldn't even see. How was I going to do this? How was I going to spend my life seeing you married? Seeing you pregnant with his child? Seeing you living your life with him? And then I realised what was upsetting me the most. You were alone. You had gone there alone and it seemed like such a hard thing to have to do alone. Such a scary thing. And I wanted to call you and tell you I'd come with you, just to hold your hand. I didn't want you in there alone.'

I feel the heat of the tears building in my eyes and before I know it I can't see. I try to push a sob back into my throat with my knuckles but it escapes anyway. The flat of his hand is on my cheek and his mouth is close to mine as I say, 'You were there? You were outside?'

He nods, pushing my tears with his thumb. I kiss him so suddenly that we crash teeth and I feel how surprised he is for a second before he is kissing me back, deep and sweet and full, leaning into me, my hands on his face and his hand on my hip, my leg. I push his shoulders until he lies back on the bunk, climb on to him with my legs either side of his hips, pulling off my T-shirt while he watches me, knocking my arm on the upper bunk in a way that reminds me of Ventura. Then I am pushing up his shirt so that my hands are on his skin while I feel the tension in his stomach as he reaches back to pull it off the rest of the way. He drops it on the floor and turns back to me, kisses my neck, but I push on his chest until he lies flat. And then we are still and I am just watching him. One of my hands on the side of his face, thumb against his beautiful parted lips, one hand just where the pretty line of moles on his throat spills down over his chest, marking the way to his heart. I don't realise that there must be something in the expression on my face until he whispers, 'What is it?' and narrows his amber eyes.

'I thought I knew you,' I tell him, shaking my head.

'You do,' he says, frowning. 'You do know me.'

My head just keeps shaking.

I shift until I am lying next to him, facing away. I feel the way he lies there, shocked, for a moment, before he presses his face against the back of my neck. 'Even if you never believe anything else, believe this,' he says. 'From the moment I met you, I knew every moment I'd ever spent with Annelise was empty. Even just talking to you, being around you, I felt more alive than I had ever felt. I had never known love and suddenly I knew it. I knew all of it. And I knew my real first time was still in the future. And I was right. Man, was I right. Because our first time – that was my real first time. That was the moment I realised how it was really meant to be, how it was really meant to feel, what it was really meant to mean. It was easily one of the best things that ever happened to me, and it'll stay that way for ever, for as long as I'm alive to remember it.' As he says this he has his fingers, his palms, his hands on my hips, gripping them in, pulling me in, and his mouth moves up the back of my neck, into my hair, close to my ear. 'Nothing ever felt like that.' And I hear it in his voice, all of it. And this is what makes me turn back to him, pull him to me, let him kiss me as he breathes in deep through his nose. And just for that moment I am not angry with him, how could I be? Right then I am back there in that moment, that long breathless moment just afterwards when he held my eye and I held his and I felt tears burn because there was too much love inside for me to hold in.

But suddenly it feels as if maybe it wasn't quite the way I remember it.

And so this is why, right now, despite the smell of his skin, the feel of him against me, the fact that all it does is make me want him closer, as close as two humans can get, despite all this, I manage to push him away and shake my head and, even though I'm out of breath, tell him, 'That's the worst thing about it, Dom – that that beautiful thing that happened to us wasn't actually what I thought it was. It was something else. And I guess that's OK. But what hurts is that you knew and I didn't. And we just weren't feeling the same things.'

He is shaking his head. 'You're wrong. We were feeling the same things. We were. Seren, you're the only girl I've ever loved.' But, even though maybe I should, I don't believe him, I can't, not even with the way he is looking at me, so sad, so sweet, skin golden and perfect even in the low, greenish light from the strip bulb.

'It's not just this.' Something hard jamming in my throat. 'It's all the things I thought were true. It's the fact the whole basis of us is not what I thought it was. How can you say I know you when you've kept some of the most important things that have happened to you secret from me? Does it really matter that you've done it because you don't want to make me sad? You keep secrets from me, Dom, huge ones, and I *never* keep secrets from you. I tell you everything. Every little thing. Maybe way too much. Probably way more than you want to know, but I put everything out there, no matter how ugly, because

I trust you to love me anyway, and honest is all I know how to be.'

'And I love that.'

'So why can't you do that for me?'

He presses his face against my shoulder and sighs there, spreading heat along my skin.

'Estrellita, I didn't tell you because, from the moment I met you, you made me see everything differently, even myself. You were the only good decision I ever made. Was it so wrong that I wanted to forget it all and be the guy you thought I was? Without the lost jobs and the black eyes and the grievous violence charges and the probation and the sex with a girl I didn't love because I thought it was the closest I would ever get?'

'The closest you would ever get to what?'

'To love. To loving someone and them loving me back.' He shakes his head slowly. 'I didn't know that you would come along and change everything.'

It's lovely. It's a lovely thing to say. So how come it just sits on my heart like a stone? I should say something but I can't; instead I just let him look at me as if I am a well with an answer written in the bottom of it, way down where it is too dark to see.

Chapter Seventeen

I fall suddenly out of sleep so that I jolt in Dom's arms and wake him, just enough so that he loosens his arms from around me and turns on to his back. He sleeps like that most of the time, on his back, hands on his lower stomach, mouth slightly open, head turned just a little to the side as if he is listening for something. The frown is new.

I crawl to the bottom of the bunk and around his legs, then up on to the bunk above, where I stare at the ceiling, at the slowly turning air vent I've seen so many times before and never thought I'd see again. It even has the same Earth manufacturer name: Santex Systems. I give up on the idea of sleep and head outside.

The sky is the purple-grey of a cloudy dawn and I look down over the settlement for a moment without seeing anyone or anything move. I turn my back on it and head into the forest, into the dead spaces between the trees where nothing seems to grow. The only thing I want to do is run. So that's what I do. I just let my feet follow each other. Until

I am hot and my hair is sticking to my neck and the air is burning in my throat and lungs. Go, go, go, in my brand new, way too big Concordia trainers. The ground is soft, almost hollow beneath my feet, as if there is this whole world down there that none of us can know about.

It's been too long since I did this, and too long since I had a full night's sleep, and too long since I ate like a normal person, so before I know it I am dizzy and slowing to a stop and bending at the waist and spitting into the dry brown dirt underfoot. Then I am sitting, holding my spinning head, leaning back against the rippled wall of the tree trunk behind me. And this is when I look up and see them. The glow-flies we saw at the river, their light pale in the rising day, utterly still, sleeping. Here they are, gathered on the underside of the branches above so that I am under my own personal sea of stars, and it is so silent, perfectly silent, in a way I have come to love about Huxley-3. I close my eyes and let my head drop back, eyes closed.

And then suddenly it isn't silent. Suddenly there is a noise, very quiet at first but rising rapidly, filling the air around me. And it is almost like ... music. Except it can't be. Except it is. I look around me, peering into the trees.

'Hello?' I call, getting to my feet. 'Hello?'

Now I've stood it seems to have grown quieter. I go back to the tree. Louder. Lay my head against it – louder still. Almost as if it's coming *out of the tree*. I lay my ear there. It makes no sense, but I'm standing there holding my head in my hands and I can still hear it and I have to know, so I drive my nails into the bark, push my fingers around a ridge of it and pull. Pull and pull and pull until there is this fibrous rending noise and I have a decent-sized flake of it in my hand. The exposed wood underneath is pale and wettish. I lay my hand on it.

'Hello?' I call. 'Is there someone in there?'

I can still hear it.

I drive my fingers in as far as I can under another bit of the bark and pull, wrenching my own shoulders and driving little bits of wood in under my nails and into my skin. I don't stop, I can't, I keep going, even after I am bleeding and crying with the effort of it. There is just something about this. I have to know. I have to.

'Hello?' I call again, hearing the fear in my own voice, and then suddenly arms are closing around me tight, pulling me back.

'Seren?' It's Grace, frowning at me, trapping my arms so that I can't keep tearing at the bark, struggling to get me to stop. 'What are you doing?'

'Music,' I tell her. 'I heard music, from in there.' But as soon as I say it I can't hear it any more. It is gone, as if it was never there. 'I can't ...' I look at Grace, at her wide eyes, at the way she is swallowing. 'I can't hear it any more, but it was real, and it came from in there.'

She shifts her eyes to the tree. 'Music?' she says. 'You heard music coming from the tree?'

I nod.

She runs her palms down my arms and holds my hands out so that they are between us where we can both look at them, at the bloody mess I have made of my nails, at the way they are shaking.

'Seren, I . . .'

And just from her tone and the way she is shaking her head I know more or less what she is going to say so I walk away, but she follows me.

'I know you're going to tell me it's all in my head,' I yell back over my shoulder. 'So we can skip that part because I've heard it all before.'

'I was only going to say that you've been through so much—'

I cut her off. 'That's another way of saying the same thing!'

'You're right,' she agrees, which makes me stop and turn to look at her. She closes the gap between us, hands up as if she surrenders. 'You're totally right. If you tell me you heard it, I believe you. But there are easier ways of getting inside one of these trees. We've got machines over there that'll turn one to sawdust in about eight minutes. And it'll save your hands.'

There's a smile on my face then, and one on hers. I only look at her properly now and realise she is in what looks like their rec uniform, and is sweaty, flushed in the face.

'What are you doing out here?' I ask her.

'I was running,' she says, pushing sweat off her top lip with her forearm. 'This is one of my favourite routes. I just ... sometimes it's the only way to think. To get my head clear. Apart from attacking trees, what were you doing?'

But I don't get time to tell her before the pain hits, sharp and angry, driving through me like a hot knife so that I almost black out. Or maybe white out – it is more as if my eyes just fill with white and so do my ears and there is no sound except this whistle in my head even though I can see that Grace is talking to me, or trying to.

I am holding my side, my hip, and so she pulls at my top then until she sees it, the coral scar, the way it is lumpy and hard and bruised.

'What is this?' she asks me, and by now the pain has subsided enough for me to hear again. 'How did you do this?'

I puff out a few breaths before I realise I am OK, that the tide of it has washed away again, for now.

'We cut ourselves on coral, back on the island,' I tell her.
'We?'

'Ezra and me. His is worse than mine, actually.'

She pulls my top up again, frowning. 'Coral?' she says. 'Like a coral reef?'

I nod.

'Was it phosphorescent?' I just go on looking at her, so she says, 'Did it glow?'

She watches me nod again, pulls my top down.

'We need to get you to Jason.' She takes my arm.

'Who's Jason?'

'He's the doctor. We need to get this checked out. This stuff is … ' She scratches her head. 'We've been researching the phosphorescent life forms on this planet since we got here and, I mean, we still don't know much. One thing we do know is that some of them are very … unusual. They have unusual properties on a quantum level. Here, put your weight on me – I'll help you.'

'Wait!' I step away from her. 'What "unusual properties"? Oh my God, is this killing me?' I hear the panic in my voice.

She holds my arm again, shushing me. 'No, no, it's nothing like that. It's just that the molecular structure of them is … unique. But then, it would be, wouldn't it?' She's smiling, but it's one of those smiles people give you when they want you to be brave about something. 'Seren, really, I'm sure it's nothing to worry about, but I want to take you to Jason right away, just to get that wound checked, OK? He's dying to meet you anyway.'

'He's dying to meet me?'

'Of course. Everyone is. But especially Jason, because he's met you before.'

I frown at her.

'Back on Ventura when you were a baby,' she clarifies. 'He came here with me.'

Chapter Eighteen

We walk a few more steps before I say, 'You ran away with him? Because you were in love?'

She laughs. 'No, it was nothing like that,' she says, and then she looks sad. 'It was a series of events that brought us here. A stupid series of events that started happening, snowballing, and, at some point it just was too late to ... turn back the clock.'

I go on watching her as we walk in the gloom under the trees.

'I haven't talked about this for so long, Seren. I'm not sure I even can.' She shakes her head at the ground in front of her as if she might cry, but then sighs and says, 'I was in our quarters. You were asleep in your cot next to the bed. You were such a good baby. You slept well and you smiled a lot and you were happy to be held by just about anybody. You were small, so the doctors would weigh you and worry but then they would see you smiling and they'd realise you were ... perfect.' She looks at me now with this smile on her face as if she can still see the baby she's talking about.

'Dad ... Jamie ... never told me anything like that,' I say. 'He never talked much about when I was a baby.'

She loses her smile. 'I guess Grandma helped to look after you quite a bit, though, right?'

I swallow. 'Um, I think so, but ... '

'But?'

'She died when I was five.' I just get it out, quick. 'Of PEST.'

She stops so suddenly that I walk on a few paces before realising and looking back at her where she is nodding, pushing tears in her eyes, whispering to herself, 'OK, OK,' and forcing deep, shaky breaths.

I think of something. 'But I spent a lot of time with Great Granny Bea – she only just died last year – and she was ... well, you know, she was pretty cool.'

She keeps doing those breaths but she smiles a little, too, and I reach for her hand, squeeze it. She looks down at it, then up at me, then starts walking again.

'I don't know why it still hurts when I lost her, lost all of you, sixteen years ago. I mean ... ' She scratches her forehead and this expression crosses her face that scares me. 'I've done so much grieving for everyone I lost. You ... I suppose you know what I mean?'

I do, but I also wonder if a lot of mine is still to come. 'I'm guessing it was worse for you,' is what I say.

She doesn't answer that at first, then she nods, pressing her lips together, clears her throat. 'I was in my quarters when I got a call on my pod, and it was Kat Von Buren or, no, wait, what was her married name? Marshall's name? Lomax. Kat Lomax. She was a captain's aide. Already, at twenty. But she was absolutely devastated to find herself pregnant. And with identical twins, too, so that everyone knew it was a natural pregnancy. She was so funny. So embarrassed. She had just had them when she went back to work, leaving them with her little sister to take care of. Not many people did that, but in Kat's case it was probably the right thing to do. She would have just been frustrated by it. We were friends, you see, or . . . I thought we were.'

I frown at her.

'She had been called to Coms for a situation, because Captain Lee was unavailable. I think the truth of the matter was that Lee was drunk. There'd been a party for your grandfather's birthday earlier that evening. Anyway, Coms was a pretty quiet place most of the time. It was where I was working before I had you. Never more than one of us on shift and most of the time there was nothing to do. We had been out of range of everything and everyone for so long. And then suddenly, this one night, someone was communicating with us.'

Even though I know what must be coming, it still gives me chills. 'Who?'

'Concordia. But of course, they were communicating in Russian. Which is why Kat called me, because I knew a little. I'd learned it from my dad and grandfather . . . '

She sees me nodding in the corner of her eye.

'Well, of course, you know that. She didn't tell me much, but enough to get me to realise she needed me, so I went there and of course it was just mind-blowing, because these were the first people that weren't on Ventura that we had ever heard from or known anything about. And I got them on audio and was just talking to them, so frustrated by my terrible Russian, but we got there, and I realised that there was so much about this situation that was not good.'

'Like what?'

'Well, Concordia were in distress. They were losing crewmembers to an infection, a flesh eater. The worst part was that it is entirely treatable if you have the right drugs, but they didn't have them. They were missing this one vital ingredient needed to make the medication. And we had it. We had it and we had the ability to make more of it.'

'So, how did you get it to them?'

'I was translating all this for Kat and the whole time she was shaking her head, and then she said, "We need to just walk away from this," and I was telling her we couldn't. I mean, we couldn't just walk away from hundreds of people and let them die when we could save them. What if this were us? But she was insistent that we couldn't let them come to us, we couldn't risk this infection coming anywhere near us, which I understood, but since we could treat it – what difference did it make? But what if they were wrong? So we called Jason, because he was a medic and also a good friend from Education. I translated everything I could from the audio, from test results they sent through on the data, and by the end he was holding his head in his hands and saying he was pretty sure that they were right about this ingredient and that we needed to get it to them. Kat was still so against it and at one point she said, "You do realise they're passing us? They left thirty-seven years later than us but they're travelling so much faster that they're passing us." And I realised then just how much Ventura meant to her. She would let hundreds of people die rather than let them overtake us? It was partly the coldness of that that led me to do what I did. Because she said that if anyone went at all it would be us, Jason and me and Gus, the guy who was on shift in Coms at the time, and it would be now, and nobody would know about it. Of course, I told her right away that I couldn't – how could I? I was a mother of two young children. I couldn't go on a high-risk off-ship mission. I couldn't. But there was part of me ... '

She breaks off and looks at me before saying, 'This is hard for me to admit, but I want to be honest with you. There was part of me that was excited, thrilled really, that this was happening to me. That something was happening to me.'

I nod, taking that in.

'So, I don't know, we just stopped thinking and started doing. Jason got everything we needed, the drugs, hazmat suits, and Kat swiped us through into the docks, which were empty. It was the middle of the night but there would usually have been someone there, so I have no idea what she did to get rid of everyone, but she was very keen that this had to be kept quiet. The most important thing was that there was to be no panic on Ventura. When we got back and everything was OK it would be different, but . . . ' She shrugs. 'Javi, a pilot Kat knew, was waiting for us in the shuttle, and I was the next to climb in there—' She struggles, cuts herself off. 'I have thought about that moment so many times.'

We both wait in the silence she leaves.

'That moment that I got in there, willingly, knowing you and Pandy were waiting for me . . . ' She shakes her head. 'I have no idea what I was thinking, Seren, except that everything would work out just the way we thought, but it was never . . . it was never going to do that.'

And I'm thinking, *Pandy?* But all I say is, 'Tell me what happened.'

The sun comes out, pink, beyond the trees somewhere.

'It took us about ten hours to get to them. I can't even tell you how it was when we saw their ship for the first time – so weird. You live on Ventura and you just have no sense that there is anyone else, anything else at all, and then suddenly there it is. And it looked so different to Ventura – so long and sleek – you could see why it was overtaking us. Docking was terrifying, suiting up, not knowing what we would find on the other side of the lock when it opened.'

'What did you find?' I ask her.

'People whose faces we'd never seen before, which was crazy enough. But they were scared, so scared. Most of them were ill to greater or lesser degrees, with open wounds, sores all over them. We didn't plan to stay long, we couldn't risk it and they knew that. The problem was what happened with Gus.'

'What happened?'

'I still don't know whether it was brought on by the situation, by the stress, or what it was, but suddenly he was on the floor, struggling to breathe, clutching at his chest, and there was nothing for it but to get him out of the suit and treat him. We took him to their medical unit, which was completely overwhelmed anyway. I mean, the scene in there was just ... a horror show. Zombie apocalypse. People with half their faces gone, so that you could see right through to their skulls, jawbones. And Gus was lying there in among it all and it came to me: the dread, the feeling that this was doomed. Gus had had a heart attack. We couldn't move him; we couldn't leave, not without killing him. I found Jason then, out of his suit, treating people. I asked him what he was doing. He didn't see the difference now that Gus had been exposed. We'd just have to all four hope for the best and treat ourselves at the first sign. And I just ... stood there. Feeling it all falling apart around me, feeling it unravel. There was no way this was going to turn out OK.'

We have come to the edge of the forest, where the trees end and the settlement begins. There is nobody around. She comes to a stop and stands there, looking over everything blankly.

'I panicked. I asked them if I could contact Ventura. Kat was waiting in Coms. I told her everything, which is exactly what I shouldn't have done.'

She looks so scared right now, reliving this.

'She didn't even say goodbye. She just told me that any craft that approached the Ventura had been ordered to be destroyed under the deadly infectious diseases act, and disconnected.'

I gasp. 'What? That was it? She wouldn't let you come back? But it was a disease you knew you could treat! That makes no sense.'

'It turns out not everyone responds to the treatment. It's a genetic lottery. Gus was ... ' She swallows. 'Gus was gone in three days.'

'But she didn't know that then.'

'That's true. But there are some things she did know,

189

and I've come to believe she made her decision based on those.'

'Like what?'

She sighs. 'She did it in the interests of Ventura. To protect them from a disease that probably would have claimed precious lives. To protect them from knowing that they had become an outmoded technology, launched ahead of its time and being passed. Something like that could be as corrosive on the whole structure of a ship's society, its philosophy, as a disease.'

I can't believe she can talk about this so calmly. 'But why let you go in the first place?'

She takes my arm and we start to walk over the mud to the buildings of the settlement. 'Maybe because there were people dying and she knew we could save them. Maybe because if we didn't it would get back to Earth or to other travellers and Ventura would be in trouble for that. Or ... she may have just taken an opportunity that was presented to her.'

'An opportunity?' I'm frowning so hard it's giving me a headache.

'I'm pretty sure that she thought Jason and I were two people Ventura could do without. A few people thought that about me, actually.'

'Why?'

'I was never political, but it bothered me that Ventura was being run on the completely wrong ideology: do your duty. It's not just that it was repressive but it was ineffective, too – or I thought it was going to be in the end. Captain Lee was such good friends with my dad that he would listen to me, or he acted like he did, anyway. People thought I was a dangerous influence, I guess. Especially Kat. She hated the things I said. I held meetings in the drill hall of people who felt the same as me, and they were getting bigger. I remember her telling me that was going to get me killed. That was while I was pregnant with you.'

We walk in silence.

'She was right, I guess. It probably would have got me killed.'

'It did,' I say suddenly. 'It did get you killed.' I turn to her. 'You were dead. And none of this seems like a good enough reason for it. These are all stupid reasons for me and my sister to end up with no mother. For my dad to think you killed yourself because he couldn't make you happy and spend the best part of his life sad and lonely. Why didn't you try to come back?'

'I did.' Her eyes fill with tears. 'Our explorer was completely dead. Remotely immobilised. Concordia had been constructed with only unmanned explorer drones, for speed of passage. In the end it was all Jason could do to stop me trying to swim through space to get back to you.' The tears spill. 'I would have done anything to get to you. It took a long time for me to stop trying.'

We have come to the clearing in the middle of the

settlement, next to the river. Their mess tables are lined up here, under a huge reflective tarp that waves slowly in the wind. We both watch it, listening to the unmistakeable kitchen noises that come from the nearest building.

I think of something. 'Ventura remotely immobilised the explorer?' I frown. 'They can do that?'

She nods. 'Which is why I was so amazed you guys got here.'

I think about that for a moment.

She is wiping the tears off her face with the back of her hand. 'Is it too much to ask you for your story?'

I shrug. 'Compared to yours it's actually pretty straightforward. I was supposed to marry Ezra. I fell in love with Dom. I tried to live without him but I couldn't. They locked me up and were trying to have him killed. We had to escape.'

'You did it for love.' She reaches for me then, pulls me into a hug where her hand is cupping the back of my head, pulling me in really tight, and I can feel the way her chest is heaving as she says again, 'You did it for love.'

A speaker attached to the nearest tree chimes three times.

'That's breakfast,' says Grace. 'Think you could manage something before we find Jason?'

We are sitting down at one of the tables and she has already introduced me to the guy on mess duty who brings out steaming bowls of that same brown grain by the time she says, 'So, I guess I know why Mariana came with you, but what about Ezra?'

'He came because he knew we would probably die if he didn't. She's the captain now, his mother.'

Grace nods slowly, a strange smile spreading. 'Of course she is,' she says, just as these two guys arrive behind her.

They greet her in Russian and she jumps, laughs a little before turning and half getting up to kiss them. They are both ridiculously tall; one of them is her age, with a shaved head and a tattoo all across his chest that shows at the unbuttoned neck of his polo shirt, the other a little younger than me, dark hair fanning up like a brush, skinny, big green eyes looking at me nervously.

'Seren.' Grace takes a deep breath. 'I want you to meet my partner, Pasha.'

The older guy takes my hand and holds it between his. 'So happy,' he says, with this thick accent.

'And this is Kirill,' she says, picking up the hand of the young guy while simultaneously picking up mine. 'He's your brother.'

Chapter Nineteen

The first thing the new half-brother I never knew about says to me is, 'It's true you stole explorer vehicle?' – because of course he speaks pretty good English.

'I guess. Though I never quite thought about it like that.'

'Cool.'

Grace sends someone for Dom and the others, and although Pasha asks me a lot of questions, I'm distracted, watching the rest of the settlement arrive to breakfast. Nobody here is much older than Grace, or much younger than me. Kirill may be the youngest person I've seen so far. They're all tall, they have a thing about tattoos, and they all have one of only two types of hair – the straight black kind that Kirill has, or blond. They all wear their pods attached to their ears. There are way fewer of them than I expected, and way more men than women. I wonder if the women are just somewhere else. Most of them stop by the table and look at me before they sit down, talking to Grace in Russian a bit before nodding at me. They don't smile a lot.

When she sees I'm not eating, Grace gets up.

'We need to get you to Jason.'

'Won't he be eating?' I look around.

'He never eats breakfast. He'll be at Med.'

Some kind of land vehicle, huge and running on tracks, is coming down the hill as we arrive at the Med building. Ezra and Mari are helping Dom get down the dropped ramp at the back. I feel them all watching me but I don't look back.

'Where were you?' says Dom, in the end. 'We were pretty worried.'

'I was running,' I say. 'Needed to clear my head.'

'It's my fault,' says Grace. 'Seren and I bumped into each other, and we had a lot to talk about.'

The door of the building behind her opens then, as if whoever was inside heard us. The girl who looks out at us is beautiful – big green cat eyes, long black hair, uniform sleeves rolled up to reveal the arm muscles of a marble sculpture. She doesn't say anything or ask why we're there before standing aside to watch us pass through the door, while Grace speaks to her in Russian and she nods.

'Irina's my niece,' Grace says, once we're inside, then, seeing my face, 'Well, I should say, she's Pasha's niece.'

I watch her as she goes to Dom, takes his arm, helps him sit on the metal bench that is affixed to the wall and then starts unravelling his already pretty dirty-looking bandage, glancing up at him as she does, smiling shyly in a way I both recognise and don't like very much.

The inner door opens suddenly and a sandy-haired guy in his thirties comes out, whistling and absently drying his hands on a towel, before freezing.

'Oh my God,' he says, and he stands there, literally losing colour out of his face, doing the most accurate impression I've ever seen of someone seeing a ghost. He reaches his hand out to the side and it hovers in the air for a moment before Grace takes it in both of hers. 'Oh my God, Grace,' he says again, and they look at each other, shaking their heads before looking back.

Ezra shifts his weight, looking uncomfortable while they both stare, because it's him they're staring at.

'I'm sorry,' the guy says, after what seems like for ever but is probably only a few seconds. 'I'm ... I'm Jason Page.' He steps forward, takes hold of Ezra's hand to shake, but then just holds it.

'Ezra Lomax.'

'And this is Seren, Domingo and Mariana,' says Grace, snapping Jason out of it so that he blinks and comes to me, taking my hand and nodding but clearly completely distracted so that he ignores the others and pretty quickly goes to the desk and sits down at it heavily. 'Grace, please tell me you have something to drink.'

She laughs.

He hangs his head and runs his hands over it, laughing at himself. 'I'm sorry, it's just … you look so much like Marshall. I mean, seriously, it's … ' He looks back at him again. 'So weird.'

I look at Ezra, trying to picture it. From what I remember of Marshall Lomax, which isn't a lot, it seems hard to believe there's that much resemblance. I guess that has something to do with the fact that he was dying of PEST for almost the whole time I knew him. I remember that he limped; I remember that my dad said he drank too much. I guess all this goes to show that knowing someone when they're dying (at thirty, which is awful now I think about it) doesn't tell you a lot about what they were like at sixteen with everything ahead of them.

'We were all at school together,' says Jason. 'Me, and both your sets of parents. God. Even saying that is weird. Marshall's still twenty-one in my head.'

'You and Dad were good friends?'

'Yeah,' he says, laughing darkly, letting it turn into a cough. 'He … never mentioned me?'

'I don't remember.' Ezra shrugs. 'I mean, I was ten when he died. I don't really remember that much about him. He was sick for so long and then he was gone. And then, I don't know, it's not as if my mum ever talked about him that much. I wish I'd known him better.'

Jason looks like someone watching a movie, a really sad one.

'You even talk like him,' he says, then shoves his chair back. 'Excuse me.' And he leaves, not back through the inner door but out into the day, banging the door closed behind him so hard we all flinch a little.

Grace looks at the closed door, then at us, before she says, 'Just give me a minute,' and disappears though it herself.

'What the hell?' says Ezra, laughing.

I give him a look. 'Your dad must have been a really good friend of his – I guess it's just . . . too much. They're not used to having to deal with the past, are they?'

Just then the door opens again, but it's Kirill. He talks to Irina in Russian, but afterwards I feel as if I should say something so I say, 'Um, this is Kirill. He's . . . it seems he's my half-brother.'

And they all just look at me.

It's Ezra who is the first to recover enough to offer him his hand, make the right kinds of noises, say the right kinds of things. Kirill goes to Dom and Mari too and all the time all I seem able to do is stare, all the time thinking, *You're my brother, one of the closest blood relatives I'll ever have, and yet I feel nothing.* And in fact, it's less than nothing, it's worse – it's a creeping, insidious dislike, just a shade above indifference.

The door opens and Jason and Grace come back in.

'Sorry about that,' says Jason, going to Dom and Mariana and shaking their hands. 'I'm Jason Page, formerly of

Ventura.' He does this one loud laugh, leaving them looking more baffled than ever. 'Gunshot wound, right?' he says to Dom. 'Alexei and Vasily can be like that if you surprise them. They've been at the outpost, guarding us from non-existent threats, for too long. Irina should take another look at that for you.' He turns back to Ezra and me but without looking at us. 'So Grace tells me that you've had a run-in with some of the local wildlife? Come with me.'

We follow him through to the other room where lights flick on and there are blue Concordia-branded blankets draped over bulky shapes and it is more like a warehouse or a storage room than a Med unit. He pulls a blanket off something behind him to reveal what looks like a human-size oven, with a tray to push a human in on.

'Damn dust gets everywhere,' he says, shaking his head as he's folding up the blanket, and then stabbing at buttons to get it to come on. It does, eventually, after he swears at it a bit, humming into life.

'Who wants to go first?'

I don't mean to look at Ezra and swallow the way I do; I mean, it's more as if I'm just gathering my courage, but Ezra says, 'Look, what's this for? You can't just make us do things without explaining.'

'Quite right,' says Jason, and he smiles at him for a beat too long before he says, 'Simply a body scanner, just like the ones on Ventura. They looked a bit different but the principle's the same.'

'I'll go first,' says Ezra.

'It's OK,' I tell him, sitting on the bench, which is cold, and swinging my legs up. They both walk behind the nearby screen, which I guess is for protection from whatever's about to hit me. I try not to tremble while the bench rumbles into the tight, coffin-like space and it whines around me, hums, buzzes, the sound settling into a deep pulse that enters under my skull plates and ends up calming me, so that by the time they rumble me back out I am blinking, semi-conscious.

'It's not that bad,' I tell Ezra as I pass him.

Standing with Jason, I watch the screen in front of us, an image of Ezra, an X-ray map of him, scrolling through him layer by layer, like sliced meat, then zooming in on where the coral sits like a series of interlinked lightning strikes, several of which dig deep into his abdomen.

'Biological matter affecting mainly latissimus dorsi,' mutters Jason. 'But with minor penetration to liver or lung a possibility.'

'Is it hazardous?' I ask him.

He looks at me briefly before going back to studying the screen, and muttering, zooming in on a place at the base of Ezra's neck. 'Small secondary growth of biological matter at collarbone.' I realise then he is dictating to his com device. I sit on the low stool behind me and it is oddly warm beneath me. When I press my fingers against the side I find out why – it's made of wood.

When the scan's finished Jason goes straight to the door and says something in Russian before coming back in, followed by Grace and then Dom, who is leaning heavily on a wooden crutch. Mari peers round the door.

Jason looks around at us all. 'I've sent for Maxim – one of our science guys. I would need to get their opinion on this. There's quite a lot of it, the coral, and it looks as if it's still living, growing even, inside you. At the moment it seems to have taken hold mostly in muscles and subcutaneous areas but there is the possibility of it affecting organs at some point.'

'How quickly can they have it removed?' asks Dom.

Jason does this weird shrug. 'Removing it could be very complex,' he says. 'This is why I need the physicists. They've been studying this stuff for years.'

Irina comes in with a guy with an asymmetrical haircut. He's young, twenty-two at the most, pushing his sunglasses up off his impassive face.

'Maxim Kreznev,' he says. 'Science specialist.' He reaches to shake hands with everybody.

Jason slips easily into Russian to explain everything as they go to study the scans on-screen.

I feel Dom looking at me, looking at me the way he does when he wants me to come to him. I almost do, and when I don't he frowns, shifts awkwardly on his crutch and then comes to me, crashing into things and forcing everyone to move out of the way. When he gets close he puts his hand on my neck and shoulder.

'Are you OK?'

So much of me wants to melt against him like I normally would, but I don't. Ezra and Mariana and Grace watch us, pretending that they're not.

'Not really,' I say to him, hugging my arms across my stomach. 'How can I be when there's a weird alien growing inside me?' I try to laugh but it dies.

Jason and Maxim come back, still talking.

'Tell him about your ... experience ... this morning,' says Grace. 'In case it's important.'

Suddenly everyone is looking at me.

'I heard something, in the forest, a sound coming out of the tree, like right out of the trunk.' I look at the expressions on their faces. 'It's not the first weird thing though, and it's not just me, is it, Ezra?'

He looks surprised. 'Wait, what? Don't bring me into this. I haven't been hearing tree music.'

'But the lights,' I say to him. 'What about the lights in the sky, the shape we thought was a boat, the cave in the forest? We both saw those things.'

He makes a face. 'We just ... I don't know ... we were exhausted, dehydrated ... ' But he's starting to look unsure.

'It's got to be to do with this ... hasn't it?'

'Let me see if I understand,' says Maxim, a finger on

his mouth like someone considering something. He has this deep voice, this way of speaking that makes you listen. 'You've been having hallucinations – auditory and visual – during the time the ALF2 material has been inside you?'

'But how can it be hallucinations if we both see the same things?'

'I should take them with me to the facility,' says Maxim to Jason, but he shakes his head.

'You have no medical capabilities whatsoever at the research facility.'

Maxim laughs and gestures around. 'You barely have them here, Dr Page.'

Jason looks annoyed but only says, 'We need to monitor them, until we are sure what kind of effect this is having on their system.'

'I am pretty sure my father would prefer it if this kind of activity took place outside of the settlement. He has always—'

'I don't think we need to involve your father just yet,' says Grace, stepping closer to Maxim. 'Do we? The commodore needs his rest right now, doesn't he?'

Maxim sighs.

'In theory,' says Jason, 'if we wanted to bring on a hallucination, what would we need to do? What made them happen in the past?'

Ezra and I look at each other, but draw a blank.

Maxim folds his arms across his chest. 'ALF2's activity is enhanced by a number of stimuli – exposure to other ALFs mainly – but it can also be activated by low intensity laser.'

Irina and Jason share a look, and Irina leaves.

'We have one of those,' says Jason. 'We have one of those for stemming blood flow in flesh wounds.' He moves down the room, pulling blankets off equipment and beds like a magician. 'We can get you comfortable, get you fully wired up so we can monitor everything carefully and then try to trigger something.'

'Why would we do any of this?' says Dom. 'It's growing inside her. It's just going to keep growing. It hurts her already, sometimes. We need to get it out before it damages her. That's the issue, not any of this other stuff.' His hand grips my shoulder tight.

'I think you're absolutely right,' says Grace. 'I think it's important that we understand exactly what it is and the nature of its involvement with them first, though, at the risk of doing more damage.'

Dom makes a face. 'What does that even mean?'

Irina gets back with the laser, which pretty much looks like a gun, but all the same I manage to say to Dom, 'They're trying to help me. I'll be OK.'

He doesn't look even a little bit convinced, even as Ezra and I are lying back on the metal sick bay beds in our underwear. Irina and Jason then spend ages sticking these little sensors all over us and talking to Maxim in Russian, while Dom and Mari stand close by and frown. Dom reaches for my fingers and squeezes them, but I only let him have the tips.

'Right,' says Jason. 'This won't hurt.' He takes one final look around at all the little screens he has wired us up to – heart monitors and blood pressure and brain activity – and he talks to Irina a little and then he fires it at me. He's right. There's no pain, really, not beyond a vague heat, there's just the low hum of it, overlaying a slight crackle, and a faint smell like thunder on the island. Everyone watches me but I'm just lying there, looking over my own shoulder at the screens, at the way things are seeming to spike a little, but probably only because I'm scared.

He moves on to Ezra, doing it a couple of times before saying, 'OK?' and that is exactly when everything slides and melts and spirals down a hole, into me, out of me, into the floor, into the ground beneath me, beneath this place, a thousand miles down and still going. The world becomes like one of those paintings I've seen where it's all just dots, splashes, but pulsing, pulsing, becoming sound, becoming light, becoming sound again, talking to me. Pulsing. Pulling at every part of me until I am sure I will be torn to pieces, to an infinite number of tiny pieces that will float up and out and into the air and become a part of everything around me. And then it is happening, it has happened, I am gone, I have disintegrated, and everything is quiet, everything is still. My ears fill with silence. No, not quite silence. It is fuller than that, richer. A swooshing in and out, bubbling, like water. My eyes fill with blue, light in shards, a chopped-up sun. It is the ocean and I am underneath, looking up.

And then it all comes crashing in. Heat, sound. I'm on the floor of the Med unit under the bed I was lying on, and Dom is, weirdly, all the way across the room, head in his hands, sitting near the door, lunging across the floor when he sees me, calling, 'She's back! They're here!' in a way that seems to make the room fill with people.

Dom kneels next to me and pulls my head on to his lap. I look over at where Ezra is, twitching hard on the floor nearby like someone having a fit, while Jason and Irina try to steady him.

'Where were you?' Dom asks me.

'Where – what?'

His face is tight, bent by a confused frown. 'You disappeared,' he says. 'You were gone. Estrellita, you've been gone almost half an hour. Where were you?'

But I can't answer, can barely even hear, let alone speak, can't do anything except tremble with fear, the pain in my hip the only thing that anchors me to the real world, hotter than hell and twisting in my flesh, pulling a stifled scream from deep inside me, completely against my will.

Chapter Twenty

'Are you OK?' Dom keeps asking me, holding my face between his palms as I roll my head against his legs. 'Talk to me, Seren, please talk to me.'

I'm trying to, but nothing's coming out. In the end I manage to get myself up on to my elbows, to push his hands away and twist on to my side where I can find air, where I can breathe, where I can finally bring my eyes back into focus. I see Ezra then, completely out, Jason pulling up his eyelids and shining a light there as he leans over him, saying his name over and over.

Grace kneels in front of me, talking, while I stretch to peer round her at Ezra who is blinking and opening his eyes, with Mariana pushing hair back off his face and looking at Jason, who sits back on his heels and breathes out a long breath.

'Now do you see?' yells Dom, over everybody, everything. 'You need to work out how to get this stuff out of them.'

'That's not what I see,' says Maxim, who I hadn't even noticed was standing there, above me, until now.

Ezra coughs and then spits on to the floor next to him before sinking back to the ground, flat on his back. 'Jesus, Hemple,' he says. 'Did you feel that?'

'Dom says we ... disappeared.' But I can't seem to get any more out than that, so he glances at me through a slit open eye.

'It was ... I don't know ... different that time ...'

'Dom says we were gone for half an hour.'

'Man, it only felt like a few seconds.' He swallows; I watch his Adam's apple drag all the way up and then down. 'But I was definitely somewhere else, weren't you?'

I notice the way Jason is staring at him. Rapt. That's the word that comes into my mind.

'No,' says Dom. 'No, this is crazy. I don't care! I don't care about any of this! Didn't anybody see what I just saw? Didn't you see? They vanished! They were ... just ... gone. To who knows where. We need to cut this stuff out of them, no matter what it takes. It doesn't matter what it is or what it does.'

'Domingo, is it?' says Maxim, stepping towards him. 'I understand your concerns, but there's a bigger picture here. We have been studying Alien Life Form 2 for years at our scientific research facility and we have reason to believe that it is a multi-dimensional being.'

'A what?' It's Dom who says it, though we are all thinking it.

'That it's able to exist in more than one dimension at a time.' He squats next to us. 'We believe it does this through a process called quantum entanglement. Possibly, on some molecular level, it is influencing you to make a temporal-spatial shift. A displacement.'

'Tell us what happened,' Jason says to Ezra.

Ezra sits, rubs his face. 'I mean, I don't know. This time wasn't like the others – it was a more like ...'

'Falling down a hole?' I supply.

'Yeah, but also ... the other times it was like looking through a window at something, where this was more like opening the door and going in.'

'It's acting like an antenna,' says Jason. 'An antenna to another dimension.'

'OK, this is crazy,' says Dom. 'Wasn't anyone else here just now? Didn't you see what happened to them? They were gone.' He closes his eyes against the memory for a second. 'They were here and then they weren't. That can't be good for their bodies. It can't be.'

'Any further research would have to be carried out up at the research facility,' says Maxim to Jason, who nods.

'Further research?' Dom tries to stand, fails. Grace hands him his crutch but, after trying to use it once, he throws it away and struggles up without it, his leg held stiffly out to the side. 'You go ahead and do whatever research you like, but you won't be using Seren as your lab rat. You're going to operate on her and get it out, all of it, right now.'

'I should go,' says Maxim. 'My father will hear of this and I will need to explain.'

After watching him leave, Jason says, 'An operation to extract the matter would be complicated, Domingo.'

'So you're suggesting she just keeps it in there for ever?'

'Not for ever, but until such time as we can work out the best way to do it, and the extent of its involvement with her, it may actually be the best option to leave it in situ.'

'While it grows some more? And becomes more involved?' He almost falls over. 'Are you even a real doctor?'

Irina goes to Dom and hands him his crutch, surprising him, but then makes sure he's steady before stepping away. I notice then how tall she is, only about a half head shorter than Dom.

'You're a medic too?' he asks her, tone gentler, and she nods. 'So what do you think?'

She sighs and crosses her arms before answering, tilts her head. 'Before machines lost contact, readings were OK.' She has the same heavy accent that Kirill has, like a movie villain. 'We check them over now to make sure, but they seem fine.'

'You think it's OK to let that thing grow inside her?'

I lie back on the ground then, listening to them talk over me. I press my hand over the place where the coral is, hot and hard as a bony, burning spider. It's all I can do not to sink my fingers in around it and haul it out. I imagine myself doing that and holding it up to them all, covered in my blood and flesh and hanging with ribbon-like nerves.

'How can you be such an idiot, Suarez?' I hear Ezra say. 'We can't just get it pulled out. Not now. Not now we know what this is. I mean, jeez, communicating with another dimension? It's too important.'

Dom shakes his head. 'Not to me. Not more important than Seren's safety.'

'We will monitor her,' says Jason. 'Very closely.'

'How?' laughs Dom. 'How will you do that if she disappears?'

Jason raises his eyebrows. 'Speaking of which, we should check them over. I'll get what we need.' Irina follows him, looking back over her shoulder once.

Grace and Mari help me get to my feet while Dom says, 'There is no way that thing is staying in you another day.'

And I find myself saying, 'You don't get to decide about my body.'

He looks shocked but says, 'Well, I think, if you're ill and you're not able to do it for yourself, then I do. I have to.' He steps close to me. 'Because I love you, and I have to protect you.'

I shake my head at the floor between us. 'You don't have to protect me. I can do that myself.'

'No you can't. Clearly you can't. This should never have

happened in the first place. You've never been a strong swimmer. If I'd been there for you then like I should have been we wouldn't even be having this conversation. I'm not letting this happen; they are operating on it today – now.'

I turn to walk away. He follows me.

'Don't you follow me,' I yell, turning on him so fast he almost loses his balance. 'Everything's on your terms and I'm sick of it. You don't get to tell me what's important, or what matters. You don't get to control what I know and don't know about the past, about my own goddam story. And you CERTAINLY don't get to tell me what I want. It's MY body and it's MY decision and nobody gets to tell ME or ANYONE ELSE what to do with it.'

'Seren, you're not making sense,' he says.

That's it. That's the button.

'Leave me alone, Dom,' I say, feeling the twist in the face I'm making.

'Estrellita, all I'm trying to do ...'

'I said, leave me alone!' It's so loud that the others all freeze now and watch us.

Dom looks at me for this long moment, a frown forming, before shaking his head at me, turning to go, struggling on his crutch before throwing it to the floor again, limping towards the door and out of it, without looking back, and I turn to where Mari, Grace and Ezra are watching me silently.

Chapter Twenty-One

Even though I have no desire to stay there at all and it has this horrible tangy electrical smoke smell because seemingly we managed to fry his heart-rate machine with some kind of energy surge, Jason is pretty insistent that we stay in Med for observation the rest of that day and overnight. Observation means us being on an IV drip and Irina coming in regularly to take blood pressure readings and check we're still alive. They put Russian movies on a screen for us. Kirill appears at one point with food in bowls, and it's the same grainy thing as the last two times, which makes me start thinking. He sits on the stool near us to eat his, watching the movie.

'Kirill,' I ask him. 'What is this?'

'We call it lebeda,' he says through a mouthful.

'Is there ever anything else on the menu?' says Ezra, which is what I'm thinking.

Kirill looks confused. 'Menu?'

'Do you have other things to eat sometimes?'

He looks back at the movie. 'This year, no.'

'This year?' Ezra almost yells, but Kirill just shrugs, laughs at something on the screen.

When he's gone Irina comes back in to mess with our IVs and take our blood pressure again and then she says, 'Domingo asks to see you.'

Which makes my heart beat in my throat.

'Tell him I'll see him tomorrow,' I say.

She slow blinks. 'Then I go to walk with him.'

'I'm sorry?'

Ezra laughs.

'I help him to walk to go home.' Another slow blink of her pretty eyes. 'Dr Jason Page is here for staying the night with you so I finish my shift now.'

I nod, shrug, and she leaves, stopping just before she does to take the band out of her glossy ponytail so that her hair unravels down her back.

'I don't know how Suarez does it,' says Ezra, shaking his head, and I throw my pillow at him. 'No, I mean it. Man, if I had half his pulling power, I could do so much more with it.'

'Shut up, Ezra,' I say, but it does make fear prickle on my neck and leave a taste in my mouth, not dissimilar to blood.

'Why are you so mad at him anyway?' asks Ezra, his face turning serious as he says it.

'I'm not mad at him.'

'Then you do a really great impression of someone who is,' he says. 'Usually you love his whole overprotective husband thing.'

I watch my fingers drawing circles on the blanket in front of me.

'Personally I think he's wrong about this,' he says, and I frown up at him. 'You know there's something amazing, and important, going on.' He gestures at this bandaged ribs. 'You know we need to know at least a bit more about it before we panic.'

'Tell me what you saw,' I say.

He shakes his head. 'Man, I don't even know if I *saw* anything, but I definitely *felt* something.'

I stare at him, knowing what he means.

Just then, Jason comes in. 'How are we all this evening? Up to seeing Mariana? She's pretty insistent.'

But oddly, once she's in, sitting on the stool between us, she's almost silent. Weary and sad faced.

'This place is weird,' she says eventually. 'I mean … isn't it? Maybe it's just because most of them don't speak English, but they seem, I don't know, a bit off. And doesn't it seem as if there should be more of them, and as if they should have got a bit further than this in nine years? You realise it's their anniversary this week and they're actually getting ready to have some kind of party to celebrate? And that Maxim guy has some spooky dying father guy who seems to be in charge but who nobody ever sees. It's more like one of those Halloween movies than a real place.' She sighs. 'How are you now, anyway? This morning was . . . actually I don't even want to talk about it.' She tucks her hair behind her ears, then frowns at her hands in her lap. 'Why are you so mad at Dom?'

Ezra laughs. 'See.'

'I know he can be overprotective sometimes, but . . . '

They both watch me. 'He . . . hides things from me,' I say, finding that's still what bothers me most.

'Like what?'

But I don't answer, I just get a little cold and pull my blanket over my lap.

I wake up once in the night, sitting up suddenly to find Jason just turning off the screen.

'Am I going to die?' I ask him, half asleep.

He comes to the side of the bed and touches my hand. 'It seems as if there have been a lot of close calls with that already, Seren, and yet you're still here.'

'That's noncommittal,' I say, and he laughs.

As he turns to go I see the way he looks at Ezra, moves the arm that hangs off the side of the bed back on to it, making him stir and turn on his side.

Jason is asleep slumped over his desk in the morning. Ezra touches his shoulder and he jolts awake, wiping his mouth.

'We OK to go?' he asks him.

Jason blinks at him for the longest time, then says, 'I should do your obs again.' He goes to stand, then flaps his hand. 'Last ones were fine. Go get some breakfast.'

'You coming?' says Ezra, from the door.

'Ah no.' He smiles. 'Don't do breakfast, but thanks.'

We're early so Dom and Mari aren't there. Maxim comes to sit with us. There's something plasticky and artificial about him, with his even tan and sunglasses.

'Feeling better?' he asks, and we nod. 'I hope you'll let me give you the tour of our settlement today. Two days from now will be a special day for us actually – our ninth anniversary.' We all look up at the guys who are balancing on the top of ladders at the edge of the clearing, threading coloured lights into the lowest branches of the trees. 'We celebrate our founding day every year. You'll like it. Music, drinking, dancing. Traditionally we give a gift to someone we care about too.'

'Why is your English so good?' I ask him.

'Your mother,' he says, turning back to us. 'And Jason. My father wanted them to teach me your language, when they joined us. I was six.'

I watch him chew his food while I think about that. Him learning English from my mother.

'Why, though?' says Ezra. 'What was the point?'

'Acquiring an additional language develops executive function,' he says without missing a beat. 'Useful for a future commodore.'

'A future commodore?' Ezra frowns. 'What . . . as in . . . you? You're taking over from your old man when he . . . ?'

Maxim nods. 'It's understood that that's how things will be.'

'Wow,' says Ezra. 'That's . . . traditional . . . historical . . . weird . . . stupid.'

'How was your commanding officer chosen?'

'Assigned by the other members of Command at the time.'

'Does that make more sense?'

Ezra laughs. 'Well, yeah, of course. People who know what the job entails choosing the person with the experience and skills to do it? Yes, it makes more sense than just passing it down to someone because of sheer genetic accident.'

'But who could do a better job than someone who's been preparing for it all their life? And anyway, who says Command would make the right decision? Maybe some things are better left to fate to decide.'

'That's the stupidest thing I ever heard,' says Ezra, and Maxim just smirks.

Dom and Mari arrive, him leaning on her heavily. While they're on their way over to us, Maxim says, 'So, are you ready for the tour?'

'Yeah, let's go.' I get up. 'We're just leaving,' I say to Dom as he arrives next to me, without looking at him.

'Where are you going?' he asks.

'Tour of the settlement. We can wait if you like,' says Maxim.

'He has to have his dressing changed,' says Mari. 'And he can't really walk.' She helps Dom sit down and puts his bowl in front of him.

'Another day for you, then,' says Maxim. 'But will you come?' He smiles at Mari.

She seems thrown. 'I ... '

'She needs to eat,' says Dom.

'I'm not hungry, actually.' Mari makes a face, her hand going to Dom's shoulder. 'Will you be OK, *primo*?'

As we walk away, Dom couldn't seem any sadder, alone at the table, dirty-bandaged leg shadowed with blood. I feel my steps slow, stop. He twists a little on the bench to look at me but something makes me turn away anyway.

We walk over to the biggest structure first. There's something almost animal about it, the way it lies across the land, half made, like a rotting corpse fading into a skeleton. There's something familiar in the vast rusting riveted girders that reach out from its near side as I read the giant, fading text along it: Concordia.

'It's your ship,' says Ezra, slack-jawed. 'You took your ship apart.'

'Exactly,' says Maxim, proudly. 'Pioneers are built of component parts so that they can be disassembled on-planet. All our habitation units are constructed from our ship.'

'Well, you're not going anywhere, then, are you?' says Mariana, laying her hand on a charred metal edge. 'Ever.'

Maxim puts his foot on a tree stump near her and folds his arms across his chest. The sun glints off his sunglasses, turning one lens red and one blue. 'Where would we go? Once she landed – through passive entry, very difficult operation – she was never going anywhere again. She was constructed in Earth orbit, with no launch capabilities. She is a pioneer. This is what she was built for.'

Ezra wants a tour of the ship, so he ends up heading into the bowels of it with one of the deconstuctors, while Mari and Maxim and I carry on to a field covered in leafy little plants, no more than shin height, growing in rough rows. We follow Maxim down the gap between two rows.

'This is our main crop. We call it lebeda; it's been genetically modified to contain the essential vitamins and minerals. Last year it grew well.' He bends to pinch the tip of a leaf for a second as if he's admiring it, then keeps walking.

'What else do you grow?' asks Mari.

'We have one other crop in production at the moment – I show you now, because I don't know what you call it.'

'But two crops doesn't seem like much.'

'I suppose it doesn't. We've had more, many more. All failed, or died, or became diseased.'

I watch the way his steps slow a little. Mari looks back at me and I can tell we are thinking the same thing.

'Is that what happened to the people, too?' I say, deciding to just come out with it.

He stops, turns back to us, looks up at the sun. 'I'm sure Grace told you that we lost many to the C1 bacteria, including my own mother. Our initial on-planet phase was also ... costly in terms of personnel.'

'Costly?'

'You know yourselves that Huxley-3 can be a difficult place for humans. Year One cost us over one hundred lives to malnutrition, infection and exposure.'

'Exposure?'

'Four months ago, where you are standing was under three metres of snow.'

'What?' Mari and I say at the same time.

'And a few weeks from now it will be so hot you will want to peel your skin off for relief from it.'

'That doesn't sound very nice,' I say.

'It's not,' he concedes. 'Heat exhaustion was something we simply had no experience of. Many more died. My brother among them.'

'That's awful,' says Mari, shaking her head at the ground.

'Pioneering involves a certain amount of loss,' is all he says, and he turns to keep walking so that we follow him along the line of shrubs. 'Our breeding programme has been compromised by these problems, as you can imagine. There haven't been children for many years.'

'Why not?' I see Mari stiffen.

'C1 left many survivors infertile. And even with those who are still able, problems with our medical provision have made the process hazardous.'

'Hazardous?' Mari says and I put my hand on her shoulder as we walk.

'The partum process is high risk. We had to concentrate on fortifying our existing population and not losing too much more of our gene pool. We suffered further losses, so we suspended breeding until Year Ten, next year, when we will hopefully re-establish our programme.'

Mari looks back at me, wide-eyed. I'm about to ask more about it when we reach the end of the row and are looking down into a broad valley. Another field begins about ten metres away but this one is home to an infinite army of two-metre-high flowers, their broad brown faces framed by vivid yellow petals all turned to the sun, up and to the left, and there are so many of them and they are so beautiful that it messes with my eyes. Maxim walks to the first row and hooks one down, bends it.

'Sunflowers,' I say, because suddenly I remember them, from Production, from the day Great Granny Bea took me there.

'Funny how they grow even though there is no sun,' she'd said that day. 'Like you.' I swear I can still feel the way she touched my face.

'Very versatile.' Maxim hums appreciatively and I feel

my own hand on my cheek. 'Seeds are nutritious, and the oil can be used as a fuel. This is our second successful rotation.'

Past the end of the sunflowers, dark reflective panels climb the valley side to where it peaks in piled grey rocks and towering windmills line up along the ridge, scything at the air.

'On-planet power sources are now becoming more reliable. The research station, where I work, is up there.' He points to the ridge.

'Why's it so far out of town?'

'Just a precaution.' He turns, so he doesn't see the look Mariana and I give each other.

As I look back in the other direction, all the way to where the sunflowers end, I see another big structure, this one half built, so tall that it clears the trees, its top part half of what will be a giant, smooth metal bowl.

'What's that?' I ask.

'Long range com,' he says.

'Why?'

He shrugs. 'We came equipped with it. Eventual purpose to communicate our progress to origin. It wasn't on the priorities list but my father OK'd it last year. If you want to know more about it you should ask Grace. It's her project.'

I look at it again. There's something so beautiful about it, about the way it catches the light.

'Just one more important thing to show you,' he says, and we are walking along the gap between the fields to where there is this oddly triangular building, clearly made up of haphazard bits of viewing windows from the ship. 'Agriculture Facility.'

Inside it's intensely hot and damp, water dripping down the insides of the windows, off the ceiling in fat drops, like rain. It reminds me so much of the island for a second that I slow my steps. The ground is ploughed into rows and there are all these plants, each one different, sprouting at intervals. Someone is bent low, tending to one, and it is only when we get close and he pushes his sunglasses up, stands, that I realise it is Kirill. He and Maxim shake hands.

'A talented agriculturalist who I believe you know.' Maxim clears his throat, as if picking up on how awkward I suddenly feel. 'Let me show you something.'

We follow him a few rows over to where there is a tiny, frondy plant lying along the ground like splayed feathers, which we all squat next to.

'This is a local species,' he says, then, 'Touch it,' to Mariana.

'What?'

'It won't hurt you. Don't you trust me?'

She touches it gently and it makes her jump when it contracts from the contact, squeezing its fronds together until it is almost invisible, all folded up.

'Cool,' says Mariana.

'Cool indeed,' he says. 'Our next project. Working out ways we can cross the genes of the plants we brought from Earth with the local plants. For strength.' He reaches out to run his finger along one of its closed fronds just as Mariana does the same. 'Genetic variety is the key,' he says.

I watch them for a moment and then feel something behind me. When I turn it is just Kirill, standing leaning on a spade, looking away when I look back, slinging the spade over his shoulder.

'Is it only you working here?' I ask him, and he stops. I get up and take a few steps towards him.

He nods. 'We need more workers.'

'Seren's good with plants,' says Mari from behind me. 'She was the only one of us who found things that were edible on the island. She could tell which ones were poisonous and which weren't.' She laughs. 'She was mostly right, anyway.'

'It must run in the family,' says Maxim, and it brings about this epic silence, into which something blue, iridescent and insanely beautiful silently flies.

Mari gasps. 'What is it?'

'A butterfly,' says Kirill. 'You call it a butterfly.'

We watch it, hardly daring to breathe, in case it evaporates. It flaps its blue wings fast, slows them, glides, lands on the roof where it hangs by its legs, closing its wings so that the ethereal blue is hidden, showing intricate patterns of brown and grey on their underside.

'You brought animals from Earth?' whispers Mari.

'We have genetic material,' says Maxim, sheepish. 'These are our only success as yet. They help us with cross-pollination, but not much else.'

'But it's so beautiful,' says Mari, looking almost as if she could cry.

'It is,' agrees Maxim, looking from it back down to her.

'What other genetic material have you got?' I ask.

'Eggs in a stasis facility,' he says. 'From other insects. From some small birds. From fish.'

'Fish?' I look at Mari and see it on her face too. 'Fish?' I don't know why I say it twice except that I just know so fully and completely that Dom could do this and it is as if I see it all already, playing out.

'They're difficult,' he sighs. 'Sensitive. We've had several farms. All have failed. We have no experience with living things really so ... wait, Seren, where are you going?'

I'm leaving before I even realise it. 'I need to see Dom,' I tell them, because it is burning in me suddenly so hard I can't even stop to explain. And then I am running, leaving them behind.

I guess it's because I know how happy it will make him that suddenly nothing else seems to matter. I can only feel my feet as they pound on the path between the fields, as I sprint along between the rows of lebeda until I get to the

Concordia, where the sound of drilling is echoing all the way out of it as if it is a giant, dying sea creature.

At the edge of the settlement I stop, look around at the buildings, unsure which one is the Med unit, waiting to orientate myself. The nearest door opens, and Dom comes out. I'm about to go to him when I realise Irina is following him, both of them stopping in the doorway to talk, her leaning her shoulders against the door frame, hips forward, reaching for his wrist and circling it with her fingers for a moment before they both laugh.

He turns then, sees me just before I leave, calls my name, but I don't stop.

Chapter Twenty-Two

The night of the anniversary party is the first warm evening we've had. Lights have been strung through the trees and there is music coming through the speakers that normally just play the chimes for meal times. The first people I notice when I get there are Vasily and Alexei from the outpost, and when we get to them they pat Mari and me on the back and make noises as if we're these old friends of theirs, which I think is weird until I notice how drunk everybody is.

I see Dom next, standing down next to the river talking to people, and I notice the way the focus of his eyes shifts from them to me so that he is watching me over their shoulders, even though he is still nodding at what they are saying.

'Talk to him tonight,' says Mari, noticing me watching him. 'For my sake? He's been driving me *loca*. He hates it when you're angry with him, you know he does.'

'Yeah, he looks really depressed,' I say, watching him

finish his drink and wipe drips off his chin while the guys he's standing with laugh and so does he.

She gives me a look and seems to be just about to say something when Maxim and Ezra come to stand with us, each handing us a cup. I peer into mine.

'What is this?'

'Some kind of moonshine Pasha makes,' says Ezra. 'It tastes awful but it does the job.'

'You can have mine,' says Mariana, passing me hers.

All this time Maxim's been staring at Mariana as if nobody else exists and now he says, 'I bet you're a great dancer.'

Which makes her laugh. 'No,' is all she says.

'No?' He smiles.

'I'm not the worst in the world but I'm not great.'

'I'm a terrible dancer. Come on, let me show you.'

'You want to show me what a terrible dancer you are?'

'Yeah.'

They keep eye contact so long that Ezra and I end up looking away, then at each other, then back, and they are still watching each other.

'OK,' she says in the end. 'Show me your worst.' She follows him over to where the tables and benches have been cleared to the side and people are shuffling around under the lights. I'm about to say something to Ezra when I realise he's looking at Dom over my shoulder, so I turn to where he is now standing with Irina. She's handing him a guitar that's made of reddish wood and old-looking. Dom really couldn't look more amazed and happy about it if he tried, and they have this whole exchange where, even though I can't hear it, I can guess that he's asking if she's really giving this to him and she's saying she is and he's ridiculously happy about it and thankful and also kind of embarrassed.

'Oh man, she's so into him,' says Ezra, so that I turn back and glare at him. 'What? She is. What a waste, man. Why can't she be into me?'

Dom's pulling the guitar strap over his head now, strumming at it a few times, so much delight on his face. She's saying something to him again then, her hand on the shoulder of the guitar. He nods at whatever she's asking. There's something about it I can't bear so I turn and walk towards the tables, feel Ezra following me.

'Seriously, can't he put a word in for me?' says Ezra. 'Like: sadly I'm unavailable but can I interest you in my far better-looking friend? Something like that?'

'Why don't you ask him?' I sit on a bench with my back to a table so I can look down at the moonlit ripples on the water. 'I don't particularly want to talk about him, to be honest.'

Ezra sits on the bench next to me. 'How long are you going to stay mad at him? I think he's pretty clear on the fact that you don't want him making decisions for you.'

'It's not just that.'

'OK . . .'

I haven't actually talked to anyone else about this, not even Mari, but for some reason I hear myself say, 'He was sleeping with Annelise.'

I look at him and he shifts his eyes to the side. 'And?'

'He didn't tell me.'

He laughs. 'And you didn't just assume? I mean, come on, what did you expect?' He pulls my head in against his shoulder and strokes my hair, hard. 'Aw, that's so sweet. Poor little innocent Hemple.' And I'm fighting him off and he's laughing and right then Dom arrives, holding the guitar by the neck and making this face as if he's asking me if I can believe it.

'So cool, right?' he says, slurring a little. 'Apparently they had a couple on board and nobody can play, so . . .'

Ezra says, 'Cool, man,' but I only smile a little, which seems to make Dom remember that I've been ignoring him for most of the last week. His smile fades.

'Well, Irina wants to hear me play it, somewhere quieter – want to come?'

'No thanks,' I say, surprising myself. 'I'd rather stay here.'

And it's only circumstantial that Ezra still has his arm around me but I can feel myself being glad that it's there as Dom clocks it and then says, 'Lomax, how about you?'

He's just taking a drink but shakes his head and when he's finished adds, 'We'll come and find you in a bit.'

And Dom leaves then, slowly, making his way over to where Irina has been waiting for him and when he gets there she puts her hand on his back, glances at me.

Once she looks away I roll my eyes. 'He's not exactly trying that hard to get me to forgive him, is he?'

'He's pretty drunk, and it's not as if he can refuse to play for her when she just gave him a guitar.'

'I know, but . . . ' I growl into my hands.

'Being mad at Suarez is a waste of time.' He hands me his drink. 'It doesn't change anything. It just makes life harder for me and Mari because of his incessant whining. So just tell him you forgive him and let's all just get hammered and enjoy ourselves for once.'

And he's right. And this is why a little later I am heading down towards the water, stepping carefully among the roots because I've definitely drunk a little too much, when I nearly crash into someone and when I look up it's Dom.

'Hey,' he says.

'Hey yourself,' I say, and then I realise he is out of breath. 'Are you OK?' I ask.

He shifts his eyes to the side. 'Yeah of course,' he says. 'Just . . . ' Shakes his head. 'It's hard to get around with my leg like this.'

He's drunk too, clearly, even drunker than me, his smile wide and lazy, and suddenly it's as if everything is forgotten and I want it to be. He has the guitar slung across his back.

'I got you a present, too,' I tell him.

'You did?'

'It's not exactly a thing, but more something I wanted to tell you.'

'OK.'

'They have fish, fish eggs, at the Agri Facility.'

His eyes intensify and flick between mine while he takes this in. 'They do?'

'I thought of you when they told me. They haven't managed to make them work but ... I just know you could. I know you would. So I thought you should know.' I turn to go but then I turn back. 'And Dom ... I don't want to be angry with you any more.'

'Really?' A smile of delight. 'Really?'

I nod and he takes my hands in both of his. Then I watch his smile fade, which isn't quite what I expected.

'I want you to know how sorry I am,' he says, super serious. 'For everything. I've been so scared, Seren.'

'Scared?' I frown.

'Scared that you didn't love me any more.'

'Dom, I always love you. Even when I'm angry with you I still love you. I always will, no matter what.'

'No matter what?'

I reach up to move his hair back from his forehead, trail the back of my hand down the side of his face afterwards. I'm expecting him to kiss me but he doesn't, yet; he just looks at me, bites his lip.

'What is it?'

He smiles. 'I just love you so much, that's all.' He takes my face between his hands and kisses me, lips closed, once, before pulling back to look at me again.

It's me who can't take it any more, who gives in to it, who grips the front of his shirt and pulls on it until he is low enough for me to press my mouth to his, to taste him again, and even though it's only been a few days it feels like for ever. When he kisses me back, when he moves, it builds like a wave in me, unstoppable.

'Take me somewhere,' I say, against his mouth, breathing hard.

He looks around in the dark. 'Shall we go home?'

'Too far.' I kiss the skin behind his ear, his throat, feel his blood coursing beneath.

He takes my hand and leads me away from the lights, lifting the guitar off and leaving it at the door to the deserted kitchens, where I lean back on the edge of a table while he lifts me on to it, kisses me.

I slide my hands inside his shirt as I lie back and he leans over me. I don't know why I need it like I do right then, but I do. I need everything he can give. I'm not sure any amount of close will ever be enough. Which is why it makes me so crazy when he stops kissing me, stays completely still, looks at me as if I'm this raging ocean he is simultaneously amazed and terrified by. He studies me so long that I end up saying, 'Tell me what's wrong.'

I watch him shake his head, one half of his face pulling up into a smile. '*Nada.*'

'You get Spanish when you're drunk. That's hot.'

Because it's so dark and because of the way we are, the glow from the coral is making its own light, shining up through the skin on my hip and on to his stomach. He reaches for it, runs his fingers along it, pressing a little.

'Don't say it,' I warn him.

'*Yo no voy a decir nada.*'

And I am willing him to kiss me, and he does.

Chapter Twenty-Three

I come to slowly, realising I am in Dom's arms, smiling to myself and then, as he wakes, at him.

'Good morning,' he says, then yelps in pain because I've just moved my leg against his and ended up kicking his gunshot wound.

'Oh my God, I am so sorry,' I say, and I am shushing him and holding his face in my hands and kissing him just lightly all these times on his lips as he gets over it. 'I'm so sorry.'

'Don't be; it's OK.'

'It's not. I'm so sorry.'

'I'm just so happy you're here, estrellita.'

'I've always been here.'

'No, I mean here. Right here.' He nods down at where I am lying against his arm. 'This is where you belong. You know that, right?'

I pretend I'm thinking about it but then say, 'Yes I know,' and as I sigh and feel the way he pulls me in tight from behind so that we are tucked close, tessellating, I look across the floor at where we've left our uniforms strewn across it, and even just the fact that I am seeing the room from this angle again, from his bed, makes me smile a little more.

We walk down to breakfast with Mari and Ezra.

'Jesus, that wall is thin,' yawns Ezra. 'You kept me awake last night, Romeo and Juliet.'

I cringe.

'Me too.' Mari smiles, shooting me a sideways look. 'It was *way* more information than I ever wanted about my own cousin, but I am glad that normal service has been resumed anyway.'

Even though I am flushed I am smiling, but when I look at Dom he isn't. He's pale, and suddenly says, 'Excuse me,' and runs into the trees a little way before leaning his hand on one and heaving up the contents of his stomach.

'Are you OK?' I ask, as he coughs a little before wiping his mouth on his forearm and coming back, nodding.

'I'm not even a little bit surprised,' says Ezra. 'Suarez, you were wasted last night.'

'Yeah,' he says, looking off into the distance before looking back at me, squeezing my hand.

Down at breakfast, Dom can't face food so he sits while I eat mine with his arms around my waist and his legs either side of the bench where I'm sitting, with his eyes pressed hard against my shoulder. After a while he groans, and I laugh.

'You'll feel better later,' I tell him.

Just then Kirill comes and sits with us, nodding at everyone. He spoons in a couple of mouthfuls of lebeda before studying Dom and saying, 'My cousin Irina is the same this morning,' and I feel Dom tense up.

After breakfast, the others leave but Dom is now slumped all the way over the table with his hands over his head as if the sky might be about to cave in on him.

'Want me to take you back to bed?' The lights from the party are still strung up in the lower branches, looking sad and dirty in the sunlight.

He shifts until he is looking at me, one-eyed, through his fingers.

'Estrellita, I ...'

'What's up?'

He growls, turns his face back against the table, tightens the lacing of his fingers in his hair. 'Oh man, I can't do this.'

I frown and touch his shoulder. 'Dom, what ...?'

He sits suddenly, sighs, looks up at the trees, then around at the way the place is emptying of the few people who actually made it to breakfast.

'You know you said that you wanted me to be ... completely honest with you? Would you still want me to be honest about something when I am sure, absolutely *sure* without even a shadow of a doubt, that the world

238

would be a far better place without you knowing? Would you still want me to tell you then?'

I manage to swallow. 'What is it?' And this is when he finally looks at me, actually meets my eye, and it stills both of us. I am staring at his mouth but not the way I do when I want him to kiss me, but the way I do when I am waiting to see what he will say, and right now I am so scared that I swear I am flinching.

'Ah man, estrellita, you have to understand, I was so wasted. I swear, seriously, I hardly even knew what was happening and then when I did, it was too late and it had ... kind of ... already happened. And I am so sorry. You are never going to know how sorry I am.'

'What are you ... what are you talking about?'

He pulls me into his arms even though I am not sure I want him to, and then he says, into the hair above my ear, 'Irina,' struggling to get the word out. 'She ... we kind of ... kissed last night.'

And I stammer a few times before I manage to say, 'What?' and then, 'She ...? You ...? What?'

'And even though she kissed me, I mean, *she* completely kissed *me*, I can't tell you it's not at least a little my fault because I knew she liked me, she's made it so obvious, and yet I went back there with her anyway and there was this part of me that let it happen, because I hoped it might make you jealous and make you want me back. And I know that sounds crazy, and it is crazy, but that's because I've been crazy these last few days – that's what even the thought of life without you does to me. Seren, I know how messed up it is, believe me. But I am so sorry. I am so, so, so sorry.'

All this time he has arms around me and he is leaning his head against mine and he is saying all of it to my hair and I am so shocked that I am not even reacting at all. It's as if someone took me away and replaced me with a doll of myself. A dummy.

'I was going to tell you right away. I was coming to tell you. But then you were there and suddenly you weren't mad at me any more. And I have been so sad and so scared these past few days. And I just couldn't. I couldn't face giving you another reason to be angry with me when you had come back to me. Can't you see that?'

He leans back to look at me, at the dummy version of me that flops in his arms.

'It was nothing, Seren. She kissed me and I was so surprised I didn't really stop it as quickly as I should have. It was a stupid drunken moment.'

Dummy me isn't able to feel anything, isn't able to speak.

'Seren?'

Still nothing.

'Talk to me please.'

'You . . . ' I am shaking my head. 'This can't be true. It can't be. You would never do that to me. You just wouldn't do that to me, would you?'

And I wait for him to take it all back, to say it's all been some kind of mistake, because Dom, my Dom, would never ever kiss someone else. But he doesn't. Instead he watches me as if he's watching a slow-motion accident he's powerless to prevent and all he says is, 'I am so sorry.'

I get up, stepping over the bench and almost falling in the process. He's the reason I don't fall, taking hold of me and steadying me, but his hands on me makes me yell, 'Don't touch me!' and it is such a shriek that everyone around is now watching us. 'Don't you touch me!' I am staring him out, both of us wide-eyed. And then I am leaving, walking away as fast as I can, and I hear him struggling with his bad leg to get up and follow me, to catch up to me, and when he does I wheel on him.

'No!' I am screaming at him, feeling it surge in me so hard that I go for him, slam my hands into his chest and shoulders as hard as I can and he flinches and staggers but takes it, lets me do it again, while he's watching the tears form in my eyes. I feel someone behind me then, taking hold of my arms just as I go for him again, stopping me.

'Hemple, what are you doing?' It's Ezra. 'What happened?'

But I don't answer him. I just listen to the way I can hardly breathe and I wrench my arms out of his grip and I plunge off towards the trees, away from them both, and I don't stop.

Chapter Twenty-Four

I hear him following me, hear him calling, and I know I just can't look at him right now. All I want to do is crawl inside the ground and hide. I see the long-range com structure through the trees, the gleam of its metallic curve, and it seems as if he won't think to check there. I run for it.

I don't know whether I wanted her to be there or not, but she is. Grace. Standing there talking to some big guy with a dark tattoo on the side of his neck.

'Seren,' she says when she sees me, and she looks like Pan standing there, Pan but older, tilting her head at me. It's like a dream. 'I'm so glad you made it here – I really wanted to ... what's the matter?'

I swallow it, or try to. 'Nothing,' I say. 'I'm fine. Show me round.'

She speaks to the tattoo guy in Russian so that he goes into the dark doorway behind him and she comes to me, lays her hand on my shoulder.

We both hear Dom then through the trees, calling me.

242

'I don't want to see him,' I say, spilling tears and turning too late to hide it.

'Why not?' she asks. 'What happened?'

I just shake my head. He calls again, getting closer.

'He ...' I try, but something blocks my throat. 'I can't even ...'

God only knows how he managed it, but Dom arrives then, hobbling on his leg and using trees for support, the new bandage stained again with blood and dirt, hair dripping with sweat. He half collapses in the dust before he makes it to me.

'Seren,' he says, shaking his head. 'You know I didn't mean for it to happen.'

He tries to take my hands but I snatch them away.

'You ... you're disgusting. You're disgusting. I mean, you let ... everything that happened last night ... you let all of that happen all night long and *then* you decide you have a conscience? *Then* you decide you need to be honest with me? Seriously? What would you think if you were me? What would you think?'

My skin is literally crawling with it. I can feel it itching on me, like bugs, the memory of his touch.

'I know, it's ...' He pinches the top of his nose. 'I should have told you straight away but I was just so happy that you weren't angry with me any more and I was drunk and it just seemed as if maybe you didn't need to know. It seemed as if maybe it would just cause unnecessary pain and problems and it should just be ... I don't know ... forgotten.'

Something occurs to me. 'Wait.' I narrow my eyes. 'You only told me because you thought maybe someone else had seen you. I'm right, aren't I? When Kirill mentioned Irina you thought maybe he was hinting at something.'

His eyes are wide. 'No.' He's shaking his head. 'No, that's not it at all.'

'Or you thought maybe she would tell me, didn't you? God, Dom, when did you get like this? Who are you?'

'You know who I am,' he says, stepping closer, and now his hand is on my face and I am looking at him, looking into his beautiful eyes, the eyes I have known and trusted most in all my life, and suddenly it all feels different and I am clutched by a horrible panic, a fear I can barely breathe through.

'I thought I knew you,' is what I say, panting, and barely getting it out.

'You do. You do know me,' he says, his mouth so close to mine that I could kiss him. And God I want to. I want to kiss him because he's mine. I want to kiss him because I want everything to be how it was. But it never will be. And suddenly I feel as if, if I kiss him, I will die of just how sad that is.

'Maybe everything's just different now,' I say, past hiccups of fear and grief, stepping back so I am looking at the ground between his feet and mine.

'Estrellita.' He comes to me again, glancing at Grace over my shoulder, whose existence I had completely forgotten about. 'Just come with me to the farmhouse. Let's talk about it, talk about everything, just you and me. I need to make you understand.' The smell of him is so deep and rich around me that I take huge breaths of it, that I almost, nearly, let my face drop against his chest.

Instead, I take these backwards steps, and even though they are tiny, each one is heavier than the last.

'I just can't be with you right now, Dom.' As I am saying these words I am hearing them from outside myself, I am hearing them as if someone else is saying them. 'I need you to just leave me alone for while. Please.' And I stay there, outside myself, while I watch him, while I watch his reaction, raising his hand to his forehead and pressing it there as if maybe if he does it hard enough this won't be happening.

And he says, 'Estrellita, please,' but when he goes to come towards me I yell, 'No! I can't even look at you right now. I just can't,' and I am walking away, around the back of the base of the long-range com, where I fall against it, slide down the metallic surface, into the long grass, face in my hands.

It's only a few seconds before I hear footsteps and look up just enough to see Grace's feet in front of me.

'Want to tell me about it?' she asks, squatting down, her hand on my arm.

I shake my head.

'I hope you don't mind if I make an observation, Seren.' She is looking at me, wide-eyed, so open that the words I want to say die on my lips, and I end up sniffing against my arm, so that she says, 'Your life seems awfully complicated for someone who's only sixteen years old.'

'I'm seventeen,' I say, swallowing something hard.

'Oh ... Oh yes, your birthday's in January so ... yes, seventeen. But ... still ... even for seventeen – complicated.' She watches me. 'Don't you think?'

'My life isn't normal,' I tell her. 'It never has been.'

I can tell from the way she looks at me then, motionless, that she thinks I'm having some kind of swipe at her. She nods a little.

'I should have told you by now how sorry I am that I wasn't there for you,' she says.

'Well, whether you're sorry or not, you weren't.' I surprise myself. 'You weren't there. And you don't know anything about any of it.'

'OK, so tell me. Tell me about it. I want to know. How long has Dom been your boyfriend?'

'Boyfriend?' I almost laugh.

'He's not your boyfriend?'

'He's ... ' How can I explain how much more to me he is than that? That I could never sum up all he is to me with a word that sounds so easy and comfortable and tame?

She gives up waiting for me to answer and says, 'Listen, Seren, when you're young it can seem like these attachments are the beginning, middle and end of the world, but as you get older, you put them into perspective.'

'Perspective?' I narrow my eyes at her.

She lays her hand back on my arm. 'From what I just heard, Domingo's doing the kind of thing eighteen-year-old guys do.'

'You think that's OK?' My voice gets loud.

'No, of course not, but ...' She shrugs, looking at the wall behind me as if what she's about to say is written there. 'Maybe it's for the best if you take some time apart. Cool off. Maybe the whole thing has just ... run its course. I mean, as far as I can see, it's not making you happy. I'd really like to see you able to just enjoy your life at this age. Attachments can come later.'

I stand so that she is looking up at me. 'Like I said, you really know nothing about it.' And I turn to go.

'Don't I?' she says to my back. 'I do know that a teenage girl who's been raised on Ventura wouldn't have the first idea how to tell the difference between love and a heavy dose of lust. I know that no man is ever worth giving up your whole life for. I know that if I'd been there to advise you, I would have told you to step back and think things through a little before making any drastic choices.'

'You're one to talk about drastic choices!' I say, wheeling on her.

There is a silence before she says, 'I thought I'd be gone for a couple of days at the most.'

'It was basically a suicide mission from the beginning. I would never have done what you did.'

Her mouth falls open in shock. 'But you did! You did exactly what I did, and worse – because you knew you were only going one way.'

'But I don't have children!'

In the long silence that follows she fixes me with her dark eyes. The ones that I suspect are probably the same as mine – heavy with dark lashes and eyebrows and difficult to read.

'I guess someone told you about what happened to Javi ... ' She shakes her head. 'The pilot who flew us to Concordia? Those first few weeks were just ... so bad. He didn't make it.'

'Didn't make it?'

'He couldn't get past the fact that he would never see his family again. He had kids. He ... couldn't live with it.'

'And you could?'

'You know, some people would say that I couldn't live with it either,' she says. 'Some people would say that was obvious from what I did.'

'Which was?'

'I got pregnant within two months.'

I don't say anything. I just watch her, while my scalp shifts beneath my hair.

'I couldn't rest, couldn't live, couldn't even breathe until I had a baby back in my arms. I spent weeks craving you, pining for you, thinking it would kill me. When I realised I couldn't ever get you back, when I realised you were gone, I knew there was nothing I could do but try to replace you, and so that's what I did.'

I'm stoppered up by the awfulness of this, but finally I manage to say, 'How touching. Do you tell Kirill this bedtime story, too?'

I walk away, shaking my head, stumbling a little on the rocks beneath the grass.

'Seren?'

I keep walking.

'Seren?' I stop, but I don't turn around. She talks anyway. 'Why are you so angry with me? I know it's late to start trying to be there for you, to start offering you advice, but I'm here now. I thought maybe you'd be glad of that. God knows I'm happy to have you back, to have the chance to be your mother again. You have no idea. It's like . . . ' She's breathless, maybe tearful. 'It's just like the most amazing gift from the universe, isn't it?'

I stare at the ground. 'Is it?'

I feel her come to me, her hands hesitating just a second before making contact with my shoulders. 'Of course it is. You have no idea how much I have longed for you, Seren, and now you're here. It's the most precious, perfect miracle I could have hoped for.'

'Except it's not.' I shrug her off. 'It's not a miracle. It's just chance. It's just … a ridiculous coincidence.'

I don't stop again, even when she calls me.

I have no idea what time it is when I hear Mariana calling me, but it's getting dark, getting cold, and I am laid in against the root of a tree, my face against its bark. I'm just sitting up and thinking about answering when she gets to me, drops to her knees in front of me, holds my face in her hands.

'I was so worried about you,' she says, out of breath, and then, 'Where've you been?'

I see Maxim then, behind her, stopping a few metres off to watch us.

We walk back down to the settlement, even though my feet feel so heavy I can hardly lift them.

'He told me,' she says, tripping over a root. Maxim switches on a small solar light he pulls off his belt and shines it forward under our feet. 'He's an idiot,' she continues. 'I'm so angry with him right now, you have no idea.'

'I don't even want to talk about it, to be honest.' When she sees the look on my face she doesn't say any more, and I feel her hand on my back.

Which is when it starts to rain. We pick up the pace, but not enough to not be completely wet by the time we get back. When the dinner chimes go off they gurgle in the speakers. I hadn't even thought about the fact that they must eat inside when the weather isn't dry, but of course they do, and so everyone is in the kitchen building, crammed around the metal tables, elbow to elbow while the rain drums on the roof.

I feel Dom more than see him, as if he's a spot on my radar. Because he is way over in the corner it is easier to sit as far away from him as possible, with Mari and Maxim. Ezra watches us, from his seat next to Dom, eyebrows raised. It's only then that I see Irina, the back of her anyway, sitting at their table, carefully spooning her food, diagonally opposite from Dom.

I'm about to tell Mari, but when I turn to her she is talking to Maxim and there is something in the way they are smiling at each other that stops my words. Instead I sit and stare into my bowl of lebeda, then up at the slowly turning vent in the ceiling, and the ugly bare light bulb next to it that flickers once as I watch.

I stand so suddenly that Mari turns to me.

'Where are you going?'

'Nowhere.' Then I realise. 'Running.'

'It's raining.'

I shrug.

'Can't you eat first?'

But I just step over the bench. 'I'm fine,' I tell her, and I feel the way they watch me leave.

I take a path I've never noticed before, leading downhill

in pretty much the opposite direction from everything else, so narrow and winding and criss-crossed by giant roots that it's difficult to pick up any pace. Out here in the falling night and the steady rain I start to realise this wasn't my best idea and I'm almost on the point of turning back when I see a clearing through the trees, pale shapes set in rows along the ground.

I walk right into the middle of it, almost trip over a row of rounded stones before I can make my eyes and brain understand what they're seeing. Once I do I back away fast, slam against a tree so hard that I squeal in fright at the contact. Each of the stones has writing on it, in Russian, but something makes me know right away that they are names, that they are graves. This is where they bury them; this is where they put them in the ground. And there are so many of them. So many. Way more people dead and rotting in the crust of this planet than there are walking around and living on it. I didn't notice this stop on Maxim's tour, and I'm not surprised. Seeing it like this, a tally chart of death and loss on an almost unimaginable scale, is appalling in the truest sense. How is it even possible to go on believing in a future, with this as your past?

I suppose that's the kind of thing you just have to live with when you have no choice.

Chapter Twenty-Five

After what happened at the Med unit, Jason has told Maxim we need two weeks to recover before we try anything up at the research station. I don't even know how the time passes but it does. This is mostly because I have stopped being me and started being this robot version of myself that walks and talks and acts like me but isn't.

Ezra lets me switch bunks with him so that I sleep in the room with Mari and he sleeps with Dom. I think he does this because he is tired of hearing Dom begging me to talk to him when I can't. I mean, I try to a couple of times, but I just can't. Not even when he pleads with me so long and hard that Mari ends up pulling him off me and yelling at him to give it up. Not even when he comes back so drunk he can't see and passes out on the floor next to my bed. Not even when he gets up one morning with his arm bandaged and his face covered in blood because he ended up in a fight with Pasha. Not even when Ezra arrives at the door soaking wet, carrying the guitar, dumping water out of it on the front step and throwing it on to Dom's bunk before saying, 'It's an Earth artefact. Tell him throwing it in the fricking river isn't going to get you back.'

Grace comes to sit with me at meals a couple of times, but as soon as she opens her mouth to talk I pick up my bowl and move away.

The only place I can stand to be is up at the lebeda fields, where the plants need thinning. This means spending the entire day on my knees in the dirt, prying up the little plants gently and replanting them further apart so they have space to grow into the two-metre-high crops we hope they will become. The added benefit is that the seedlings are edible, too, so for a short while we get salad with our lebeda at dinner.

After dinner I play cards with Mari and Maxim and sometimes Kirill. Listening to them laugh is like sitting in a room on my own and hearing music coming through a wall.

I am so empty.

One morning I am working on the edge of one of the fields when I hear the whine of a vehicle struggling in the mud, signalling its own arrival. Maxim winds down the window.

'Mari wants you, Seren,' he says. 'She's with Jason at the clinic.'

When I get to the Med unit door I stop. I almost can't go in after how scared I was last time I was here. I breathe through it, but it doesn't get much better, because the first person I see when I enter is Irina.

She looks up when she sees me, and we both miss a beat before she says, 'Please come in,' and points at the doorway through to the main Med unit. I feel her watch me walk past her, feel her follow me.

The room is dark and I have to edge past the damaged equipment from the other week to get to them. Mari is lying on one of the benches, but both she and Jason are staring intently at a screen, the light from it illuminating slight smiles. Mari glances at me quickly.

'Look, Seren,' she says, and Jason makes space.

I've never seen one of these baby scans before so at first I'm just looking at the grey shapes and wondering what they are. I even start to tell her it's great, because I'm getting embarrassed that I don't see anything, but then Jason moves the paddle thing on her stomach around a little more and suddenly there it is – a baby – little and ghostly and bent and hollow-eyed, but a baby. And, as I watch, it shifts, moves.

'Wow.' When I look at Mari she is smiling so hard I hear her lips move over her teeth.

'See this, here,' says Jason, pointing at a little flashing spot. 'This is the baby's heart beating, and it looks nice and strong.'

We watch it flashing away.

'In fact, I think I can ...' he switches something on

255

the screen and suddenly we can hear it – a high pumping sound, faster than I was expecting, like a little plunger, but so relentless, so determined.

'That's so cool,' I say. Mari has this look on her face I don't recognise, and she is wet-eyed.

'And everything looks good and perfectly healthy,' says Jason. 'Very early stages still, but . . . '

'Very early stages?' I say.

'Yeah,' he says, the heartbeat sound stopping as he takes the paddle off and hands it to Irina to dry the sticky gel. 'From these measurements I'd say no more than eight or nine weeks.'

I look at Mariana, and I can tell that both of us are thinking the same thing. Irina goes to dry the gel off her stomach but Mari takes the cloth from her and does it herself.

'But that means . . . ' I frown at her as she sits up slowly, pulling down her top, and it all passes between us without me having to say any more. Jason clicks the lights back on and we all blink in the harshness of it.

'So I'll have to register this on the settlement record now,' he says, moving his wooden stool over to where there is a terminal on the wall and sliding on a battered pair of clear glasses. 'An unauthorised natural. But a healthy one. The commodore will have to approve it, but I don't foresee him taking issue. I mean, we need children here. Who shall I identify as the father?'

There's something about the way he says it that makes me think he knows the answer already. Irina is motionless too, watching her. The moment goes on for ever.

'I don't want ...' She looks at her hands in her lap. 'Look, how do things even work here with this? Can't I just do this on my own?'

Jason studies her over his shoulder. He pulls off his glasses and sighs.

'We haven't done this for a while, but the fact is that family units are as important here as they were on Ventura. Maybe more so. We're building a society after all – a permanent one. We need this community to function. We need it to have a future. Without rules ...' He shakes his head, but then he adds, 'Listen, I don't like it any more than you do, but there it is.'

And I wonder what that means.

'I'm going to need to register a father here,' he says, sliding his glasses back on and looking at the terminal. 'You've been on-planet since before you conceived, so it's only one of two possibilities, right? If you need a genetic test to determine ...'

'Oh my God, no,' says Mariana, making a face. 'No. God. Gross. No. Domingo's my cousin!'

He glances back over his shoulder again.

'So I'll record Ezra as the father?'

'No, don't, please,' she says. 'Please don't. Not yet. Just

don't do it yet. I haven't told him. He doesn't know. I don't want him to know.'

'Why not?'

She is messing with her hair, trying to put it back into a ponytail but missing bits out. 'For a lot of reasons. Because he's sixteen. Because this only happened at all because we were ... I don't know ... lonely. Because he's Ezra. Because I just want to do this by myself.' She gets frustrated by her hair and growls, leaving it down.

Jason looks at her steadily for the longest time, before speaking in Russian. Irina answers him, and puts down the equipment she's cleaning to leave. She is beautiful, with her long elegant neck. The thought that I can see why Dom wanted to kiss her sticks in my ribs, almost manifesting in a weird desire to kiss her too, which I have to blink away.

Once she is gone, he says, 'I'll leave it blank for now, though it will raise questions, so you won't have that much time. You'll need to tell him.'

'But I just want to do this by myself.'

'You can't raise a child alone.'

'She won't be alone,' I say. 'She'll have me.'

Jason sighs. 'When I came here, once I got over everything that I'd lost, and the fact that I was never going home again, I started to be hopeful that things would be different. The rules on Ventura were so hard to live with for some of us. I genuinely think some people are OK with having their lives mapped out that way, but then there are those of us who are tortured by it for whatever reason ... for our own reasons ... ' He loses track a little, then stirs himself back on to it. 'But the reality is, with space civilisations ... these aren't our lives. They're our jobs. We're expected to do our jobs.'

'But this isn't my job,' says Mariana, getting up. 'I just ended up here. I could walk back out of here right now and make my own goddam rules out there in the woods.'

We watch her, both of us thinking the same thing that Jason is the one to eventually say.

'You can't have a baby out in the woods, Mariana.'

She crosses her arms across her chest and bites her lip, the same way Dom does when there are so many things to say that it's difficult to know where to start.

'I don't even know what the commodore will want to do about this, to be honest. I guess he would have preferred to have you all assigned into the breeding programme properly, but ... ' He shakes his head.

'What?' I say. 'Wait, nobody's getting assigned into anything.'

He looks at me. 'Seren, you know the reality of our situation.'

'That's not my problem!' I'm getting loud.

'Believe it or not, I'm on your side.'

'I'm finding it a little hard to believe that at the moment, to be honest.'

'I can imagine.' He goes on looking at me steadily and calmly. 'But I know exactly what it's like to live a lie. To live a lie and have it bother you every minute. I was married, on Ventura. My life partner, Eden, was wonderful, but somehow that only made it worse. Because I loved someone else and I couldn't stop, no matter how hard I tried. And ... the person I loved ... he felt the same about me.'

We are both still and silent, watching him, waiting for him to go on.

'We were friends, best friends, and so for a long time nobody ever really suspected anything when we were together. We had been getting away with it for years, right through both of us getting married, him having kids. But then we almost got caught, and it scared him. He was significant, you see, to those in power. The consequences were ...' He just shakes his head.

'Well, I guess we know what the consequences were,' I supply. 'You ended up here, didn't you?'

He does an almost laugh through his nose and looks at me for a long beat. 'Yeah. You might say that.'

'What happened to him?' asks Mariana quietly. 'Who ... who was he? One of us must have known him. Maybe we can ...'

'No, I ...' He frowns. 'I ... already know what happened to him. He died sometime after I left.' He nods, but you can see how sad it makes him, and we are all quiet for a moment, before he says, 'My point is, I don't like enforced partnerships any more than you do. I've always wondered if there's another way to map our genetic future without actually deciding the course of our lives. But I'm not in charge here. Far from it. I'm just some foreign immigrant doctor with no say in that stuff.'

'Who does have the say?' says Mari.

'The commodore, his Science team maybe, Maxim even, I guess. But ultimately . . .'

'Ultimately what?'

'In my experience, in the end these guys will just follow the rules, and they'll expect us to do the same. And how we feel about it won't matter. Because in the grand scheme of things, it doesn't.' He turns away from us to study the screen. 'And this place is all about the grand scheme. I'll give you a little time before I submit this, Mariana, but that's all I can do.'

'Thanks,' she says, but it doesn't sound as if she means it.

On our way out through the outer room, we pass Irina and I feel my skin shift under her gaze before she says, 'Seren, can I . . . it's possible I can talk to you?'

And before I can say anything Mariana says, 'No you can't. Don't you dare talk to her! Don't you come near her! If I even hear you say her name again you'll be sorry.' And she has her hand so tight around my wrist that it hurts when she pulls me out of the door after her, and I have

261

to laugh just a little when I get a glimpse of the shock on Irina's face.

'I don't even have words for what I think of her,' says Mari, pulling up the hood of her newly issued Concordia jacket against the rain, and not dropping my wrist.

'Where are we going?' I ask, stumbling after her.

'I don't know,' she says. 'Anywhere, man. Anywhere but here.'

I notice now how the people who are in this part of settlement (a guy up a wooden ladder fixing a light, someone leaning against the side of the doorway to the canteen) watch us as we pass. The two crazy foreign girls. The deserters. I keep sliding in the mud. I pull Mari to make her stop.

'Just talk to Maxim,' I tell her. 'It seems as if maybe ... you're friends. Aren't you?'

She shakes her head. 'We're not friends.'

'Tell him about the baby anyway – see what happens.'

'He already knows.'

'You told him?'

'Yeah.'

'But you're not friends?'

There's this slight smile in her eyes then, only in her eyes, but it fades quickly. 'Jason's right. These guys always follow the rules. I just ... ' She throws a growl at the sky. 'How have we ended up here dealing with the same crap we've dealt with all our lives? What was the point in everything we did, in risking everything, losing everything ... if we were just going to end up right back here?' When she looks at me there are tears in her eyes. 'God, Seren, it's just ...'

And there isn't anything to say to that, nothing that'll make it better anyway, so instead I say, 'We'll figure something out,' but right now so much is unravelling I don't believe that even a little bit.

Chapter Twenty-Six

Ezra and I sit in the back of one of the Concordia trucks, heading up a narrow corridor between the trees, only just wide enough for the vehicle, powering up a slope so steep the engine whines. I peer through the window of the cab at Maxim and Jason, but all you can see is the backs of their heads and they couldn't be more anonymous.

'How long do you think you can go on ignoring Suarez?' Ezra asks.

I can't think about that right now, let alone talk about it, so I just tighten my grip on the metal bar behind me and look up the slope to where we're headed. He doesn't take the hint.

'I've got to hand it to you – it really takes some determination to avoid someone you're actually living with. To be honest, I can't take much more of him myself, the crap he's been pulling lately. You know they asked him not to come back to his job in Deconstruction? He kept turning up still drunk from the night before.'

I swallow. 'Where was he last night?' I say, but it is so quiet it is stolen away on the wind and I have to ask again. It still bothers me when I walk past their room and see the moonlight falling across Dom's empty bed like I did in the dead of last night.

'No idea,' says Ezra. 'You think he tells me anything?' He leans in close. 'Why don't you do us all a favour and let him make it up to you? I know you've always believed he's some kind of celestial being but – newsflash – it turns out he's not. He makes mistakes like anybody else.'

I shake my head, look up at the treetops tossing in the wind.

After another ten minutes the trees open up on to the rocky peak of the hill we've been climbing. There are three squat, windowless, brushed-steel buildings and an absolute fleet of huge black windmills, standing to attention, chopping at the air. The vehicle grinds to a halt in the stones in front of one of the buildings and Maxim and Jason get out.

'We're here,' says Maxim, raising a hand in greeting at the tall guy who walks out of one of the buildings behind him and stands watching us. He's pale and scary-looking and Maxim introduces him to us as Karim. He greets us in Russian, says something to Maxim.

'He says "welcome",' he translates, but from the look that passes between them I guess it was probably something else.

Inside, lights hum on down the length of a laboratory. The walls have the same dull sheen on the inside as they do on the outside, meaning there are ghostly reflections of us as we follow them across the room. The weird detail I only notice now is that the inside of the building is cross-braced with pale, knobbly beams. I reach out as I pass one, touch it. Wood.

'New construction method,' says Maxim, more than a hint of pride. 'My own idea.'

Ezra walks around questioning them on what all their different machines do, but I find myself heading for a door in the back wall, ending up outside at the back of the main building, looking at another building that sits among the trees. I'm walking over to it when I hear Maxim's voice.

'Alien life samples,' is all he says. 'It's kept climate-controlled. Heated. Because they came from the tropics.' He laughs. 'Like you, I suppose. Maybe we should keep you in there.'

'Can I see them?'

'You already have. We collected most of them from the subtropical maritime region. We haven't found anything else that could be classified as living.'

I look at the door, unconvinced. He walks over and fingerprints us in.

It's dark, billowing hot air out at us in a way that reminds me far more of the laundry rooms on Ventura than anything to do with the island. There are four vast floor-to-ceiling tanks ranged across the dimly lit space, the first empty apart from a branch and a small, sad group of glow-flies, gathered on its length. I press my face to the glass, breathing on it.

'Glow-flies,' I tell him.

'We call them ALF1,' he says. 'They're pretty ubiquitous, even on the northern continent.'

He gestures at the second tank. 'You're already very familiar with ALF2.'

A chunk of reef the size of a felled tree sits diagonally in the tank, partly obscured by a wall of bubbles, oxygenating the water. It shimmers, light bouncing off the ceiling. I touch my hip on instinct.

The next tank is filled with water, the bed pale sand. I squint in and then turn to him.

'ALF3. They're not visible unless agitated. I can stir it if . . .'

'It's OK.' I glance back in at the dark water. 'I've seen them before.'

The sea stars. It's too much. I lean my forehead against the back of my hand and squeeze my eyes shut.

I hear him shift his weight behind me. 'Are you . . . are you OK?'

What can I say? There is no way to explain the enormity of the gap between the last time I saw the sea stars, out on the beach, and now. So I just say, 'I'm fine, I just need some air,' and I go for the door, leaving him there.

Outside I blink in the light, feel the wind move across me, head for the corner of the building.

'Where are you going, Hemple?' It's Ezra.

'I'm just . . . ' But I'm not sure, so I don't answer, I just keep walking, and I hear him following me, footsteps on the stony ground, until he has hold of my arm.

'Are you scared?'

'It's not that.'

He makes a face. 'Why aren't you talking to me any more?'

'What do you mean? Of course I'm talking to you.'

'Hemple, you may not have realised this, but you're not really talking to anyone. You're getting pretty close to giving up talking altogether.'

A gust of wind moves his too-long hair over his face so that he pushes it back as if he's angry with it, and it's such an Ezra gesture that it makes me smile, but he flinches, holding his side.

'Are you OK?' I ask him, suddenly getting a flash of pain myself.

He is wincing.

'Let's go inside and find Jason,' I say, but he shakes his head.

'No,' he says. 'Walk it off. I want to walk it off.' He plants his hand heavily on my shoulder, pressing down on it as we take a few steps.

'Tell me something,' he says. 'What did your mother

say about how they ended up here? Jason said a bit, but he's always weird with me. I get the feeling there's stuff he's not telling me.'

I try to form words that make sense. 'In a way, I guess it was all just a dumb accident.'

I stop walking and turn to him, so he does too. He has his navy Concordia jacket zipped all the way up so that the stiff canvas collar covers the bottom part of his face and I can only see his eyes.

'I guess,' he says, muffled. 'Well, whatever, I mean, you must be happy that she's alive, right?'

I watch the hair blow across his eyes again and reach up to push it away while I think about it. 'You need a haircut,' I tell him.

'Your feedback on my hairstyle is noted as always,' he says.

We walk on, reaching higher ground, steps slowing, unsure, while the landscape shifts, panning oddly, spreading out below like something unnatural.

'Wow,' I say, before I can even figure it out.

We keep walking, under the shifting sky, and in front of us the earth beneath our feet makes itself, unmakes itself. We are nearing an edge, a dizzying, dropping edge, the edge of the world, as if the planet itself is ending and ready to topple us back out into space.

'Holy crap,' I say.

'I know, right?' breathes Ezra, like someone in church.

And it is like that. It's an experience. It burns my eyes. It must be a drop of a thousand metres, straight down, so far that the trees down there are tiny, like toys, like something in miniature.

I stand as close to it as I dare. I try with everything I have not to fall off, not to jump, not to imagine myself falling a kilometre through that air down there, all the way, hitting the ground at the kind of speed I've never known.

'It goes on for ever.' Ezra is looking away from me, facing into the wind, looking along the line that marks the edge as far in either direction as we can see.

'Do you think they've ever been down there?'

'I don't see how,' he says, and then, 'Wait, what's that?' He points.

I follow his finger but can't see anything but trees, small clearings maybe, a line among the forest.

'A road?' he asks.

I shake my head. 'Must be a river or something.'

'And that? God, what's that?'

My eyes are tearing so much in the wind that I have to rub at them to get any kind of proper sight of it, and even then it is so far away it is hard to make out. But I see it. I see it. It's a tower, some kind of tower, pale but catching the light, unmistakeably unnatural and created.

We look at each other, both open-mouthed, before I say, 'It must be theirs. Concordia's. Something they just haven't shown us yet.'

'You think?'

'Of course.'

The wind pushes at us suddenly, and so hard, that we both back away from the edge on instinct.

'Jesus, how could they not tell us this was here?' Ezra stomps away. 'What if we'd stumbled over it in the dark?'

'Why would we be out here in the dark?'

'That's not the point.'

It's only as we turn to head back that I notice the sky, the colour of it, the deep orange and pink, even though it's still morning. Was it like this when we first came out here? I don't have time to ask Ezra because right then he says, 'How did we get so lost?'

And I pan down to where we are standing, alone among the rocks of the peak, where there are no buildings, no turbines, no nothing. Just us and the sky and the wind and the endless fall to nothing.

He turns a circle. 'We didn't walk that far, did we?'

But when he looks back at me, we both know.

I look up again and he follows my gaze.

'The sky,' he almost sighs.

We look at each other for a long moment before he says, 'But how . . . how did we . . . ?' He looks around.

I shake my head, swallow hard. 'No idea. I really don't know.' I feel it come over me, creeping, a panic I can't contain, can't control, seeping into my bones. He takes hold of my arms.

'We're not going to freak out,' he says.

The tension in my throat is about the size of a fist, impossible to swallow round, but somehow I manage to get the words out. 'What if we can't get back?'

He steps towards me. 'Hemple, we don't know anything about what this is. We can't panic right now. We just don't ... I mean ...'

I'm not listening any more. I struggle away from him, head for the trees.

'Where are you going?' he calls after me.

I run for the treeline, stumbling on the rocks. The trees stand thicker here, but I see a gap and when I get to it to it I realise it is a stream. Since it's the easiest way to get in the direction of where the settlement should be I run to it, follow it, kicking up the water as I go.

I pick up my pace, running, stumbling on the uneven, loose rocks and the slippery streambed but so determined to outrun the fear, the panic. There's this little waterfall in my way and I manage to go crashing down, face-planting into the pool at the bottom and then the obvious thing happens and Ezra does it too, landing right on top of me, his knee hitting my hip. And before I can scramble up and away, he gets hold of my wrists and is tight in behind me, gripping them while I twist and struggle.

'Let me go!' I am shrieking at him, screaming even though his head is right against mine, his chin pressing into my shoulder, and the water is slimy and foaming around us while he says, 'Hemple,' right against my ear and nothing else, and he has his hands on my arms, holding me from behind, making it impossible to move.

'Get off me!' I tell him, but he won't and so I shriek, 'Ezra, get off me!'

But he doesn't, he pulls me in against him, wraps my own arms around my ribs so that I can feel the way they are heaving too fast, too hard, so hard the world starts to spin. When he speaks his mouth is so close to my ear that it's all I can hear; everything else fades out.

'We're OK. For all we know we just got a little lost up here. We're here together and we will work it out. We've got out of worse scrapes than this before, Hemple, and we probably will again, so just breathe with me now, OK? Just breathe. All you need to do is breathe.' He holds me tight, pulls me into him so that I can feel his stomach and chest pressed into my back, his rib cage and my rib cage expanding as we breathe, in then out, slower, slower, slow, and he has one forearm across the front of my shoulders, one across my stomach, anchoring me, and suddenly it is OK. I am nodding and over my shoulder I feel him nod too and he says, 'You see? It's OK, you see?' and at this point he loosens his grip, and there is some part of me that doesn't want him to. In some way it feels as if that is all that was holding me together.

I stand and step away before turning.

'You've done that before. Do you remember?'

His eyes hold mine as he says, 'I do.'

Because of the white noise of the stream I don't hear it right away, only as we walk back up in the direction of the peak and leave the stream to head through the trees.

'Do you hear that?' I ask Ezra, reaching to take hold of his arm.

He cocks his head to listen, and is about to tell me no when I see his expression change.

'What is it?' he says, stepping towards the nearest tree, laying his hand on it.

'That's what I heard the other day,' I tell him.

There's no easy way to describe it. A whisper that's just a shade too low to actually hear, but in more of a rhythm than talking, so it is almost like poetry, or music. And it's coming right out of the tree.

Ezra frowns, sticks his finger in his ear and moves it around a little as if he could pry it out. Then he gives up on that and lays his head against the tree, eyes moving while he listens.

'OK, I don't get that at all,' he says. 'And I don't think I want to.'

'What if . . . ?' I take a steadying breath. 'If the coral is letting us travel to another dimension – is that . . . what this is? Is that where we are?'

He looks at me, then up and around at the trees.

'Well . . . ' He shrugs. 'It would be pretty cool if it was, right?' But I can see the fear in him, too.

I swallow.

'The talking tree dimension. Pretty random.' Then he looks as if he remembers something. 'That tower,' he says, heading back to the drop-off.

I follow him, but suddenly it is so much harder to walk, my steps slowing, as if I am losing power. I call to him but my voice doesn't carry. It is the weirdest thing because with each step it is as if the air is thickening, time seizing up around me.

'Ezra!' I try again, but he is too far ahead and doesn't hear me.

I fall to the ground but it seems to take minutes, during which time I look up at the sky and watch the colours that pass along it – red, pink, even a little green. The particles of coral seem to burn inside me; I can feel their heat. All this goes on so long I wonder if I will be stuck here for ever just like this, and I know more certainly than ever that if that happens, I will go insane, that it will be a torture no human could endure.

When I realise someone has hold of me, has hold of my shoulders and is pulling me into a sitting position, my first instinct is to scream and fight them off. It is only after doing this that I see it is Jason and I am so relieved that I wrap my arms around him and bury my face against his neck.

'You're OK,' he says. 'Thank God you're OK. Where were you? Where did you go?'

I open my eyes to look over his shoulder then and realise it is dark, dead of night. I have to blink a few times to believe it.

'Jason!' Maxim's voice through the trees. 'He's here. Come quick!'

He tries to get me to my feet but I can't, so I tell him to leave me and watch him run to where I can see Maxim's torch lighting up Ezra, who is face down on the ground, not moving.

'Are you OK?' I can hear Maxim asking him, and I see him shift, see him stir.

'Ezra?' Jason's voice now. 'Talk to me. Do you know where you are?'

Ezra just makes all these noises, as if his mouth or his throat or maybe his brain forgot how to talk and for this moment I am gripped by the terror of it, right up until he says, 'Man, I feel like crap.'

And I fall back against the ground, breathe there, focus on the tiny irregular shape of stars I can see between the treetops, high above.

Chapter Twenty-Seven

I wake up on one of the bunks in the research station, sun streaming in on my face. Karim is in the middle of the room, pulling his T-shirt on over his tattoos, when he notices that I'm awake and says something in Russian.

When I step out of the door the sun is sitting just above the horizon, its light bouncing off the distant sea and making me squint. Cold wind wraps the outer walls of the lab, and I slide my arms up my sleeves, tightening my arms around my ribs.

'Morning,' says Maxim, making me jump. He sits on one of the wooden stools, up against the front wall, blanket round his shoulders, expressionless in his sunglasses.

'It's cold,' I tell him.

He unpeels the blanket and hands it to me. I think about refusing but then take it, pulling its warmth around me.

'It's the wind off the mountains. There's still quite a lot of snow there. Climb one of the turbines and take a look.'

The door opens and Ezra stands there, hair in his face, hunched shoulders as he leans against the doorframe, shivering in his T-shirt. When the sun hits his eyes he steps back, raising his hand to shield them.

Maxim watches him for a minute and then sighs. 'I'll make coffee.'

While he's gone, Jason comes out carrying two more stools and puts them down, sitting on one. He chafes his hands together between his knees before he looks across at us.

'Well that was ... unexpected.'

I've lent Ezra half the blanket so that we are sitting on the stools huddled under it, teeth chattering.

'Do you feel up to telling us what happened?'

'How long were we gone?' I ask Jason.

He looks at me steadily. 'Think it was just over seventeen hours in the end.'

'Seventeen hours?' Ezra shakes his head. 'Jesus.'

'How did you find us?'

'I heard you,' he says to me. 'You were calling out. You were calling for Domingo, actually.' He glances up at me. 'Would you like me to send for him?'

'No,' I answer, as quick as I can, though this huge part of me feels exactly the opposite.

Maxim comes back out with metal cups of coffee that he hands to Ezra and me. We wrap our hands around them for warmth. It smells odd; nothing like I remember the coffee from Ventura. Karim appears in the doorway, arms folded, watching us.

'You were triggered by the ALF samples,' says Maxim, taking the fourth stool. 'My fault for taking you in there. I had no idea the reaction would be so instant, and so extreme.'

'We assumed you just ran away at first,' says Jason. 'Got spooked. I called a few people down at the settlement though and nobody had seen you.'

'Didn't you assume we'd maybe stumbled over the cliff edge you never told us about?' says Ezra with a laugh.

All three of them look at us blankly.

'What cliff edge?'

We walk three circuits of the wind field, under the turbines. Even though the ground does descend on that side of the ridge, there is no sign of the giant rift we looked out over, the drop into nothing.

'This is the first time that you were able to explore the new environment like this?' Maxim asks us.

I swallow and nod.

'And there was a tower,' says Ezra, his eyes lighting up with the memory of it. 'Remember, Hemple? Remember?'

I only nod but he is pacing back to roughly where we stood on the edge, and pointing. 'There! Remember? It was right around there. It's not there now, but ...'

Maxim squints at the distant point. 'It was ... man-made? Artificial?'

'No question. At the time, we assumed it was something to do with you guys, but . . . ' Ezra turns to look at us and his eyes are wide. 'Oh man, do you know what this means? Hemple, we need to get back there again, we need to.'

I am already shaking my head, backing away. 'No way.'

'Man, what do you mean? This is the most amazing thing that ever happened.'

'No,' I say louder. 'I don't want it happening to me again. Ever. I was scared, Ezra. At one point it felt as if . . . I don't know. What if the next time we can't get back?'

He does this big dramatic shrug. 'And? What's so great about your life here anyway?'

I look down at my feet and think about that for a moment. 'Nothing, I guess,' I end up saying. 'But it's not just that – I don't think our bodies, or our minds, are meant to be doing this. I don't think we're up to it.'

'I should tell you,' interrupts Jason. 'That when I examined you last night – the nature of the fresh bruising – there was some evidence of internal bleeding. Seren is right. This displacement or whatever it was, it was hard on your bodies.'

'You see! Ezra, I don't want to die; I don't want you to. How could it ever be worth it?'

He's making faces. 'We won't die. We aren't going to die. And this is . . . Jesus, Hemple, it was amazing – it was the most important thing that's ever happened to either of us, maybe to anyone. This is so huge. We can't just walk away from it. We need to keep going. And the tower! You saw it. If there are beings there, we have a responsibility to find out – to make contact with them.'

Jason is watching Ezra through this whole speech, but then he turns to Maxim. 'To be honest, after last night, I'm not sure I can sanction this research. Its results are so unpredictable. As a medical professional, if it is my opinion that you are endangering your test subjects, I have to let you know. For safety reasons, I think we need to suspend the research and the matter needs to be removed as soon as possible.'

Maxim is nodding slightly, while Ezra shakes his head.

'No,' he says. 'No way! Not now, when it just got interesting!'

Karim has spent almost the whole time we've been talking scanning the area of low ground in front of us with his binoculars and he says something in Russian now as he points out towards where the tower was. Maxim answers him and they talk for a while and nod a lot before Jason says, 'None of that is the point now,' and shakes his head.

'What's not the point?' asks Ezra. 'What's he saying?'

Maxim reaches a finger in behind his sunglasses to rub his eye. 'He's reminding me that this area, where you saw the tower, has been previously identified as a field of very strong and very unusual energy. We've been there to take readings in the past.'

Ezra shades his eyes and gazes back out at the land down there, where it opens up into grassy clearings before rising again.

'Maxim, you can't endanger people's lives in the name of scientific discovery,' says Jason.

Ezra laughs. 'Seriously? Did you hear what you just said? We only exist at all in the name of scientific discovery.'

Jason watches him in silence, eyes sad. 'Just because we live for it, it doesn't mean we have to die for it.'

'How soon can we take it out?' I ask him.

'Tomorrow, if you like.'

I nod, while Ezra says, 'Hemple, no. I know you. You're braver than this. You want to know as much as I do.'

But I shake my head, walk away, feel him following me.

'Where are you going?'

'I want to climb a turbine,' I realise as I say it.

'What, now?'

We walk away from the others, making our way to the first turbine fifty metres off. He stands at the base of it, looking up at the swooping blades high above.

'How did you plan to climb it?'

I lay my hand on the surface of it next to him, where there is the outline of a door that is slightly less than my height. It's completely flush, no handle, but I try a push and it releases open with a sigh.

Inside it's barely big enough for a person and the

narrow ladder rungs that run up one wall. I get a third of the way up towards the perfect circle of light I see at the top when I hear his voice, oddly loud and close in the confines.

'You're not really going up there?'

I laugh. 'That's what I came to do.'

Up at the top I have to hang off the rungs to open another identical door just behind me. I step across and out on to a narrow platform, made of metal mesh, which wraps itself around the turbine, just under the blades, like a collar. The blades are about ten times more immense than I thought they'd be, dividing the air in great thrumming circles an arm's length away, separating me from the ground far below. As I complete a circuit, edging round, I see the mountains out over the carpet of treetops to the north up along the ridge. Snow, just like Maxim said. They are high and lonely and far away, gathering the snow among them like a secret. I imagine myself there, or try to, in all that white and silence.

Ezra flops awkwardly out of the door behind me and sits, knees pulled up to his chest, pale and damp with sweat.

'Look.' I point out the mountains.

He barely looks, but nods.

'You can't see them properly from there,' I tell him. 'Get up and come over here.'

He shakes his head. 'Can't.'

'Why?'

'Can't move my legs.'

I start to laugh but then the look on his face stops me. 'You're scared of heights?'

'No!' He tries pretty hard to act affronted.

'You are!' I do laugh now. 'You're not scared of inter-dimensional displacement, but you're scared of heights!'

'Can we just go back now, Hemple?'

Later, sunset, the colours so vivid they have begun to scare me, and I am sitting on a wooden stool out the front again when Jason finds me.

'You're making the right decision,' he says. 'And maybe he'll come round.'

'He won't.'

He sighs.

'I'll drive you up to the farmhouse soon. I'm sure you're keen to see Domingo. He'll be glad you've made this decision.'

I shake my head, look into the wind to hide the tears in my eyes. 'Things are ... different now.'

He doesn't ask any more; he just watches me, nods slowly, then says, 'It turns out to be complicated, you know – love. It starts out really simple. That's why they call it falling, because it's easy to do. And then life happens around you. At first it feels like it's only the two of you who even exist, and then you realise that it isn't.

With me and . . . the boy I loved . . . we tried to end it so many times. It was so impossible, so dangerous – what was the point in torturing ourselves with all these little moments we managed to steal together if it was never, *could* never, be anything more than that? And every time I saw him with her it hurt so badly. And we argued about it so much. Was he just a lot better at pretending than me, or was he actually happy with her? I wasted a lot of time before I realised that it didn't matter. It didn't matter how he was with her when I wasn't around; it didn't matter that he and I would never share a life together beyond those moments. Those moments were the best thing in my life. Even if that's all they were ever going to be, they were worth it.'

I look at how he pinches his nose and looks away, rubs his hands over his face.

'My situation is different,' I say.

'Of course it is,' he says. 'But my point is . . . don't expect it to be easy. Just expect it to be worth it.'

He reaches to put his hand on mine, then seems to think better of it for a second, before changing his mind again and doing it. I try to smile but I can't, and he mirrors my mixed-up expression. Just as he is getting up to leave, I say, 'Was it . . . ' I swallow. 'Was it Marshall Lomax who you loved?'

He freezes mid-movement, then he sits back in his chair and looks at me, silently, and I know.

'I don't think Ezra should know, do you?' he says.

I turn away to think about this. 'I'm not sure.'

'What would be the point?'

'Sometimes I feel as if we all spend too much time hiding things from each other, when all we really want is the truth,' I say, not even realising it's what I think until I hear myself say it.

And he says, 'I think you're right.' He pauses, then adds, 'Have you told Mariana that, out of interest?'

But I don't answer, so we both look out at the sickening pink swirls of cloud trapped in the sunset light.

Chapter Twenty-Eight

I go out running early, go back to the farm once I know they'll all be gone so I can shower alone. And still I manage to walk into the main square just in time to see them sitting together at breakfast, Irina and Dom, her laughing and leaning her forehead against his shoulder for a moment.

It stops me, right in my tracks. The heat they've all been telling us about is in the air this morning but suddenly I am so, so cold. I swear Dom must feel me there because he turns and locks eyes with me, stays locked as I cross the entire length of the area on my way to the Med unit.

I am aware of him getting up to follow me, still awkward on his bad foot, but Ezra is passing at just that moment and gets to me first.

'I suppose there's no point in asking you to not to do it,' he says, standing there holding his bowl, sun in his eyes.

I shake my head.

'I'm standing here thinking of ways to change *your* mind,' I tell him.

'No chance,' he says.

Just then Dom gets to us and even though I feel him standing behind me I don't turn, I only stand, keep my back to him, hoping that he'll leave, and when I realise, after so long, that he won't, I turn, I watch him bite his lip, that self-same tic that used to make me want him so bad, and all I feel the urge to do is roll my eyes. And so I go with it.

I keep waiting, and when he doesn't speak I ask, 'Did you want something?'

And he says, 'Yes, actually, I did,' but then doesn't continue, and though I stand there looking at him, waiting, nothing happens.

So I roll my eyes again and say, 'Excuse me,' and go to leave, then find that his hand is on my elbow.

'Don't touch me,' I say, but it comes out almost like a question and I am left wondering if I mean it, and we are standing there in the process of walking past each other but not, and it is the closest we have been in what feels like so long, and it is almost like getting a prolonged electric shock; it is like endurance. Which is when I look down at his hand, his wrist, the pieces of string he still keeps there, and this is when I see that he has this huge tattoo – a tattoo! – along the inside of his forearm, and though I can't make it out right now, it looks like a Russian word.

I'm still reeling from this when he says, 'Want me to come with you?'

It's amazing how he knows I do, knew from all the way across the square, without even talking to me, but I just say, 'No thanks,' and then, 'Nice tattoo,' and raise an eyebrow. He smiles, but looks embarrassed, and opens his mouth, maybe to explain, but I leave before I change my mind.

'You're going to need someone to look after you while you recover,' Jason says to me while I'm sitting in a chair across the desk from him. 'To make life easier, I've asked Grace. She knows what she's doing and her place is close by.' He watches me shake my head and says, 'What's the problem?'

'I haven't really been speaking to her.'

He sighs. 'She didn't say anything about that.'

'Can't Mariana do it?'

'I thought she was feeling really sick at the moment?'

Which is true; these last few days she's mostly been sitting green-faced while everyone eats around her, before running off to throw up.

'Grace knows what she's doing,' he says. 'She's an adult, she has help. You can stay here in Med if you prefer, but there might be people in and out. It will take you a couple of days to be able to walk and do other things, I imagine.'

Just then the door opens, and Irina is standing there.

'What's she doing here?'

Jason looks surprised. 'She ... she'll be assisting me with the operation. She's our trained anaesthetist.' He shifts his gaze from me to Irina and then back again. 'Is that OK?'

I don't say anything, but he gets up anyway.

'I'm going to get cleaned up while Irina gets you ready. You're going to be OK, Seren. Don't worry.' He tries a smile, fails.

Irina hands me a white nightdress thing, similar to the ones I remember from Ventura, and I go into the next-door toilet to put it on. My hands are shaking so badly I can hardly get my zip down, buttons undone; it makes me want to shout at my hands for betraying me. I try deep breaths but they are so rattly it seems to make it even worse. When I finally get it sorted and walk out on wobbly legs, Irina takes my folded uniform and places it gently on a chair.

'I know this is not right time,' she says, in the understatement of the millennium, 'but I am sorry for what happened.'

I don't answer. What is there to say? It's OK? It's OK you kissed the love of my life and now I can't even look at him?

'The feelings I have for him are very confusing for me,' she says, almost unbearably pretty as she looks at her fingers twisting together. 'It's the first time I felt like that. In my life.' She looks at me as if she expects me to do something with this information, other than punch her perfect nose.

'It's none of my business any more,' I say, dizzy with it for moment.

She frowns. 'You mean this?'

I nod, even though the thought of her with him makes my body want to shuck my skin, shrivel into nothing.

Thankfully Jason calls us through at just that moment and I follow her to where one of the metal benches is set up in the middle of the main room, surrounded by machines, flanked by tables full of gleaming metal instruments, whose blades whisper at me as I pass.

I manage to get all the way laid down on the bench before I see the big round light above me, the one that he will use to see the thing that is inside me, and it is just like the one in Fertility back on Ventura and it all closes in on me, closes in on me hard, and I am up, getting up off the bench so suddenly that I kick one of the machines and it crashes to the floor but I don't care; I am standing in the corner and they are coming at me and I am shaking my head no.

'I can't,' I tell them. 'I've changed my mind. I can't do it. Just leave it in.'

'Seren, it's OK,' says Jason, then he tells Irina something in Russian and she leaves. 'I've sent for Grace. Just ...'
He's holding his hand out to me as if I am a wild animal.
'Just take it easy, OK? You're going to be sleeping the

whole time. It's not going to hurt at all. You won't know anything about it. You'll go to sleep, and when you wake up it will all be gone, and you'll be back to normal. Doesn't that sound good?'

But all I can feel is it rushing in on me, closing down around me.

'You won't … you won't be able to get it out, not properly, not without killing me.' I am pressing at it through the thin nightdress, pressing at the place on my hip where I can feel it, tracing it under my skin around to where it has begun to creep across my back, a little further each day so that I have become too scared to check on it. It's almost reached all the way to my spine now, and it makes me gasp. 'I'm trapped,' I say, feeling the threat of tears. 'If I leave it in it'll probably kill me, but taking it out will too.' I search his face and all I find is fear. 'I'm right, aren't I?'

'No,' he says, but he's not even slightly convincing.

'Oh God, I'm right.' I blink, trying to adjust to it.

'Seren, no.' He shakes his head. 'No. Come and sit down. Let me talk to you.'

'No.' I shake my head. 'There's no point.' I cover my face.

When I hear the door opening I don't look, don't move, not even when I feel her hands on my wrists.

'Seren,' is all she says at first, but I shake my head.

'I don't want to die.' My voice is hardly even there.

'You're not going to,' she says. 'I won't let you.'

'I don't want to be cut open.'

'I know you're scared, but you've done things that were a lot scarier than this before. I know you have.' She pulls my hands off my face and makes me look at her. 'I heard what happened up there. I've seen what it's doing to you. You need to get this out, and you need to do it now. You're making the right decision. I wanted to come and tell you, come and talk to you but . . . you were so angry with me.'

My breathing has levelled; I can see straight again.

She tries a slight smile and, over her shoulder, Jason says, 'All you need to do is go to sleep. Let me do the rest.'

They get me to lie on the bench somehow, even though I can't look, can't open my eyes, can only do it by pretending that none of it is happening at all, that I am not even here, that I am somewhere else. I can feel Grace's hand in mine, warm and pliant; in fact I think I am probably holding it too tight, hurting her. I can hear her talking to Irina in Russian. I let them sit me up as if I were a baby, pull at the nightgown until it is up around my chest and my whole bottom half is naked, and when they lie me back down they cover me with a sheet. I feel Irina's cold hands while she fixes sensors on my chest and forehead. She warns me about the needle before she feeds it into the back of my hand. I guess I expected their anaesthesia to be the same as ours – a gas they gave you in a mask – because I don't realise that this will drag me under as quickly as it does. And it is only then, right in that second that she is telling me I will sleep now and I am sinking under the world without trace that the truth comes to me and I only just get time to call it back up to them, to force my eyes open, to gasp one last time into consciousness to say, 'I want Dom to be here,' but then it's too late and my eyes are closing, and the last thing I feel are the tears that fall out of the corners of my eyes.

When I come round, it's as if I'm surfacing out of water, sudden and gradual at the same time. I'm covered in several puffy Concordia blankets but still shaking hard with cold.

Grace is sitting studying a screen in her lap but when I shift a little she reaches under the blanket for my hand and smiles at me, wet-eyed. 'Jason says everything went perfectly.'

I know the drugs are still affecting me pretty heavily because I am utterly calm, with no desire to move or run away at all. I only nod.

'First body scan shows no remaining parasite,' says Irina. 'We check again in few days.'

'Isn't that great?' says Grace.

I watch Irina go through to the other room. I try to move my hips and feel the pain then; it's far away still, kept behind a door. When I try to reach under the blankets with my hand I realise there is a plastic tube in it, feeding me from a drip. I use the other hand and feel only a mass of bandages, hiding me from myself.

Grace is watching but only says, 'Once you can walk a little, I'll get you to my place where you can rest.'

'I don't think I want to go to your place,' I say, even though it's rude. The drugs must be like a truth serum.

'Don't worry, we'll make you comfortable,' she says, absorbing it, and then, eyes shifting, 'Just before you went under, you said you wanted to see Domingo.' I turn my head away but hear her say, 'Do you still want to? Shall I send for him?'

I shake my head, so it can't be that much of a truth serum. If it was I would say yes, I would say that all I want to do is pretend that what happened didn't happen so we can be us again, even if I have to go on pretending all my life.

'He's been here three times asking to see you, by the way. Just so you know.'

And I nod, without looking back at her.

It's dark by the time she and Jason help me hobble over to her place, taking almost all my weight by holding my arms. There must be a storm, but somewhere far off, because the purple night is illuminating in flashes above the trees, distant rumbles in their wake.

When we get to their place, Kirill and Pasha are standing, looking disorientated, and I realise they have been asleep in their chairs, waiting up for us. Grace barks orders at them in Russian until they come, Kirill relieving Jason and walking me through to one of the bedrooms, helping me on to a lower bunk, even though I have to bend in the middle to get on it and it sends knives of pain into me that make me cry out.

'OK?' says Kirill, shifting the pillow under me as I finally lie flat, something like fear in his eyes.

I nod, just to make him feel better.

'Water?' he offers, and I nod again. He leaves and is replaced by Jason, who kneels by the bed, hands clasped together close to me, almost as if he is praying.

'These guys will take good care of you,' he says. 'And I'll be over as often as I can to check on you, too. I'm so glad everything went well.' And just before he leaves, he takes my hand and squeezes.

In the morning I see I am in Kirill's room. He has plants, ranged all along the wall that catches the early sun from the window, potted into anything he has been able to find – tin cups without handles, broken buckets, cracked vacuum packs. In among his clothes there is a toy shuttle lying on the floor, left over from when he was a kid. I try to imagine him growing up here, in this room, with my mother, his mother, coming in each night to kiss him goodnight.

Just then he leaps down lightly off the top bunk, straight on to the floor, scaring the life out of me so that I shriek a little, and he turns, smiling, bending all the way over so that his face is upside down as he says, 'Sorry to scare you.' He stands up to pull his T-shirt on. 'I go to get breakfast for you, OK?'

'I don't think I want any,' I tell him, but he goes anyway, saying something in Russian as he leaves which makes Grace come in.

'How was your night?' She kneels close to me. 'I wanted to have you in with me, but I only have one bed in my room and Jason thought I might knock you by mistake.'

'I slept fine.'

'No pain?'

'A bit.' It's a lie, it hurts like hell, and she sees it in my face, goes and comes back with a cup.

'Jason gave me this for you, for the pain.'

I peer into it and see a couple of centimetres of a bright green liquid.

'Don't think about it.' She laughs. 'Just knock it back. Always the best policy.'

It's hard enough even to lever myself up enough to be able to drink, and then the stuff itself is unbelievably vile. So bad I want to rake at my tongue with my fingers just to get rid of any trace of it. I realise then that Pasha is standing leaning in the doorway, filling it almost, laughing at the look on my face. Grace speaks to him and he leaves.

'I asked him to get you some water,' she says. 'He'll be back.'

'He seems nice,' I say, more for something to say than anything else.

'He is.' She looks down. 'It's been ... what ... sixteen years we've been together now, so ...'

I nod through the awkwardness.

'Domingo's been here looking for you again this morning,' she says.

I hand her back the cup. 'Was he sober?'

'Look, I know it's none of my business.' She looks at me warily before she continues. 'But you should consider the role Irina plays in all this. She doesn't know an awful lot about how things work. I mean, none of us do, do we? We see these movies and read these books but our lives are ... different. And she's always been very confused by her own feelings, her own desires. He might be a victim of circumstance here, just a little.'

I sigh hard, letting out all my breath. 'That's her excuse, but what's his?'

She doesn't answer that. Pasha comes back with water and hands it to her, and I struggle to pull myself up again before she helps me, and Pasha slides a pillow in under me.

'I wish you didn't have so many things to contend with,' says Grace. 'If that helps.'

'It doesn't,' I tell her, and Pasha laughs.

Chapter Twenty-Nine

It takes a long time to get anywhere when you feel as if you risk tearing your body open with every step. Jason says I will stop feeling this way soon, that the scarring won't feel so tight once the swelling goes down. The good news is that the body scan still shows nothing.

'There could be trace elements,' he says, squinting at the screen, the light from it glinting on his glasses before he pulls them off and looks at me. 'Which, in theory, means it could begin to grow again, so we'll keep an eye on it, but as far as I can see ... there's nothing there. Do you want to see it, by the way?'

I'm not sure that I do, but I manage to nod, and he reaches for a metal tray on one of his shelves and slides it on to the bench next to me. Lying inside are two slender antlers of coral, pale and bone-like, branching into smaller and smaller offshoots, reaching. I'm still staring at them, picturing the way they must have grown inside me, when he says, 'You're lucky, actually, because yours was a lot more isolated than Ezra's. His is much more diversified, spread throughout his body. Almost as if it broke up somehow.'

His words steal down my back, like a physical touch. 'It did break up,' I say. 'I broke it up. We thought it was poisoning him. We thought we were helping.'

'It probably just broke up on initial impact.'

I shake my head. 'We pounded at it with a rock.'

He puts his glasses back on and sighs. 'It was a sound theory, and may well have been the right thing to do at the time.' He studies the screen again, but I get the impression it's just an excuse not to look at me.

'But it wasn't the right thing, was it? It was completely the wrong thing.'

'You were four kids in a survival situation, Seren. It's a miracle you're still alive. I'm so impressed by you; you have no idea. You have such courage.'

He wants me to wait for Grace to come and get me but I won't.

'I haven't had time alone for so long,' I tell him. 'Please.'

So I walk off up the track to the Agri Facility, even though I basically take one step every million years. Everyone's at work so I don't see anyone, only the dead spaces between the trees, which is just how I want it. Grace has been off work to look after me, bringing me my food from the canteen so I can ignore it, changing my dressing, getting me water, feeding me the weird green liquid, worrying so much that I might be bored that she tries to translate Russian books for me out of their library. Turns out translation is harder than you think. It's been more fun in the evenings with Kirill and Pasha at home. Pasha's the guy to know in settlement, because of the still out back where he makes his alcohol, which he drinks a reasonable amount of too. There are generally a couple of extra guys in the main quarters at night telling loud stories, while Kirill sits on the floor next to my bed, leaning his back against it and showing me his favourite Russian TV shows, helping me follow their not-that-intricate solve-a-crime plots. Or he helps me sit up so we can play computer games against each other, as warring gangs in the back streets of St Petersburg. He laughs like Pan, smiles like her, but only when he's winning.

I get to the Agri Facility and I guess Mari must see me through the windows because her hand is wiping away the steam and condensation on the inside before the door flaps open and she comes to me, hooks her arm under mine as if she's just doing it to be friendly but I know it's because she sees I can barely walk.

'What are you doing here?' she says. 'Shouldn't you be resting?'

'Couldn't I say the same to you?' I squint at her in the strong sun. Out from under the trees there is a rich heat in the sun that pours from the sky.

'What – I'm going to lie in my bunk for six months?'

Inside it's intensely hot; fat drops fall from the ceiling in loud ticks. Kirill is digging in a corner but comes over, pulling his hat off and wiping runnels of sweat from his face with the back of his hand, even though it's pointless because more just flows off his soaking wet hair.

'Your scan is OK?' he says.

And he actually looks so worried that I smile before I say, 'Yeah, it was OK.'

I sit near Mari and watch her pushing tiny plants into a row of holes. I try to help a few times but I end up pulling at my stitches and seeing stars, even just handing her a trowel.

'A bit like old times,' I say, when she takes it from me. 'Although sometimes that life, Ventura . . . it all just seems like a dream to me now.'

She sits back on her heels. 'Even the island seems like a dream to me.'

I nod. Something about that seems sad.

'You look thin,' she tells me.

'Well, the food's not exactly up to much around here.'

She laughs. 'I told Maxim that. Even got him to go to his dad with it – I'm not sure he particularly gave a damn.'

'You met his dad?' I feel my eyes widen. 'What's he like?'

'Super old. I think he was already old when Maxim was born. He's managed to live through a whole bunch of diseases, but only just. I don't think he'll last much

302

longer. It's understandable that he's pretty grumpy and stuff.'

I let all this settle, and then find myself saying again, 'You met his dad?' but this time with a smile. 'Like, he took you home to meet his family?' I raise my eyebrows.

'Shut up, Seren.' She throws a little lump of soil at my arm.

'Something I should know?' I raise my eyebrows again.

'We're *friends*,' she says, but I swear there is pink in her cheeks as she drills the trowel into the soil in totally the wrong place, messing up her line. 'Anyway it's not as if . . . Even if there were choices we wanted to make, they're not ours to make, are they?'

She sits back again and looks at me, as sad-eyed and full-lipped and pretty as her cousin.

'You still haven't told him, have you?' I ask her. 'Ezra, I mean.' I watch her shake her head, carefully fingering the soil around another little plant.

'I haven't seen him much to be honest, and when I do he's weird. He doesn't want to talk about anything except the coral thing. He's obsessed with it. It scares me. He spends a lot of time with Domingo actually, which is . . . different.'

I blink. 'They're friends now?'

'It seems like it.'

'They're not friends. They've never been friends. They can't stand each other. That's just plain weird.'

The roof sheds a few drops on to us, making dark circles on the legs of my trousers.

'It's not that weird,' says Mari, wiping water off her creasing forehead. 'They've got a lot of shared history now. And Domingo's ... well ... I think he's been feeling pretty lonely lately.'

One of the beautiful butterflies flutters silently into the space between us and lands on the toe of my trainer. We both stare at it, at its wings so vivid and ethereal it's as if someone painted them on to the ordinary world.

'He got a tattoo,' I find myself saying.

And she sighs. 'Yeah.'

I think about telling her how terrible it is that he has done that to his perfect skin, his flawless beautiful body that is, or has been, so precious to me, a work of art that is now spoiled, but just thinking about it makes my eyes burn and closes my throat, so I don't say anything at all.

Then she says, 'He's really struggling, Seren. He is so, so unhappy.'

I don't say anything, don't even meet her eye.

'You don't understand,' she continues. 'He's not as strong as you.'

I almost laugh. 'What?' The butterfly flaps off. 'Not as strong as *me*? He is the strongest person I have ever known. He is infinitely stronger than me. That's what I love ... loved ... about him the most.'

But she is shaking her head. 'He's amazing – you know

304

how much I love him. But he has a lot of weakness in him. He loses himself, and his way, very easily. He was so lost in life when you met him, Seren.'

And I feel so sad then, as I say, 'Was he?' and watch her nod.

'You were the first and only thing he really cared about. I'm worried what will happen to him without you.'

'That's not ...' But I'm so disorientated by what she's saying that I lose my train of thought.

'I know it was horrible, but it was just this one moment. And he swears that she initiated it.'

'And you believe him?'

'I do. I mean, it's obvious how much she likes him. But she must be getting sick of the fact that he spends eighty per cent of the time drunk and complaining about how much he misses you,' she adds quickly.

I grab the trowel and stab at the soil next to me, until Mariana's hand appears on mine and makes me drop it.

'You can't really be considering giving up on everything you have together because of this one little thing.'

'It's not a little thing to me.' I cover my face with my hands. 'I trusted him. I never trusted anyone or anything and then I trusted him. And this is what happened!'

'Please think about it, Seren. For me, if not for you.' She has both her hands on my knees and is leaning into me. 'You two made me believe in true love. I didn't believe there was any such thing until I saw you together.'

And I am trying so hard not to blink because I know when I do this stupid amount of tear water is just going to spill on to my face and I am going to have to do something about it.

'Do you know how angry I am with him for letting this happen?' she says. 'I can hardly look at him. But don't you think you could at least try to talk to him?'

Even though it's almost unbearably painful on my stitches I bring my knees up and rest my face against them, just so I can soak up the tears before I say, 'I thought he would never hurt me,' my throat so hard it almost won't function.

And Mari's face falls into an expression so sad I'm not sure I've ever seen it on her, and at the same time she is rubbing my leg, nodding, then looking away, and I look away too, out to where the forest is only just visible through the dripping steam on the window.

Chapter Thirty

'Just stay,' says Grace. 'Stay here. I like looking after you. And Kirill loves spending time with you, you know he does.'

I shake my head. 'It's been nice,' I tell her. 'But I'm sure Kirill wants his room back to himself, and I just . . . well, look, there are lots of reasons. Mari says Dom and Ezra are going away on a camping trip or something, so . . . it'll just be us for a few days at least.'

She's so still for a moment that I get still too, end up watching her back the way she is watching me, with our matching sets of eyes.

'What?' I ask her.

'I think you're amazing, for the record.'

I bite my lip and laugh. 'I don't think anyone's ever said that to me before,' I say.

She frowns. 'Are you sure?'

And I feel my smile fade. If anyone ever has, I know who it would be.

*

There's a beautiful sunset creeping into the sky as I climb the rocky path to the old farm. Ever since my stitches dissolved, I've been able to walk a lot easier.

I'm pretty close to the old farm by the time I hear the raised voices that make me slow my steps.

'Because it sounds like a stupid idea, that's why!' It's Mari.

'Maxim doesn't seem to think so. Doesn't that change your mind? It usually does.' Ezra.

'No! Don't you do that!' Mari again.

The quieter voice that I can't hear is Dom's.

'Then you're as much of an idiot as he is,' is Mari's response to whatever it is he said.

By the time I get to the door and push it open they are silent, and when I step in it is into the triangle of them, Mari sitting on the only stool with her head in her hands, Ezra messing with his hair by his bunk, Dom leaning on the small windowsill, standing slowly as he sees me, his eyes finding mine and making it almost impossible for me to look away.

'What's happening?' I say. 'I thought you were going on a trip.'

'A stupid trip,' spits Mariana.

Ezra laughs. 'Why don't you let her make up her own mind about that?'

'They're going to that place, the place you saw the tower when you . . . travelled.'

'When we were *displaced*,' says Ezra, shooting her a look. 'When we were displaced in space-time.'

'The place where Maxim and Karim went to take readings before, and they were off the chart?' continues Mari. 'After what happened to you, it just seems reckless.' She makes this face at me. 'Doesn't it?'

'Your boyfriend's up for it,' smirks Ezra.

'God, Lomax, shut up.' She pinches the bridge of her nose.

I frown. 'What does Jason say about it?'

Silence, and shared looks, before Dom says, 'He doesn't, strictly speaking, know about it.' Hearing his voice nearly makes my knees give out.

'And this very fact is what shows that you know how dangerous it is. You *know*, and you just don't care,' Mari says.

'I told you,' yells Ezra. 'Irina's coming! She's a trained medic, and she's fine with it, and ... jeez, it's not even as if I need to explain myself, or anything I do to you.' He turns, starts stuffing clothes into his bag, and I watch the muscles of his back shifting under his T-shirt.

Mari gets up and goes to the door, slamming it after her. I exchange a look with each of them before following her.

She is over where the ground drops away, the sky still coloured in stripes, breathing hard. I get to her and hold her shoulders and it comes to me right away.

'You need to tell him, Mari – this is it. This is the time. You need to tell him – it'll stop him going. He won't take the risk if he knows.'

She turns to me but she's shaking her head. '*Estás loca*, Seren. And you're wrong. That wouldn't stop him going. If anything, that would make him run faster and further. It would probably make him even more determined to do something stupid.'

'I don't . . . ' I try to imagine myself in her shoes; in his. 'It's got to be worth a try, hasn't it? I mean, as Jason said, he might surprise us. Something like that changes a person.'

'It does.' She nods, tearful. 'Of course it does. It changes a person . . . completely. And for ever. But not right away. Not overnight. It'll take time. He'll need time to get used to it, probably quite a lot of it. It'll be a process. And the first part of it will probably be him hating it, and hating the idea of it, and wanting to be a million miles away from it, as far as anyone can get, where he doesn't need to deal with it at all.' She is breathless, watching me in the red light. 'I've been here before, remember.' She actually manages to smile, just a little, as I pull her into my arms and lean my head against hers.

We stay like that, both watching the sun sink into the treetops, until she says, 'God, you know what, if anyone has a chance of talking him out of it, it's you. You're the only person he's ever listened to about anything.'

I shake my head. 'That's definitely not true.'

'It is true. I've got to know him a little these past months. One thing I've noticed is that your opinion matters to him. Maybe more than anyone's. You are, like, his oldest friend after all, aren't you?'

'I ... I suppose I am, in a way,' I manage. 'But I don't think he's listening to anyone right now.'

'You should go with them,' she says suddenly. 'You need to. You could be the only thing that stops him doing something crazy. God knows that *idiota* Irina doesn't really care if he kills himself; she's just along for the ride. She's probably only going because Dom is.'

This makes me swallow hard. 'I'm not going. I can't.'

'You have to.' She is wide-eyed.

'Why don't you talk to Maxim?' I ask her.

'I've tried that. He's too excited about it. About what it could mean for his research. He's spent five years or something looking for answers to this stuff. And I can't ...' She makes a face. 'I haven't told him the real reason why it matters to me so much. It's ... awkward. You need to go. That's what needs to happen. Please.'

'No.' I'm shaking my head. 'I'll tell you what – how about this? I'll tell Jason. I'll tell Grace and Pasha. They'll put a stop to it. They won't let them go.'

'It's too late for that. They leave at dawn.'

We both look around for answers in the growing darkness before she says, 'Seren, please. Please do this for me. I know it will be hard, but I just ... it feels as if you could be the one thing that makes a difference.'

Our eyes meet, but I don't say anything else. I just walk back to the doorway of the old farm and open the door, spilling light out as I step in.

Ezra is laid out on his bunk by now, Dom standing slowly from where he has been bent over, packing a bag.

'I'm coming with you,' I tell them.

'Um, OK,' says Ezra, half laughing.

Dom watches me cross the room before he says, 'You sure you're up to it?'

And something makes me say, 'Why? Don't you want me along on your romantic getaway?'

To which Ezra laughs, and when Dom's finished rolling his eyes at him, he says, 'I mean, because you're just recovering from surgery, and the ground's too soft for the vehicles, so it's a lot of walking.'

I stop in the doorway through to mine and Mari's room but don't turn around. 'Why don't you just let me worry about me, and you worry about you?' When he doesn't answer, I say, 'I'll see you at dawn,' and snap off the light.

Chapter Thirty-One

'Man,' says Dom, pulling at the strap of the guitar he's wearing across his back. 'Surely we could have brought one of the vehicles at least this far?'

We've been walking maybe an hour by this point under a high hazy sun with a cool wind skimming along over an absolute ocean of smooth, knee-high grass. To the north the mountains form a wall, snow-topped. It's beautiful, and I'm wondering when Dom got so annoying. Because of his limp and my surgery scar we keep ending up at the back, with Maxim, Ezra and Irina forging on.

'It probably wasn't a good idea to bring something so bulky with you,' I say, raising my eyebrow.

'I was asked to,' he says.

'So, even though you can't actually walk properly, someone thought it was a good idea for you to carry a guitar on a two-day hike so you could serenade them at their will?' I put my finger on my lips. 'Let me think whose idea this must be.'

Up ahead I see that Irina has stopped and is waiting for us in the grass, hair blowing prettily back, like someone on a book cover.

'She's waiting for you. Better hurry up.'

He glances back to pin me with a look. 'Seren, it's not like that.'

'Well, OK, if you say so.'

'What's that supposed to mean?' He stops so suddenly I have to sidestep so that I don't crash into him and we end up next to each other, him looking down at me while I look around at the view, the wind making my eyes tear.

Just then Irina calls, 'Everything is OK?'

And so we just hold each other's eyes for this moment, and then we start walking again.

It doesn't take long until we drop back again, left behind. Dom falls at one point, awkwardly, almost like someone falling in slow motion. I go to pass him but then stop.

'Why did you even come if you still can't walk?'

'Because Lomax asked me to,' he says, picking up the hem of his T-shirt to mop the sweat on his face. 'Why did you?'

'Because Mari asked me to. She was worried about Ezra.'

'OK,' is all he says, and then, 'Think you could help me up?'

So I offer him my hand, but he doesn't take it; instead

I feel his hand at the top of my forearm, gripping tight, hauling on me so that I nearly fall into him, so that we are close as he gets to his feet, close enough I can smell him, and as he disengages his arm he does it slowly, in stages, in a way that annoys but also completely flusters me.

We keep hiking until the sun is turning golden on the mountaintop snow and, just when it's about time to stop for the night, with no warning the flat of the land drops away beneath our feet and suddenly we see a lake, broad and still and bouncing the sky back up at itself, puckering slightly on its far edge. The others are already there, standing at the water's edge, gazing out over it.

'Did you know this was here?' I ask Maxim.

He shakes his head.

'Oh my God,' says Dom, and I turn to him, study his side profile as he looks across the water. 'It's ... ' But he doesn't finish, just smiles, shakes his head as if he doesn't quite believe it. 'Is it fresh?'

Irina squats next to it and lifts a handful to her mouth. 'It's fresh,' she says then, letting a few drips of it rest on her lips and throat as she looks up at him. Jesus.

Once we've put the tents up, Maxim, Irina and Dom spend an hour taking water samples while Ezra and I build a fire. Neither of us can do it the way Mariana can, but we get something going by the time it is just getting dark and the temperature is dropping fast, under the achingly clear sky and its mine of stars. Ezra is studying the map in his lap even though it's almost too dark, when I say, 'It's not too late to turn back, you know.'

'Turn back?' He laughs. 'Why would I do that?'

I lean towards him over my knees. 'Because this whole thing is nuts. Ezra, it's nuts. After what happened last time I can't believe you would consider doing this again.'

'I can't believe you would just walk away from it the way you did, but there you go, we're different people.'

Later I go down to the edge of the lake to fill up a pan with water and Dom follows me. I would know his footsteps anywhere.

'I think it could be perfect,' he sighs.

'What could?' I ask, irritable, swishing the pan in the water.

'This place, for a fish farm, in the future.'

I don't answer, just watch my hands in the water, feel the cold locking my fingers.

'I'll need someone to help me with it,' he says.

And though he's obviously not finished his sentence, I get up to head back towards the fire and say, 'I'm sure you'll find a willing volunteer.'

And I feel him watch me go, probably in shock more than anything else. I follow the glow of the fire through the gap between the tents to where the others are. Maxim points at my bowl where it sits with Dom's near the fire, and I go to pick it up. When I sit down near her, Irina says, 'Where's Domingo?'

And I don't answer, but just then he arrives, biting his lip before sitting down near Ezra, and just as he is about to take his first mouthful of food, Maxim says, 'You play guitar when finish food or not?'

And even though I can tell he doesn't want to, Irina says, 'I'll get it for you,' and springs up.

When she gets back she doesn't sit where she was, next to me; she sits right next to Dom, laying the guitar down in front of him, taking his just empty bowl from him and leaning all the way in to say something that makes him smile a little even though he doesn't meet her gaze. All the same it gets into my head, the sight of them together, the way she is as beautiful and long and lean and extraordinary as he is, as if they were a matching set – a male and female version of the same thing. I'm sure nobody ever looked at Dom and me and thought that; nobody ever could.

'Are you OK?' This is Ezra, watching me with narrowed eyes.

'Yeah, of course, why?'

'You were talking to yourself just then.' He pushes his hair back off his face. 'Well, in fact you were shaking your head at yourself, but it amounts to the same thing.'

I don't answer, just shrug.

Dom only plays a few chords before Irina grins in recognition, and I end up wondering if this is what he played the night he kissed her. His hair flops over his face because of the way he looks down at his guitar, the way it did on Ventura. This is part of what makes him so good to watch when he plays – he lets you look without looking back. All this beauty and he asks for nothing in return. I shift my eyes to Irina for a moment and I swear from the way she is watching him I can almost hear her purring.

He finishes the song and the others clap, and Irina starts asking him if he knows all these songs, this huge long list as if he were an infinite jukebox, and so he is scratching the back of his head and in this position we can see his tattoo, all across the inside of his forearm.

Maxim says to me, 'I love that new tattoo.'

And I guess I show him what I think of it just by the look I give him, because he says, 'You don't like it?'

And I say, 'I do not.'

And he reads it to me: '*Zvyozdochka*,' and then yawns as he says, 'Star, little star, in English. For Huxley, I suppose. Pretty cool. I might get one.' He's smiling a little until he looks at me. 'Are you OK?'

But I can't speak, can't even answer, can't even name the feeling that takes hold of me except that it grips me tight, right around the chest, as I look at Dom, across the fire, through the flames. The only thing I ever really wanted, the person I have loved the most, the only place that ever felt like home, my one true thing. And I hardly know him at all.

'I'm going to bed; goodnight,' I announce, and there is this general silence of surprise, and even though I don't look at Dom I feel him watching me as I go.

I don't know how long I have been in the tent, balling up the sleeping bag over my ears so that I don't have to hear Dom playing, hear his voice reminding me how much I love the way he sings, when he starts another song and I know there is no way I will be able to stop my ears from hearing it, because it is the song he wrote for me, back on Ventura. 'The Light From You' is what he called it, and suddenly it means so many things to me, things it never meant before. And all of a sudden it seems like a million years ago. Back before our love was an absolute, before it became the sun and moon and stars for me, for both of us. Back before our universe imploded and it suddenly wasn't any more. When he wrote me this song he was just a beautiful boy I hardly knew; maybe that's all he ever was.

My tears drop on to the folded jacket I'm using as a pillow.

It doesn't really occur to me that Irina and I will share a tent until she crawls in sometime later and shuffles into her sleeping bag. She doesn't say anything at first but after a while I turn to her and I can see the shine of her eyes in the darkness.

'You're still awake,' she says.

'No.'

319

She lets it slide. 'If you don't want me talking that's fine, but for a long time I have wanted to tell you that it was my fault. That night. I kissed him. He didn't want me to.'

'Thanks for the information.'

'It's true,' she says. 'And I'm sorry.'

'What do you want me to say, Irina?'

She looks as if she isn't sure.

'I care about him too,' she says, eventually. 'I want him to be happy. He says he's never going to be, without you.'

'I don't ...' My voice is infuriatingly unsteady. 'I don't want your advice, OK? You're the last person I would take advice from. As if all the crap you've pulled so far wasn't enough, now you're going against everything Jason said, going behind his back and letting Ezra take stupid risks ...'

'He would have come with or without me, Seren; is it not better me here than nobody?' She widens her green eyes at me.

But I'm not in the mood, so I slide down the tent and lunge forward, pulling at the zip.

'Where are you going?' she asks me.

'Oh, what do you care?'

And I struggle out, which isn't easy with how small the tent is, and I get stuck a few times before I manage to get out into the black.

I start walking even though I'm blinded, blinking, eyes still adjusting so that I don't see him right away, even though I almost collide with him as I am pacing

320

out into the hissing grass, lit by the intense blue-white streak of galaxy above, wind buffeting as he turns around, plastering his dark hair across his face. Dom.

Even though he doesn't speak, I hold my finger up at him to stop whatever he might be about to say and make sure I get in first.

'Don't.' And I pass him, leaving him behind, although I hear him follow me, grass whispering against his legs. So I throw the rest back over my shoulder: 'Don't sing our song. Not ever. You gave up the right to do that when you kissed her.'

'SHE kissed ME.'

I stop and turn to him.

'You kissed her back.'

'I was . . . shocked.'

'You were thrilled.'

He just stands there, bites his lip while he looks at me. 'You know, if someone kissed you I'd punch them and that would be the end of it.'

I shake my head at him. 'Maybe that's the case. But it hardly matters, now we're basically strangers.'

'Seren, I still know you.' His voice feels closer to me than he is when he says that, almost as if it's moving through me.

I shake it off and say, 'Well, I don't know you at all. I leave that to Irina these days. Maybe she knows why you get stupid Russian tattoos all over your arm.'

He looks at it then, almost as if he's discovering it for the first time, and he makes a face as he says, 'I got that for you.'

'I know you did, but I don't know why.'

He pulls his lips to the side then, still beautiful, even when he's grimacing. 'I don't either now, really I don't. Maybe it was to remind myself that I'll never love that way again. Maybe it was to remind myself that I'll never love anyone the way I love you, but what good that does for either of us . . . I just couldn't say.'

And as his words sink in I lose the ability to say whatever I was going to next, swallowing hard instead. He watches me, waits, and when he sees I'm not going to speak he goes to walk away, back towards the tents behind me, and only stops just before he passes me.

'Do you know how many times I've thought about that first day I came to talk to you in Med? Thought about how, if I hadn't talked to you, you would have stayed, married Ezra, been happy there. Because you would have been, eventually, you know. And we would never have ended up here, alone, broken into pieces, lost on an empty planet. I've thought about it so many times. And yet . . . somehow, despite it all, I still know if I could go back in time I would do it again. I would do it again and again and again. I wouldn't change any of it. Even if that's all it's ever going to be for you and me . . . even if it's never ever like that again for me . . . and I know it won't be . . . it was still worth it.'

And I fight for breath, my throat so tight, and then he goes to walk away, but just before he does I take his arm, hold his forearm and stop him; hold him there, pull him back to me.

'You have no idea how much I miss you,' he says, voice broken, and after this moment when it feels as if all either of us are doing is listening to each other breathe, I feel his hand on my hair, smoothing it on to my back, and because it is the first time he has touched me in I don't know how long I hold my breath, hold it all in and just feel it, and I swear it is as if no one has ever touched me before in my life and I never want it to end. I wonder what will happen if he doesn't hold me, if he doesn't kiss me right now, because maybe I'll scream, maybe I'll cry, maybe I'll die, maybe the ground will open and swallow me so deep I'll never be heard of again.

I turn to him so suddenly that I hear him draw breath when I grab him, my arms around his neck and my face pressed to the skin at the base of his throat and my whole body pressed into his so tight. And I keep my face pressed against him until I can be sure I won't cry and then I lift it, super slow, until I am looking at his shoulder, his ear, the side of his neck, and he is doing the same, and we are both still, just breathing, my hands on his chest, his on my hips. And then we are kissing, and it is not as if he kisses me or I kiss him, but this utterly spontaneous moment where we're not and then we are, and it is noisy and wet and desperate and absolutely beautiful. He is soft and gentle and salty and warm and deep, his body something I know so well and not at all, his fingers on the back of my neck, down my spine, in the small of my back, on my hip, bringing it in against his leg, all the time breathing in and in and in, like something we have done a million times and yet also like something neither of us have ever done before, and it is just us and the boundless waving grass, the ceiling of endless stars and everything that's in our hearts. When my fingers find the hem of his shirt, when my hand finds the smoothest skin over his hipbone with a tremble I am sure he can feel, he speaks against my mouth, slowly he sighs it: 'Estrellita,' and I feel my eyes filling with hot tears.

And sometimes I am trying to talk and he will stop to say, 'What?'

And I will say, 'Nothing,' and shake my head, but not because it was nothing, only because all I want is to be kissing him again. And sometimes it will seem as if he is trying to say something and I will stop and say, 'What?' and all he will do is kiss me again, because there are all these things, I mean there are all these things that we have to say to each other and it is bursting out of us but right now the only thing that matters is showing each other that it is *you*; it has always been you.

But then the words are there again and I am pulling away and saying, 'I can't,' as I lean my head against his and his lips are still close enough to taste. 'I can't do this.' I am shaking my head. 'You don't understand. It would be too hard . . . I can't lose you again.'

And I have no idea how I have the will to say this when the feel of his body so close to mine moves me the way it does, every atom of me knowing he has been gone too long.

'You won't lose me,' he says, kissing me again, but gently, just once, asking me to come back.

'Everybody loses everybody in the end.'

'That's the kind of thing only you would say,' he says, tightening his arms. 'The only way you're getting rid of me is by killing me, I promise.'

'I mean it, Dom, I can't do this, I can't . . . It can't be like it was before. Not ever.' I pull at his arms until he releases me, until he watches me walk away from him with a fading smile.

'Why can't it?'

And then there is this long, still moment, the stillest moment in the world, when he looks at me and I look at him and he looks at me and I look at him.

'Because I can't just forget it ever happened,' is the only answer I have.

'You don't have to forget, you just have to get past it. God, Seren, we're probably going to have to get past a lot of things, don't you think?' He looks down at the ground between us, his hair dark and shining as the wind paints it across his eyes. 'I mean, two people can't spend their whole lives together without having to get past a few things.'

'Our whole lives?' I look out into the dark as the wind passes us. In the light of the moons the snow on the mountains is bright in the distance.

'Wasn't that the plan once?' he says. 'Wasn't that the whole point of coming here? Of everything?'

He turns away then, head down, and I study the curve of his back and shoulders with something halfway between intense desire and a sharp physical pain like a knife in the ribs. And then he is walking away from me, off into the riptide of grass as if intent on drowning in it.

I follow him out there, of course I do, running him down, laying my hand on his shoulder and smoothing it down his back, feeling him slow his pace, winding my body round his, under his arm until I feel him hold me, and he wraps me, kisses me, lifts me so that I can ease my legs around his hips.

'You're still the only thing that feels like real life to me,' I whisper to his earlobe, while he kisses my neck and makes me flex my toes, and we tumble into the grass, let it swallow us.

Chapter Thirty-Two

When the sun rises, making the eastern stars fade first, then turning the streaks of cloud pink, we are still out among the waving grass, under Dom's sleeping bag, fingers linked, looking at each other as if we might evaporate into the dawn if we stop. We've just decided we should sneak back to the tents when there is the sound of a zip, and it is the loudest thing I have ever heard. We can see Maxim emerging, standing straight slowly, yawning so hard he starts to tremble, before bending down to clank pots together as he starts breakfast.

Dom pulls me into him, kisses me on the edge of my mouth, and both of us keep our eyes open, go cross-eyed, merging into one, smiling into it, maybe only realising now that this was one of those nights you never want to end.

'I was just about to get worried,' says Maxim as we approach a few minutes later. 'But something told me I didn't need to.' He gives us a smile and this little half wink.

Dom sits behind me with his knees crooked up on either side of me as I try to get the fire going, helping me and laughing at my frustration when it keeps going wrong. I realise I don't want him any further away from me than this when he is about to get more kindling and I stop him with my hands on his knees and lean back into him, tilting my head back to kiss him, and this is exactly the scene when Irina steps out of the tent. She glances at us once and then looks around at the horizons with her hands on her hips.

'I hope you get lot of sleep,' she says, to nobody in particular. 'Lot of walking today.' She goes down to where Maxim is filling pans at the edge of the lake.

The land rises steadily all morning until we reach a place where there are rocks, huge ones, scattered as if some giant threw them there for a game. From here the land drops fairly sharply, so that we wind down into a forest, but not of the trees back at settlement. These are much smaller, with twisted trunks and branches, coated in a thick, dark moss.

Dom and I bring up the rear all day but we hardly notice. It probably makes it harder but we never stop talking. At one point we catch up to the others and they are sitting near a stream, drinking from their bottles, ranged on the rocks, and Maxim is looking at the portable screen in his lap.

'We're almost there. We should make camp here and walk over there to check it out,' he says.

I look around the darkness of the wood and shiver a little. We pitch the tents in the tight space between the stream and where the trees crowd together, before Dom heads off to look for firewood. I join Ezra down by the water, where he's washing his face.

'So you and Suarez are a thing again?'

I don't answer.

But he says, 'Well, thank God for that. Maybe you can convince him he needs to get a haircut. He can't wear his hair that long – it's too floppy. His whole vibe is just ... He looks like that love interest in a *telenovela* who turns out to be slightly bad news.'

We both laugh and I say, 'You've obviously spent a lot of time thinking about this.'

'Yeah, maybe too much.' He watches me scoop water up and dash my face.

'So I guess I missed my chance again,' he says, suddenly still.

'Your chance?'

'You were almost single there for about five minutes.'

I laugh it off, but when he doesn't join in I stop, my cheeks flushed. 'Ezra,' I say then, as if I'm telling him off. 'You don't want a chance. And anyway, you had it, once.'

'No I didn't.' He makes a face. 'Not really.'

There's a silence in which I am watching him wash his hands, trying to work out if he is actually serious or not, before I say, 'What about you and Mari?'

'Are you for real? Haven't you even noticed how bad she's got it for Maxim?' He pulls his shirt off to wash, which silences me and I have no idea what expression I have on my face but I am guessing it shows at least some of the horror I am feeling because he does this double take at me and says, 'Oh come on, it's not that bad is it?'

But it is.

The coral has grown so much, permeating almost his entire torso, branching all across his stomach, up on to his chest and down towards his hip. There's a new bit growing, too, a breakaway on his left shoulder that creeps up his neck and down into his armpit. I make him turn around and it has crawled, plant-like, all down and across his back, and absolutely everywhere it touches is black and blue and purple and horribly shadowed with bruise. When I reach towards it he shrinks away.

'Does it hurt?' I ask him, just as Dom arrives back and drops the firewood with a crash, before stepping carefully over to us.

'Wow, it got worse,' he says. Understatement.

'OK, so I have been thinking that I probably need to go and see Jason when we get back.' Ezra holds his hands up. 'Not to have all of it removed but maybe, at least, some. If that's something he can do.'

'I think that's a good idea,' says Dom.

'Guys, come and check this out,' says Maxim, foot up on a twisted root, and he walks in under the trees.

Even though night is falling fast there is light in the direction we are walking – blue and glimmering as if it were coming through water. Something about it makes me slow my steps.

'Maxim, what ...?' I am shaking my head when he glances back at me.

'Come and see it, Seren,' he says, laughing. 'I promise you, you'll love it.'

I hear it then too, a sound that has become a far-off memory already. I realise now it has been in the periphery of my hearing since we got to the stream. I would know it anywhere. I look at Dom.

'Is that ...?'

He nods, takes my hand to help me on the rocks, but I am frozen.

'Ezra!' I call down to him. 'I don't think you should. Not yet.' But he is already too far ahead, taking big, slightly out of control steps on the steep decline, and he isn't listening to me, and I watch the way he gets to the bottom of the slope and stops, hands by his sides, looking around, and I hear him say, 'Oh wow.'

It isn't like a real thing or a real place or a real anything. It's like something somebody dreamed once that somehow ended up existing. It's the flowers from the island, and I haven't seen them once the whole time we've been here, not even one of them, and yet here they are suddenly and there are hundreds, no, maybe thousands, maybe

331

more than that, growing so close and so thick that there is a carpet of them and we have no choice but to walk on them, even though they are far too beautiful to be walked on and it feels wrong and I can smell them a little as they break under my feet. But that isn't all, because above them, swirling, eddying, filling the air like a cloud, are countless hundreds of glow-flies, gathering on every tree, on every leaf, on every twig, so that the entire clearing is a churning riot of blue and purple light and in among it there is us.

I look at Dom, at the way the glow-flies are lighting on his hair and shoulders, and he says, 'God, it's so beautiful.' We hold our hands out in front of us, between us, and watch the glow-flies landing on our fingertips like jewels, and I can hear Irina and Maxim laughing with just the mad joy of it, but suddenly it occurs to me that it is almost too much to bear. And it begins. A light so bright it is blinding, filling my eyes, and a ringing in my ears that gets louder and louder, drowning out the flowers, drowning out everything, and this is when I spin round, turn and turn again, but all I see is blue light.

'Ezra?' But I can't find him, and suddenly I am panicking, flapping my hands in front of my face to try to make a space to see through. 'EZRA? Where is he?' I find Dom, grab the collar of his shirt and pull on it. 'Where is he? Do you see him?'

I watch the tendons in his neck as he strains to look for him. 'Lomax?'

I run then, straight in, straight into the heart of it, even though it's all fluttering so hard in my face, and it's like being underwater, being in a vortex, disappearing down a whirlpool. It takes Dom to find my hand and lead me out in the end, and when he does I am coughing, spluttering, just as if I had been drowning.

'Where is he?' I say as we both fall to our knees on the rocks.

'Gone.' He shakes his head.

'Gone?'

Maxim and Irina appear next to us, both coated in glow-flies that they try to carefully dust off. 'GONE?' I say again, louder. 'Why did you bring him here? WHY? I said—'

'I know!' says Maxim. 'I see that now.'

'You see that NOW?' I shriek. 'Now that he's gone, you see that?' I stand up and step closer to him. 'Jesus, what kind of scientist are you? You had already worked out that these things trigger it and you bring him to a place where there are more of them than we've ever seen before and just let him wander into it?'

'Look, Seren, I'm frustrated by it too. I wanted to witness him displacing. But ultimately –' he wipes a glow-fly off his cheek, accidentally killing it and leaving a streak of light on his skin – 'ultimately, there isn't much I can do anyway. I can't follow him. None of us can any more. We just have to let him do it and see what he says when he gets back.'

'*If* he gets back, you mean.' My throat gets tight.

'He'll get back.' He seems so sure it comes over smug.

'You weren't there,' I tell him, tightening my jaw. 'You weren't there. You don't know what it was like. It felt as if . . . it felt as if you could get lost in there. Maybe for ever.'

'He'll be OK.' He reaches for my arm but I shrug him off.

'And you.' I turn to Irina. 'Have you examined him lately? Have you seen how bad it's got?'

There are glow-flies studding her hair like blue diamonds. Her mouth moves before she can make words. 'I have not examined him exactly but—'

'So why are you even here? Why are you here pretending that you actually give a damn what happens to him when the truth is that you clearly don't?' But I don't wait for her answer. I climb the rocks back up to camp and leave them there.

Dom follows close behind me, but only catches me at the top.

'Hey,' he says as he takes hold of my hand. It's about the fifth time he's said it. I turn to him and he doesn't look much less worried than I feel.

'How stupid was that?' I say.

'Yeah, it was pretty stupid, but I mean, it was going to happen at some point.' He picks a glow-fly out of my hair and we both watch it fly away, up into the sky, where the stars are appearing. 'That's why we came here, after all, isn't it? You know it's what he wanted.'

'I know, but you don't get it. It was terrifying being there, and it hurt. Physically, I mean. It really, really hurt.'

The thought of him being there scares me so much that all I can do is make this noise and push my fingers into my hair, squeezing at my head as if I could crush the thoughts right out of it, and I feel Dom's hands over mine, warmer than mine, gentler. He is shushing me, helping me sit, keeping his arms tight around me so that maybe I can stop shaking, even just a little.

We sit by the fire until late, listening for him, while Maxim stays where the flowers are, on watch. He comes back at one point and stands looking at the fire, shaking his head.

'The energy is very strong here. Those flowers. In a similar way to the coral, they are ... linked to each other. Like a computer network – imagine it that way. So that rather than being individuals, they are like one super-being.'

I remember the tree music, then. The voices. Something about it is beautiful and horrible all at the same time. But that's Huxley-3.

Dom tries to convince me to sleep and I only agree to try because he comes with me into the tent and spoons in behind me. Every time I fall asleep I jolt awake as if I'm falling from a height.

Eventually I must drift into sleep, though, because at some point I open my eyes and realise it has just started to get light and I am alone. Outside the tent there is just the ring of blackened stones where the fire was last night. I stand and look at it for a minute and swallow a pain in my throat. When I look at the other tent and the door is flapped open it sends this hard pulse of fear through me because there are two pairs of feet there and neither of them are Ezra's.

I make my way down the rocks to where Dom is sitting at the bottom of the slope, looking up at me. The light from the glow-flies is beginning to wash out in the dawn and half of the flowers are closed and nodding their heads.

'You should have woken me to do a shift,' I tell him. 'How long have you been here?'

'Maxim only woke me a couple of hours ago, maybe,' he says, and I think about that, about how lonely those hours before dawn always are.

'No sign then?' I ask him, even though it's a stupid question.

I watch him shake his head and we look around in silence for a moment before he frowns and says, 'I've been thinking – when you ... displaced ...' He hesitates over the word. 'Did you return to the exact same place you left from?'

He watches me think about this. Did we?

'I can't be sure,' I end up saying. 'We didn't actually

realise we had done it at first and then ... but no, we reappeared in the woods, so no, it wasn't the exact same place.'

He looks at me long after I've finished speaking and then glances off round the woods. 'I'll go for another walk around the area,' he says, standing. 'You stay here? Just in case?'

I don't want to be alone but I agree anyway and watch him go, his limp slightly more pronounced, if anything, after the strain of the last few days. Once he is gone I look around at the nearest patch of flowers and catch the moment one ceases to make its noise and droop its star-petalled head in sleep. It occurs to me then how alive they are, far more like living things than other plants. Has Kirill seen these? I start to think about how I can get one back to him.

Which is when I hear it, off in the woods the opposite way from where Dom walked. Weak and quiet but unmistakeably in terrible, terrible pain. Everything turns cold, so cold, and I am almost immobilised by it. Then I feel it flood my legs and I am running.

When I get to him he is lying among the roots of a tree, soaking the fallen leaves with a seeping circle of black. When I lift him against me it feels as if he empties, as if he empties on to the ground as I pull him up, as if I feel the life flood out of him right in that moment. Which is almost exactly what actually happens. He is opened out, has been ruptured, all along his backbone, and when I lift him I leave behind almost all of his blood. And when I look at him he is so pale, so white, almost blue, and his eyes are rolling back in his head and he is cold beyond belief.

And I am saying, 'Ezra, no!' I am forbidding him from dying, forbidding him from doing this and not believing for a second that he actually will, especially because he has risked it all before, risked it all for us and lived. And it's also this: that he has been alive almost as long as I have – just four months fewer – and I don't understand a world in which he isn't living too. And so I am saying to him that he can't go because if he does it won't make sense, it all just won't make any sense any more, it's as simple as that; it just is. I yell for Dom and my voice fries out into silence the way it does in nightmares.

'I saw them,' says Ezra, his words bringing blood that bubbles on to his lips and nearly chokes him. 'I saw them. It was them.'

'It was who?' I can hardly speak.

'Concordia. They had a city, with a beautiful church, but it was them. I saw Maxim, Pasha . . .' He is smiling, almost laughing. 'I didn't get long enough to explain who I was.'

Dom arrives and drops to his knees next to us, pulling his T-shirt off and balling it, I guess to put pressure on the wound, stop the bleeding, but then he doesn't know where to start and we share a look. He presses it to Ezra's side in the end, as if it could ever have a hope of stemming the tide, and then he whispers, 'It's OK; you'll be OK,' and we can hear the others sliding down the rocks towards us.

Ezra's still smiling, even though the blood is starting to issue down his chin and fill his mouth. 'Everywhere we go, we just keep running into ourselves.' He laughs, or tries to, but can't, and that's when his eyes widen for a second and I see the agony on his face.

'No!' I am almost screaming at this point, his blood hot and wet and all over my lap and legs and everywhere. 'This isn't how it ends for you!' The words scrape out of my raw throat and he's frowning, the scowl, his scowl, the one he has always had, but then it fades, relaxes away slowly, slowly, until it is all gone.

For a while afterwards I can't let go; I rock him, pulling him against me while his blood cools and puddles and goes sticky against my legs, until they eventually ease him off me on to the ground and Dom pulls me up and away, and for a moment I fight, push him back because, I don't know, I guess part of me is still denying the way it is.

'Do something,' I sob, grabbing at the front of Irina's shirt. 'You're a medic – do something!' But of course she can't, so she doesn't, she only looks from me to him and then back again with the saddest eyes, because it is so clearly over.

It's the kind of absolute Ezra would have appreciated. It just is ... and that's it.

And that's it.

Chapter Thirty-Three

'No,' is all Mariana says once she knows.

We don't even tell her; we don't need to. It's obvious from the way we arrive back. It's dinner time, so they are all around the tables, and if we were thinking straight we wouldn't go blundering in there the way we do.

They see that there are four of us when there should be five. They see the zipped-up sleeping bag that we were carrying between us and have just laid out on the ground.

'No,' says Mariana again, and I don't say anything. I just watch her look down at me, at my trousers, at the way they are caked to my body with dark blood, her face crumbling into horror, and then, 'Oh God. Oh God, no.'

And I still don't say anything. I can't. And in some ways, I never will. I'll never tell her about how it was in those first minutes and hours we sat next to his body. How I stared at his face and tried to work out how much pain he'd been in. How Dom just wouldn't believe it, couldn't, and then started to freak out completely, unable to breathe, so afraid that Irina had to give him a shot to calm down, and then that was even worse because he was out of it, truth-telling, slurring his words, while we were zipping up Ezra's body. He said things that everyone could have done without hearing, such as, 'It's as if half his flesh is just gone,' while he was staring at the gaping wounds in Ezra's side and back before we closed the sleeping bag.

I don't tell her how it was for the two days it took us to walk back, carrying him, how we asked each other all these times why we couldn't just bury him where we were, why we hadn't just done that in the first place, argued about it, while all the time we knew that we couldn't leave him, that he needed to stay with us, to come home with us.

And now we are back. And the time is almost here to bury him. And I'm still not sure I can do it. Because we have always been together. We have been together all our lives. This is the first time that his path has gone one way and mine another, and I didn't even realise that it mattered to me until now. And now my path is continuing and his has just ... ended, and it's almost too much to bear.

I wake up on the day of the funeral because Dom is talking in his sleep again. He keeps doing it, keeps dreaming so hard that he wakes me, wakes himself, panting and falling out of bed, covered in sweat. It takes me ages to convince him that he is safe, holding him and stroking his hair and shushing him until he'll lie down again next to me, and when he does he is trembling, and he always apologises for it. And I guess it should be scary that he's falling apart this way, when he's always been the one who doesn't, but actually, weirdly, it makes me feel better.

We make our way to the graveyard. It's the first time I've been here since the day I first saw it. I know the others visit here and I just thought it was creepy but now, already, I know why they come. Even though today it is layered in a lilac mist, soaked with dew, draped in dark blue moss, polished pale stones standing around like the ghosts of those who are gone. And in among it all is the new hole, freshly dug yesterday, torn out of the ground like a wound, and the new, pale wooden box, with him inside, waiting.

They bury their dead here the way they did back on Earth. I can't stop thinking about it, about him in the ground, about how we could never have guessed this is how it would be for him, dead three weeks before his seventeenth birthday, dead and in the ground when he was born in space and probably always thought he would die in space. If he ever thought about dying at all, which, knowing Ezra, he probably didn't.

I'm amazed I manage to get there at all. In fact, I am kind of surprised when I find myself there, no memory of the journey. And then I am wondering how I will ever manage to make the speech they want me to make.

'Why did I agree to this?' I say to Dom, turning to him, but he only looks back at me and says, 'I think I'm going to be sick,' and squeezes my hand before sprinting off in the direction of the trees.

This is why it's only Mariana and I standing there when Jason and Grace join us, the next to arrive, and it is Jason who pulls me into his arms, sighs against my hair.

'I should have done something.'

And even though I've been thinking the same thing and worse over the last few days, I surprise myself by only saying, 'I doubt there's anything you could have done.'

'Maybe. Maybe not. And now we'll never know.'

Grace holds my face in her hands. 'My darling girl,' is all she says.

Jason is holding Mari's hands and peering into her face while she shakes her head. 'You never got to tell him?' and then he sighs, 'Neither did I.'

And I know what he means even though I don't think Mariana does.

I am talking to other people by the time I see Maxim arrive, notice him over their heads even as I'm listening to them all telling me how sorry they are. Leaning heavily on his arm is this really old, bent-over, grey haired version of himself, and this must be his father; this must be the commodore.

343

'I'm sorry to meet you like this,' he says once I'm standing in front of him; once I'm shaking his huge, twisted hand, cold in mine.

He seems older than my grandfather, so it occurs to me that he must have lived on Earth, must have been with the Concordia since it all began, must have seen all these people die. How do you do that? How do you just keep on burying people and burying people without giving up? I'm not even sure I can do it once.

Maxim helps him to the front and it is the commodore who speaks, who leads everything, probably the same way it has always been done, but who knows what that is because it is all in Russian. When the time comes for me to speak, everyone sitting on assorted benches and wooden stools and watching me and waiting, I have no idea what will come out of my mouth because I didn't plan it, I couldn't bear to, but somehow I knew that it would come.

'Ezra Lomax was my oldest friend, though I guess I never actually thought about that until it was too late. Most of you have probably heard by now about what happened to him, about how he was displaced into what we can only assume was another dimension and was killed on the return journey. Before he died he just about had time to tell me what he saw there.' I manage to look up and around at them all. 'It was you. He saw you. Concordia. Another version of you all on another version of Huxley-3. And he said: "Everywhere we go, we just keep running into ourselves."'

I almost laugh then because it's such an Ezra thing to say, and suddenly he is just the tiniest bit alive again for me. Then it burns in my eyes and when I look back out at them I can hardly see.

'Someone said to me recently that Ezra had made what was probably the most important and significant discovery in all of human history. But the truth is, I don't care about that. I don't care about it, when all I really want is to have him back. It's the most important discovery in all of human history and I don't care about it because I would much rather see him be seventeen and eighteen and twenty-one and a father to his child, and a grandfather, than have this goddam discovery, whatever it might or might not mean for us . . . '

I lose the blood in my head then, so much so that I have to cover my face and sniff into my hands, get it together before I can speak again.

'When someone dies you suddenly think of all the things you never told them that you should have,' is how I carry on, and I catch the look in Mariana's eye before she looks away, and Jason's too. 'But by the time you think about it, there's nothing you can do about it. Maybe that just goes to show that we all need to start being more honest with each other.' I catch Dom's eye then. 'Where Ezra and I came from, there were so many

345

lies. We weren't trusted with the truth, ever. And almost everyone we knew, everyone we had to look up to, was living a lie of some kind or another. I don't want to live like that any more. I don't even think I can. And what's more, I don't think we should. Everywhere we go we just keep running into ourselves. So maybe the truth is that we are alone out here. Maybe we are the only ones. And if we are the only ones, shouldn't we try to be better at it? Shouldn't we try to get it right? If we're the only life, we just need to be better, we owe it to this beautiful universe, and to each other.' Suddenly I feel ridiculous, and I laugh a little. 'I'm sorry. I didn't want to stand here and ... ' I shake my head, and find I am remembering something else. 'He told me there was a church. In their settlement, their version of Concordia settlement, he said there was a beautiful church. I'm not a fan of God, I never have been, but I am a fan of faith. Ezra was a twin; his brother Jonah was a priest, and he said to me once: "I'm not asking you to believe in God, but I am asking you to believe in something. Pick one true thing and believe in it as hard as you can. That's all faith is." I guess I still don't believe in anything, really. But I want to. So maybe we should believe in us. In Huxley-3. I don't even know what, but in something. You came here to make a new life. It doesn't have to have anything to do with the old one. We don't have to play by those rules. Maybe we should believe that we can be better. We have learned something so amazing.

346

Ezra has allowed us to learn something amazing. We have a chance. We have more chances. Maybe we have infinite chances. So we can get it right. Maybe we can be the ones to get it right, if we try.'

I don't know if I'm finished or not but I definitely can't say any more, so I walk back to the front row to where Dom is waiting for me. I don't watch when the guys who normally operate the tree clearance machinery lower the box into the ground. It's too much to think about.

I don't know why people always eat and drink after funerals but they do, and Concordia's no different, so Pasha has supplied a pretty huge amount of his alcohol and everyone, even the people who normally wouldn't, are drinking loads of it. I don't know whether it's my idea or someone else's that I end up next to Commodore Kreznev but either way I do and it soothes me, and I am pretty sure it has quite a lot to do with the fact that he reminds me of Grandpa, with his voice that makes people listen.

'Did you know Earth?' I ask him at some point, wincing after a harsh hit of alcohol.

He nods. 'I was twenty-three when we left. So many dreams.'

'What was it like?'

'Like a place living on borrowed time. The only resource it still had plenty of was people, so it used them. Take Ventura as a case in point. People said it was all a publicity stunt.'

347

'They did?' Dom is leaning over me, listening in.

'There were ... shall we say ... rumours that the signal was a fake, that it was all manufactured by the communications experts at Ventura Com for their own purposes. That eight hundred people was a pretty small price to pay for the publicity the whole mission generated. It was all anyone talked about; it was all the world talked about. For years. Even for many years after it left. It was the first of its kind. In many ways, it was a long way ahead of its time. Maybe too far.'

He coughs then, lets it take him over, screwing up his eyes so that they are hidden by the folds of his wrinkles. Dom and I exchange glances.

'But you want to know what I always thought?' He looks at us even though it's a question not expecting an answer. 'Even if the signal was a fake, there is something so noble and ... I don't know ... pure about the Ventura's mission. Communication. The quest for contact. Not like this grubby little pioneer land grab of mine.' He shakes his head, spits into the dirt nearby in a way that surprises me. 'So cheap. And yet it has cost so much.'

We all sit with that for a moment and I look over at where Jason and Grace are talking, heads close, pained expressions, his head dropping against her shoulder for a moment. Beyond them I can see Mariana sitting with Maxim, leaning back against him while he rests a hand on her stomach.

Commodore Kreznev raises his cup with a shaking hand and says, 'To the one true thing.'

'And what is that for you?' says Dom, as I pick up my cup and go to touch it to the commodore's.

'Humans,' he says, his voice soft. 'Humans. And our desire to survive against all odds. Our desire to live.'

And we touch our cups to his.

Chapter Thirty-Four

Summer settles on us suddenly, like a heavy blanket.

It's almost time to harvest the dried-up, dead army of sunflowers I walk through on the way to the long-range com. Grace is inside, sitting in a chair, looking around at the desks of instruments that don't work yet, taking a while to realise I'm there and look up at me.

'Seren,' she says, getting up and coming to me, hugging me. 'How ... how are you?' She cringes. 'OK, stupid question.'

'I'm OK,' I tell her.

She seems lost for words for a moment. 'I'm so ... I'm so sorry, you know.'

I try to smile, walk away from her, do a circuit of the room before I say, 'What's the deal with this place anyway?'

'How do you mean?'

'Why did you even build it? Who are you expecting to hear from?'

She looks around as if she's seeing it for the first time. 'You know, sometimes I'm not even sure. The idea was to get it set up so we could communicate our progress to Earth but sometimes ... I think about Ventura, about whether we could ever hear from them, about whether ...'

She doesn't finish, just runs her fingers over a control panel.

'About whether what?' I ask her.

'I always wondered what would happen if they got to Eridani and found out the signal was nothing, nobody.'

I know what she means.

'I don't like the idea of them out there, knowing it was all for nothing. Maybe, at least, if we were here, on the way back, it would be ... I don't know.'

I nod into the silence.

'She was your age, you know, when she signed up for Ventura.' She looks up at me, and I know she means Great Granny Bea. 'Can you imagine that?'

I sigh. 'Now I live on a planet I find it even harder to imagine than I did before.'

She smiles at that, watches me for a moment, then says, 'Hey, have you seen what Kirill's done?'

When I get there, I see Mariana first, knees down in the dirt. She gets up when she sees me, brushes off the soil. She leads me through to the back where Kirill is soaking a bunch of little trees in bags with the hose. He turns the

351

hose off when he sees me, punches my arm, can't stop smiling.

'So come on then, let's see what the big deal is,' I tell him.

He makes me squat down, peer in with him under the dark leaves of the little trees, until I see them – fruit. Small, but unmistakeable, hanging in pairs and rosy with juice.

'What are they?' I ask him.

'They don't have a name yet,' he says. 'They're new. First ever Earth–Huxley hybrid.'

'Oh my God,' I say on an outbreath.

'Wait until you taste it,' says Mariana from behind me.

Kirill eases one off its stem gently and holds it out to me between finger and thumb. And I mean, it's not as if I've ever really eaten much fruit before, not if you don't count the mostly poisonous things I tried on the island, so for a moment I am just studying it and then I say, 'The whole thing, or . . . ?'

'Be careful of the stone in the middle.' He is smiling so hard and he says, 'Just taste it, come on.'

And so I do. It's like being flooded with liquid warmth, or liquid light. So good it makes me dribble and sigh in a way that makes them both laugh at me, and I don't even realise I am gobbling the whole thing right off the stone until it is gone and I am wishing there were more of it.

'Oh man,' I tell them afterwards, wiping my chin on my sleeve. 'So good. How did you do it?'

'Maxim helped me,' he said. 'Had to wait two years to see if it had worked.'

'It was worth it,' I tell him. 'No question.'

Mariana and I walk over to where Maxim asked us to meet him. The edge of town, where yesterday they just cleared an area of trees. The devastation is so fresh that the woodchips still smell rich and tangy.

'Nice,' I tell him as we arrive, noticing only as I do that Jason is standing with him. 'You can almost still hear them screaming.'

'Sacrifices have had to be made.' He half smiles. 'They always do.'

Mariana goes to him and he lifts his arm over her shoulders, pulls her in against his side. Since Ezra died it's been like this; they've completely given up pretending they're not a couple, and even though I guess maybe that could upset me, it doesn't. Instead it makes me happy. It makes everyone happy.

Almost as if he's reading my mind right then, Maxim says, 'I wanted to ask what you would think if I built something in Ezra's honour. After all, he's the father of Huxley's first ever native.'

He looks at me, then Mariana, then me again.

'What are you going to build?' I ask, feeling it's important to know that before I give my answer.

'Well ... I was wondering about a church.'

He and Jason watch us in silence while we take it in.

'I know it might seem a bit weird,' says Jason. 'When none of us are particularly into religion or anything, but when you spoke about it at the funeral, I guess we all started thinking about it, and thinking that we probably should have somewhere to, I don't know, gather. Somewhere to have quiet time to think and reflect. To celebrate what we believe in, whatever that might be. We need somewhere proper to hold our funerals. And we'd hope to have more reasons to use it in the coming years. Maybe even some weddings?' He raises his eyebrows at Maxim, but he doesn't take the bait.

He only says, 'And the building would be multi-purpose, of course. We will need to get an education programme re-established in the near future, which could be housed here. Actually, Seren, I was wondering if you would like to be responsible for that.'

I nearly choke. 'An education programme? Me?'

'Yes. You. You've experienced so much already in life. And I consider you very wise, so I think in a few years ...'

I hold his gaze, challenging him. 'I wouldn't teach people to obey the rules and do as they're told, Maxim. I'm done with that.'

'I wouldn't expect you to,' he says without missing a beat, and Mariana leans in to kiss him on the ear.

He smiles down at her before looking around the clearing, squinting a little. 'I have this idea that we could build it out of wood, make it look just like the inside of the forest, almost as if it were the trees' idea to have it here.' He looks at Mariana. 'Does that sound crazy?'

She shakes her head.

I look around too, then. I can nearly see it.

The walk takes a lot less time than I expect it to. The first time I came I was still so sick after the operation, and Dom's leg was still bad. That already seems like another lifetime, even though it was only a few weeks ago.

He left before dawn, like he does sometimes, but last night he made sure I knew how to get here.

'Come up when you can,' he said. 'I want to show you something.'

When I get there, he is knee-deep in the water, arms folded across his bare chest as he looks out across the oddly pale blue expanse of water, deep in thought. He turns when he hears me, and this is what I see on his face: he wasn't really sure that I would come, thinking it might be too painful to return. So I go to him, drop my bag next to the fire and walk straight in until I am next to him, taking his hand, raising it to my mouth.

'You made it,' he says, not smiling, though there is one, a secret one, hidden in his eyes.

I look around at the beautiful jade lake in the twilight,

two hundred metres across and almost perfectly round. 'I'd forgotten how beautiful it is here.'

He nods. 'It is, but that isn't why I wanted you to come.'

I turn my face towards him, hold his gaze for so long that I know he will reach for me and he does, and I am pulling his hips against me while he kisses my neck, my shoulders, my chest, and it is only when I jump up into his arms, wrapping my legs around him, that we lose our balance and fall into the shallows of the cooling lake, him on top of me and both of us laughing for what feels like the first time in so long.

'Why did you want me to come, then?' I ask, wiping the water off his face and smoothing his hair back.

'Fish.' He smiles.

And I say, 'What?' and just about a second later I get it and I say, 'What? You mean ... in here? There are fish?'

And he is watching all this play out on my face and smiling that slow, sweet, one-dimpled smile that I love so much and then, right then, as if he planned it, just nearby, maybe two metres away, one breaks the surface, too quickly to see anything except a flash of silver scales, a tiny fin, but it is so incredible I shriek, a sound that echoes everywhere and then I am kissing him and saying, right against his lips, 'You're amazing, you know that? You are so amazing.'

'They're still so little,' he says. 'So young. It's too soon to say whether they have a future here, but it's a start.'

And I am looking at his beautiful face, at the light in his eyes he only gets at times like this.

'I'm so lucky,' I say. 'That you love me. You're this amazing person who can make life where there wasn't any, and you love me.' I shake my head.

'That's why I have to keep coming out here to check on them,' he says, looking around. 'I don't like to leave you, but . . . '

'I thought maybe you just wanted a bit of alone time. After everything.'

He kind of laughs, but sadly. He has his hands on my hips and his fingertips have found the scar from my operation, the smooth, hardening lines of it. It's just chance that it ended being the shape of a capital E, but I'm glad. Now it will always remind me of my friend, and of all the other unlived lives of the universe. Dom bends his knees up out of the water and rests his arms on them, looks down at the water. 'I still can't believe we lost him.'

We lost him. It's taken me a while to start seeing it like that. Such a clean and distant way of thinking about it, without all the details that make it even harder to bear. We lost him. That's what it comes down to in the end. We lost everything he was to us and everything he was going to be.

'He's the only reason we're here at all,' he says. 'And now . . . '

'Which is why we owe it to him to be happy, I guess.'

357

I rest my chin on his forearm and watch his sad face, his eyelashes still wet and clumped together, drops working their way down his neck. 'You know what I keep thinking?'

He shakes his head.

'What he saw ... it means, probably, that there are other – what? – dimensions, timelines, in which there are other versions of us, living other lives, right?'

He meets my eye.

'So somewhere there's another Ezra. Still alive. Still cracking stupid jokes and making snarky comments and still with his whole future ahead of him,' I say.

'If you could go in there and see him, speak to him now, what would you say?'

I've thought of it a thousand times, a thousand different ways, but all I say is, 'Get a haircut, probably.'

And he smiles, almost laughs, sighs hard as if he's shaking something off, looks around us.

'I was thinking we could live out here,' he says then. 'Might take a while to build something better than a tent.'

I look around at the lilac sky, at the mirror-flat water showing the rising moons their own reflections.

'We could,' I say. 'Or we could be a little closer to the settlement. That might be a good idea. For any number of reasons.'

'With the breeding programme starting up next year?' He raises his eyebrows. 'You don't think they've got plans for us? We don't want any part of it – we need to be self-sufficient.'

But I am shaking my head. 'I don't think we need to worry about that any more. I have a feeling things are going to be different from now on.'

Suddenly I feel the cold steal into me a little, so I stand in the water, scaring a tiny fish that had come to investigate. I offer Dom my hand and he looks at it for a second.

'Let's get out of these wet clothes,' I say.

'Now there's an offer I can't refuse.' He takes my hand so that I pull him to his feet and for a moment we are standing there facing each other, hands joined, the moons at our back, the water at our feet.

'I hope you and I still get to be together in the other dimensions,' he says as I lead him back to shore.

So I say, 'Oh I think some things are inevitable, even with infinite possibilities,' and even though I don't look back, I know he's smiling.

Acknowledgements

Thanks to Kate Agar, the unflappable and talented editor who is destined for bigger and better things. You have always kept your head when I've been losing mine, and I will miss you.

Thanks to Sophie Burdess, wonderful cover designer, as well as Becca Allen, Catherine Coe and the other talents in and around Hachette.

Thanks to Madeleine Milburn and her team (Alice Sutherland-Hawes, Hayley Steed and Thérèse Coen) for being the good sense and business brains that I don't have.

Thanks to Kristin Overmeier, Elisabeth Strandgaard, Jolijn Swager, Nynke de Groot, Marieke Woortman, Ahu Ayan, Elsbeth Witt, Anne Marie Koper, Asena Cakmak Ozdemir, Laerke Pade, Anna Carbone, Pico Floridi, Mirella Prato, Alessandro Zontini and all the other talented editors, publishers and translators who bring my stories to people in faraway lands.

Thanks to everyone who read and loved *Loneliness*, especially those who took the time to tell me why.

But most of all thanks to my beautiful little family, because it's you who have to put up with it all: the getting up at 5:45am every morning to write; the thousand yard stare when I'm thinking about my book instead of you; the fact that there's no such thing as spare time for us.

People always ask me how I manage to work full time, raise two kids and also write books. The answer is that I don't. With all the jobs I have to do I am always doing one of them badly. My girls, for the times that the one I'm doing badly is being your mum, I'm sorry. But if you think I'm working hard for this dream, you should see what I was prepared to go through for my first one. I never gave up on it, and I never would have done, even though it nearly killed me more than once. That first dream was you. And every day I spend with you just confirms how totally worth it you were.